# MISS FORTUNE COOKIE

# LAUREN BJORKMAN

miss
FORTUNE
COOKIE

HENRY HOLT AND COMPANY

NEW YORK

Henry Holt and Company, LLC
*Publishers since 1866*
175 Fifth Avenue
New York, New York 10010
macteenbooks.com

Library of Congress Cataloging-in-Publication Data
Bjorkman, Lauren.
Miss Fortune Cookie / Lauren Bjorkman.—1st ed.
p.    cm.
Summary: Erin, a non-Chinese teenager living in San Francisco's Chinatown, ghostwrites
an online advice column, but when a reply to her ex-best friend backfires,
Erin's carefully constructed life takes a crazy spin.
ISBN 978-0-8050-8951-6 (hardcover)—ISBN 978-0-8050-9636-1 (e-book)
[1. Advice columns—Fiction.   2. Interpersonal relations—Fiction.
3. Friendship—Fiction.   4. Chinese Americans—Fiction.   5. Chinatown
(San Francisco, Calif.)—Fiction.   6. San Francisco (Calif.)—Fiction.]   I. Title.
PZ7.B52859Mi 2012   [Fic]—dc23     2012006327

First Edition—2012 / Designed by April Ward
Printed in the United States of America

1   3   5   7   9   10   8   6   4   2

*For everyone who believes in the power of love*

# MISS
# FORTUNE
# COOKIE

You will have much luck and little hardship.
Or the other way around.

My friends and I were riding home from school on Muni, clinging to an assortment of slippery handholds, when Linny almost blew my secret identity. Intentionally.

"Listen to this one," she said, reading off her iPhone, a faint but smirky glint in her eyes. "'Dear Miss Fortune Cookie. My cousin thinks I'm chasing her boyfriend. Her boyfriend and I never flirt, but sometimes we text. What can I do to make her believe me? Just Friends.'"

In fact, I—Erin Kavanagh, alias Miss Fortune Cookie— had posted this very letter on my anonymous advice blog, and Linny happened to be the only person in San Francisco to know that, the only person in the whole world, except for some random administrator at WordPress. She takes every opportunity to harass me about keeping my blog a secret. "What advice would *you* give, Erin?" she asked, winking this time.

I kept my face as neutral as possible. Luckily Darren and Mei were only paying attention each other. As usual.

Personally speaking, I think nano-deceptions are a good thing. I regularly use them to protect my friends from unpleasant truths. Should I tell Linny that her favorite knit hat makes her head look like a furry meatball? Or nudge Mei whenever Darren winces at her hyena laugh? Should I have cautioned Darren that taking AP physics would wreck his grade-point average? Absolutely not. Sincere lies keep everyone happy.

I blew the hair out of my eyes. "The cousin will never stop suspecting the two of them," I said to Linny, "so *Just Friends* has to stop the texting. She could get her own boyfriend. Or move to somewhere far away like Moldavia."

Muni, a sort of bus powered by electric wires overhead, jerked to a halt. A seat opened up, and Linny took it. "Exactly!" She had the happiest smile ever, so big it barely fit on her face. Metaphorically speaking. "Mei, don't you think Erin is a natural at giving advice?"

"Hmm?" Mei said. She was somewhat entwined with Darren and therefore distracted.

"Nothing." I jabbed Linny in the ribs to get her to stop talking. Gently of course. The three of us—Mei, Linny, and me—made an enviable friendship trio. I was the lesser third, maybe because Mei and Linny were gorgeously Chinese-American, while I was just Boring-American. A Person of Irish.

Mei knew nothing about my connection to Miss Fortune Cookie. We used to be best friends, and by best friends I mean we spent every afternoon and weekend together until eighth grade, when things fell apart between us. The truth is, Mei dumped me. Then Linny brought us together again during freshman year, inviting us both to eat lunch with her, forming a little group. A few months later, I mustered the courage to bring up the dumping incident with Mei, except she didn't want to talk about it. So we became friends again without dealing with the past. Pretty much.

Except I didn't trust her like I used to.

And she didn't share as many intimate details about herself with me.

Linny beckoned me closer to whisper in my ear. "I have a question for Miss Fortune Cookie. A very personal one. But you can't tell Mei."

"Why not?"

She lowered her voice more. "You just can't, 'kay?"

I nodded. Linny usually let both of us in on every detail about her life, although lately she'd been secretive about her new boyfriend. Whatever it was, it wouldn't be boring. I turned my back toward Mei and said in my quietest voice, "Go ahead. I'm listening. What is it?"

Linny shook her head. "Not now."

Just then, the Muni driver made the sharp turn into Chinatown, and three things happened almost simultaneously: a bicyclist veered into the road, the driver slammed on the brakes, and I fell into another passenger. We came to a halt fifty feet from the stop, and the bicyclist escaped unscathed. I could tell by the vigorous way he flipped off the driver. Then I caught sight of Mrs. Liu, bundled against the fog, among the passengers waiting to board.

"Your mom!" I whispered to Mei. "She's getting on!"

Mei's eyes widened. "What the what?"

Which demonstrates a problem with sincere lies—in this case, Mei's lie to her mom about not having a boyfriend. They can be found out. Darren dropped his arm from around Mei's waist and grabbed his backpack. "Bye," he mouthed before zipping to the back and catapulting out the rear door. He's considerate like that.

3

Mrs. Liu's grocery bags thumped against the handrail as she marched up the steps. She has sharp, high cheekbones and is tall like her daughter. She and Mei both have blunt-cut hair that reaches their shoulders. Our favorite salon in Chinatown sometimes offers two-for-one specials.

Mei hurried to the front to take the two largest bags. "Ma, let me."

Mrs. Liu stretched her swan neck toward the window. "Who is that with you?"

Mei shook her head nervously. "No one. Just Erin and Linny. I invited them to help with the turnip cakes."

"No. I see boy before." Mrs. Liu believed with every sinew in her heart that a boyfriend would distract Mei from her schoolwork, ruining her chances of getting into the number one university in the country, Harvard. So when Mei fell in love with Darren last spring, she kept it a secret from her mom. For thirteen whole months. Which showed amazing ingenuity and skill on her part, but once you start a lie, it's hard to escape it.

"Who is boy?"

"Oh, him," Mei said. "Someone from AP chem. We were discussing the homework. Chemical reactions." She blinked fast. "And stuff like that."

To be fair, most people have trouble lying to Mrs. Liu. Her eyes bore right through your skull and read your thoughts as if you accidentally uploaded them onto Facebook. It's her superpower.

Linny stood up to offer her seat to Mrs. Liu. "Mr. F assigned loads of homework over the weekend. He wants us in top shape for the AP test."

Mrs. Liu ignored the seat. She had just turned forty and didn't appreciate the senior-citizen treatment. "Very good. Homework make you smart."

"Ma, please sit down. *Ni shi lao.*" That means *you are the elder*, a show of respect. It also means *you are old*.

"I am comfortable," Mrs. Liu said.

Mei continued arguing politely. Though most Chinese immigrants to San Francisco speak Cantonese, a dialect common in the south of China, Mrs. Liu emigrated from the north, where they speak Mandarin. I was fluent enough to follow their conversation.

"*Ma, ni zuo.*" Ma, just sit.

"*Gaosu wo ta de mingzi.*" *Tell me his name.*

Before they resolved anything, the driver pulled into the stop by Mrs. Liu's restaurant, and we all got off. Hay Fat occupies a prominent street corner in Chinatown. Mrs. Liu's heightened culinary sensibility has turned it into a legend, luring in the more adventurous tourists and fussy locals. She serves authentic dishes with ingredients such as fermented bean paste, whole fish with eyeballs intact, and lotus. Her menu also includes beef broccoli in case people with less sophisticated palates wander in by mistake.

We entered the kitchen through the alley. The dinner rush had yet to begin, which meant we had the place to ourselves. After setting me up with the grater and Mei with the bacon to steam, Mrs. Liu tossed a handful of sesame seeds into sizzling oil at the bottom of the wok. I closed my eyes to better appreciate the scrumptious smell.

"What should I do?" Linny asked. I looked at her appraisingly, wondering about her secret. Not that we could talk here in the kitchen.

Mrs. Liu handed her a bowl. "Cut mushrooms. Very small pieces."

I consider Hay Fat my second home. Mom and Mrs. Liu met when Mei and I were in preschool and have been good

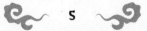

friends ever since. We live one floor below them in an apartment a few blocks from here in a quieter part of Chinatown. Mrs. Liu has always welcomed me into her kitchen, even during that black year when Mei and I barely spoke.

What I know of her life before America comes through Mom. Twenty-three years ago, Mrs. Liu studied cooking at a special school in China that trains workers for American restaurants. After finishing the program, she immigrated to San Francisco, where she met Mei's dad. He soon left her, and she has remained single ever since. Which could explain some of her gruffness.

"No lollygagging," Mrs. Liu said. The cloth she wore over her hair fell askew, and my fingers itched to straighten it. I didn't stop grating for a second, though, because sometimes when I slack off from a job she's given me, she'll pinch my arm. Not hard, but still.

Linny held out her cutting board for inspection. "Are these pieces small enough?"

Mrs. Liu took the board and tossed the mushrooms into the wok. "Almost. Watch. This is secret part. Very important. Not in recipe."

Smoke rose from the hot metal. While Mrs. Liu stirred up a storm, I took the chance to rest my aching muscles. As I was standing there, I noticed that the photographs hanging over the sink had been dusted recently. One showed four-year-old Mei holding a pen and scroll, a minischolar. Next to it hung a picture of me dressed as a sunflower for our preschool play.

The turnip cakes were for a party next week, an event to celebrate Mei's acceptance into Harvard. Mrs. Liu had planned it out a long time ago. I think she decided on which dishes to serve before Mei started high school. Last July, she bought boxes of scarlet and black decorations. She mailed the invitations a month ago. Harvard's acceptance emails, though, wouldn't go out until tomorrow, April 1, at 5:00 p.m. Eastern Daylight Time.

Now Mei just had to get in.

The three of us attend Lowell, a high school for academic types—nerds in the best sense—a rare public school that students compete to get into. At Lowell, we have a popular crowd, hipsters, and partiers like everywhere else, but we worry more about SAT percentiles and college choices than our counterparts. For us, the first of April is bigger than the Academy Awards. Tomorrow, hopes would be mangled and dreams decapitated.

Mrs. Liu spun around to face Mei. "*Meihua!* That boy on bus. *Shi bu shi* boyfriend?"

Meihua blinked. "He's not, Ma."

Linny and I exchanged glances.

$$full\ denial = a\ lie\ of\ omission \times 10^3$$

Mei's sincere lie had gone bad, turned slimy and evil smelling like leftovers jammed to the back of the fridge behind the sauce jars.

"The stove!" Linny yelled.

Flames shot upward. Mrs. Liu calmly fetched a small broom and beat out the fire in three precise strokes. She's efficient like that. "You are young. You cannot know love."

Except Romeo and Juliet were young, and though Darren had not declared his devotion publicly from the alley or climbed a trellis to the window leading to Mei's bedchamber, Romeo had nothing on him when it came to passion. I'd seen more of that than I cared to, in fact.

Mei laid the steamed bacon on a clean bamboo chopping block and commenced mincing it into molecule-sized bits.

Mrs. Liu waved her spatula. "Harvard most important thing. Future more valuable than useless boy. You tell me, Erin. Who is boy?"

My hand flew across the grater, and the mound of turnips grew. "The boy on Muni?"

Mrs. Liu growled with exasperation. "The Master say give elder no reason for anxiety."

Mei ducked her head. "You're right, Ma."

"I am not right," Mrs. Liu barked. "*The Master* is right." By the Master, she meant Confucius, the spiritual grandfather of China, born more than five hundred years before Jesus. Arguing against the Master would be futile. The main dinner chef arrived, and Mrs. Liu dismissed us. "Skedaddle. Do homework. Good-bye."

Grateful for the reprieve, I slipped out of my apron. Mei planted her feet by the stove and lifted her chin. She looked exactly like she used to long ago when we shoved cooked rice and fruit under the stove to feed the hungry ghost that lived there: scared but determined. She turned to Linny and me. "I'm staying to help Ma. Wait for me."

Which meant Linny and I would get a little time alone and she could finally tell me what she started to say on Muni.

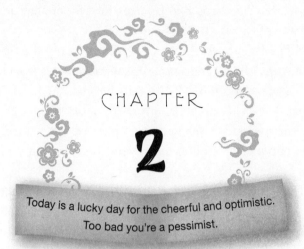

CHAPTER

2

Today is a lucky day for the cheerful and optimistic.
Too bad you're a pessimist.

Bubbling over with curiosity, I swished through the swinging door that separated the kitchen from the restaurant and sat down at a table next to a shelf crowded with cinnabar bowls. Brand-new hot-pink lanterns dangled overhead, blazing us with their cheerfulness. "So, what did you want to tell me?"

Linny took the seat across from me. Before school, she'd gathered most of her hair into a ponytail, but some of it had gotten loose, and a black cloud framed her face. "Mei should come clean to her mom about Darren, don't you think?" she asked.

I swallowed a sigh of disappointment. We'd been discussing this same topic for days. "I don't know. We're talking about Shoe Fang, here." Mrs. Liu's first name was Shufang, which conjured to my mind a pair of black Chinese slippers with long incisors. "Shin-Biter Woman."

Linny laughed. "She's not *that* scary. Darren has awesome grades and acts polite around adults. Shoe Fang doesn't have to know that he burns K-Pop mixes for Mei or that he has a weird way of eating string cheese."

I dipped a chopstick into a sauce bin and put the tip in my mouth. Yum. Mrs. Liu never serves soy sauce made from hydrolyzed vegetable protein. "If Mei tells her ma, she has to admit to lying. Anyway, Shoe Fang only cares about Harvard."

A derisive noise escaped from Linny's throat. "Mrs. Liu is so stereotypically Chinese. Harvard is all about bragging rights for her."

"That's not true," I said. Being third-generation American made Linny less sensitive to Mrs. Liu's point of view. Generally speaking, China's long and venerable history interested her less than, say, stories about our notorious classmate Gabby who, only last week, swore at the teacher who'd confiscating her cell phone. "Mrs. Liu works hard and wants the very best future for Mei. It's tradition."

"As if going to Harvard guarantees a successful life." Linny made a face to emphasize the sarcasm.

Um.

Harvard has produced nine U.S. presidents. Not to mention Natalie Portman and Matt Damon. Other amazing people went there too—Henry David Thoreau, Ralph Waldo Emerson, and Yo-Yo Ma—literary and musical geniuses with really cool names. Which kind of explained why I had applied there too.

"You haven't fallen for all that number-one-university crapola?" she said, wrinkling her nose.

"Just a little?"

During the application season, Linny had skipped Ivy League schools altogether, claiming they were snobby. Actually, though, junior year she devoted too much time to organizing protests, and her grades dropped some, which pretty much ruined her chances. My numbers were a little better than hers—still not up to Ivy League standards, but I'd applied to a few because I admired their scholarliness. Linny didn't share my reverence for academia.

"Harvard has like hypnotized the whole country," she said.

"I know, right? Who'd want to be Bill Gates?"

She laughed. "Exactly. Have you seen his hair?"

This whole discussion was theoretical, anyway, since the Ivy Leagues would reject me tomorrow. Besides, I'd gotten in to UC Berkeley, and so had Linny.

The waiter bustled over to our table. According to Mrs. Liu, he had a doctorate in plant physiology from a university in China, which kind of proved Linny's point. "What am I having?" I asked. She can make decisions faster than most girls can flip open their phones. I, on the other hand, like to ponder, take my time to consider all the options, a skill generally not appreciated by overworked restaurant staff.

Linny studied me. "Something balancing. Watercress and a bowl of hot and sour soup." After she pointed to the numbers on the menu, the waiter left, and her face changed. "So here's my question, X." *X* stands for *xiao bi, small nose,* her sweet nickname for me.

She hesitated. This had to be about her new love interest and international boy of mystery, Dub. After weeks of asking about him, I had gleaned these few facts: She met him at a gay-marriage rally at Berkeley. They'd held hands and laughed together. The band Plain White T's practically wrote the soundtrack to his life.

I tucked my hair behind my ears. "I'm listening." She usually shared too many details about her boyfriends—I had to hear about the one with a galaxy of pimples on his back and

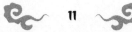

the boy who ate Pepsodent between classes—but she hadn't even taken a picture of Dub. Could there be something wrong with him? Maybe he had elephantiasis.

Maybe he already had a girlfriend. Cheating jerk.

Linny twisted her ponytail tight. "Dear Miss Fortune Cookie," she said loudly just as the waiter came over with my watercress.

I put my finger to my lips.

Linny looked at the waiter critically. "As if he would blab it all over Lowell," she said after he left us. "Besides, you should be proud of your column."

When I started Miss Fortune Cookie freshman year, I had a serious shyness problem. Like every time a teacher called on me I'd blush, whether I knew the answer or not. Things had improved since then, but I still didn't want to go public. "The anonymity gives me a certain mystique, you know," I said in a sultry voice. And by mystique, I mean credibility.

If my readers knew that I—an immature, non-Chinese high school senior—wrote Miss Fortune Cookie, they would never take the blog seriously. True, I was born in China, but my DNA was stubbornly European.

As if she could hear my thoughts, Linny argued with me. "Everyone would love knowing it's you, Erin. You'd be like the rock star of Lowell. But whatever." She pulled a handout from her bag and started writing furiously on the back.

Dear Miss Fortune Cookie,

Freshman year, my friends and I promised each other to wait for serious love before sleeping with a boy. But I'm older now, about to graduate, and I have fallen in "like" with

*an amazing college man. I want to break*
*our old pact. what do you think?*

*Too old to be a virgin*

Ack. I took a bite of watercress to give myself time to think. She wanted to . . . with Dub? The obvious answer came to me in a picosecond. *No.* Why settle for "like" when true love would come someday? Yes, inexperience would be embarrassing in college, but it would be survivable.

I closed my eyes to escape Linny's intense gaze. Then again, my knowledge about boys bordered on nonexistent. One kissed me at a dance once, but I think he did it by accident, so I knew nothing about love firsthand. I opened my eyes and whispered to her, "Miss Fortune Cookie says, eagles may soar, but rodents don't get sucked into jet engines."

Linny broke into a megajoule smile. "What does that even mean?"

"I don't know. You're an eagle? You can do whatever you want?"

She brushed her chin with her ponytail. "Mei won't approve."

I put my hand on her arm. "Tell Mei that you happen to be electric-magnetic-charismatic. Dub has stirred up your electrons, forcing them to jump into a higher orbital."

Linny's dimples deepened. "Physics nerd."

The blame for my lack of experience did not fall entirely on my shoulders. At Lowell, girls outnumbered boys three to two and most boys without girlfriends had fatal flaws. Some talked nonstop, some said nothing at all, and some had only one thing on their minds—video games.

"Did you ask Dub the Pokémon question?" I asked.

The Pokémon question sounds like a joke, but it works. For

example, boys who worship Charmander are often somewhat obnoxious, preferring to solve problems by blasting them with flames.

Seriously.

"He's never even played Pokémon."

"That's not normal, and totally perfect."

Linny drummed the tabletop with her nails. Most Lowell students have developed nervous tics from all of our coffee- and Skittles-fueled study sessions. And from sleeping five hours a night. "God, I'm dying for a cigarette," Linny said.

I dipped the clean end of a chopstick into the mustard bin. When I licked it, the sharp spice zipped up my nose.

"Don't make that face at me," Linny said, misunderstanding. "I quit smoking after Mom showed me a dehydrated lung. I'm *yearning* for a cigarette, that's all. And don't tell Mei about what I just told you."

"Sure." An easy promise to keep because Mei and I shared few secrets these days. Our friendship had never returned to normal, exactly, like when you neglect a houseplant and it wilts and no amount of water will make it lush again. When we hung out these days, she didn't want to play the games we used to. She'd outgrown them, I think. But sometimes I missed our old silly style.

As if summoned by her name, Mei emerged from the kitchen to join us. When I saw her framed in the doorway, she shone with familiar glamour. She'd become mature without me. But it seemed to me like she'd acquired a new skin too, an extra layer that covered her real self, a barrier making her a little less nice than before. Which might explain why Linny had confided in me—the lesser third—about her plans with Dub, while keeping it a secret from Mei. It was strange, in fact.

And wonderful.

# CHAPTER

## 3

You will soon experience a fortunate calamity.

Mei plunked down in the chair between Linny and me just as my hot and sour soup arrived. "I adore your coat, Lin. I'd steal it, but it would look terrible on me," she said.

Linny had on a houndstooth jacket, a patterned shirt, jeans, and spike-heeled boots. I noticed that her lapel had somehow gotten trapped under her collar. I reached over the table to smooth it. "I know what you mean, Mei. If I try to dress like her, I end up looking like a thrift-store mannequin."

Linny flicked me with her fingers. "Oh, please. Look at you in those leggings. Twenty-five cents." She fines me a quarter whenever I put myself down, to cure my self-esteem problem. She's thoughtful like that.

"If I had your calves," Mei said, "I'd wear leggings every day."

I looked down at my legs. Were they nice?

Linny crossed her arms and gave Mei the snarky eyeball. She has down-curving lids like flower petals, and delicate features that make everyone else resemble Genghis Khan. Still, she knows how to glare. "Did you tell your mom about Darren yet?"

Mei gnawed on her pinkie knuckle, a new habit she'd picked up in an effort to stop biting her nails. It looked painful. "No."

"When are you going to?"

Mei dropped her hands into her lap. "I don't see the point. Harvard *could* reject me, you know. They only let in one thousand eight hundred of the thirty thousand who apply. What if Stanford wants me? Ma can't prevent me from having a boyfriend in college, right? I could introduce them in November. Ta-da! Meet Darren! We just met at a lecture given by a Nobel laureate."

I most definitely agreed. Why upset Shoe Fang unnecessarily? Mei and I think alike. We used to be an unbeatable team in charades. She could flap her arms and cough for a nanosecond, and I'd know she meant bird flu. But arguments agitate my insides, which explained why I didn't get involved in this one.

"What if you *do* get into Harvard?" Linny persisted. "Will you tell her about Darren then?"

Like Linny and me, Darren planned to go to UC Berkeley. It consistently makes the top twenty-five national universities and is way more affordable than out-of-state schools.

Mei let out a shaky laugh. "I'll have to. If I get into both, I'm choosing Stanford. I don't want to do the long-distance thing with Darren."

Linny looked impressed. "You'll turn down Harvard?"

Mei chewed her pinkie again. "I need him nearby to stay sane."

Mei's relationship with Darren kind of amazed me, like how they'd found each other and managed to stay in love

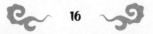

after spending so many hours together. Even my *crushes* didn't last thirteen months. And I failed at the most basic stages of flirting. If a cute boy tried to talk to me, I would start babbling about random things—topics for personal essays, what I'd planned to eat for breakfast but forgot in the microwave, or the miracle of smallpox eradication.

"Not that Ma will listen," Mei added. "She's . . . what's the right word for her, Erin?"

"Implacable?"

Linny swatted Mei on the arm. "Tell her that you're an adult. Tell her you make your own decisions from now on."

Mei shook her head. "I can't. Ma believes in the old traditions. She will always be my elder, and I will always follow her wishes." Mei understood about tradition. A person shouldn't just ignore the rules of a civilization that has thrived for thousands of years. When my ancestors were still trading ax heads, hers were writing poetry while wearing elaborate silk robes.

Linny suppressed a scoffing snort, which sounded similar to holding back a sneeze.

Mei sat up. "Just pray I don't get into Harvard. Unless we . . ." She looked hard at Linny, then shook her head. "If I told you, you'd just try to talk me out of it."

Clearly, the plan she had for thwarting Mrs. Liu fell under the heading of Plan D—D as in deleterious. A waft of cold air swirled past me like a ghost, and goose bumps rose on my neck. I believe in ghosts. Back in elementary school, when Mei and I played ghost-girls, she often chose to be a fox spirit—clever and a little dangerous.

Linny linked arms with Mei. "You can trust us. What's your idea?"

"I'll tell you later. After the Harvard Email of Doom."

Some Chinese tales tell of flower spirits that come to life

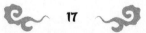

as beautiful maidens. One time, Mei painted my face pink and white and draped me in silk to transform me into a peony spirit. I appeared before a young, handsome traveler as he rode across a meadow on horseback. He proposed to me, of course, and we had a wedding, but ghost marriages only last three days.

Linny kicked me under the table. "Or you could tell us now."

Mei buried her face in her hands. "Can we change the subject, please, before I freak out?"

Linny's phone vibrated. "Your wish has been granted." As she read the text, her eyebrows kept lifting higher and higher. "You won't believe this. Have you ever heard of Westboro Baptist Church?"

Mei and I answered together. "No."

Linny's face lit up so intensely, I thought someone must've flipped a switch inside her. "You know Kevin, that boy I met in the Gay-Straight Alliance? He just texted me. Westboro is some hate group from Kansas. And get this. They're picketing Lowell on Tuesday. It's hella crazy."

I set down my spoon. "Why? They hate brainiac students? That makes *no* sense."

Linny's thumbs went crazy for a moment. "I'll ask Kevin."

While we waited for his answer, I wasted ten million nanoseconds envying Linny's iPhone. I had a TracFone with no minutes left. Plus, my computer died last week, and we couldn't afford to replace it until next month. Mom worked at home translating contracts and other documents from English to Chinese and vice versa. She loved her job, but the pay could've been better.

Linny's phone buzzed in her hand, and she read the screen. "Kevin says that Westboro people hate gays the most. But they

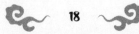

also have a thing against Jewish people, Twitter, Chinese people, Catholics, the United Kingdom, Lady Gaga—"

"I still don't understand why they picked Lowell."

Linny shrugged. "We have an active Gay-Straight Alliance? Sometimes we tweet about Lady Gaga? I don't know. For whatever reason, they're coming." Her phone buzzed one more time. "Kevin wants me to help organize the counterprotest." I could see her molecules trembling with excitement. "You should sing a song about world peace, X."

I raised my hands to my cheeks. "Have you forgotten about my vasovagal episodes?" Stressful situations can simultaneously slow your heart rate and expand your blood vessels, which lowers blood pressure. In nonmedical terms, a girl could faint. I've learned a lot volunteering at California Pacific Medical Center this year. None of it good.

Linny ignored me. "Don't you know 'Hava Nagila' on the violin, Mei?"

"It's been a while since I played it."

"Forget perfection. This is all about overcoming hate." Then Linny started talking so fast, it was a miracle her tongue didn't fly out of her mouth. "We should circulate a petition. Do you know any tech types for doing the sound system? I need help making signs. I have to call television stations. We can rehearse your song this weekend, Erin. Tomorrow."

She paused to text Kevin.

Singing with television cameras present? Everything on Linny's to-do list was on my to-don't list. I could wave a sign, maybe. Over my face. "You know I sing . . ." Like a sick dog. ". . . badly when I'm nervous."

"You have a beautiful voice, X. Twenty-five cents."

Mei slapped my hand playfully. "You're like the Avril Lavigne of Lowell, only quieter and with less eyeliner."

And cleavage. I sang the first line from Avril's song "I'm With You" in a low voice—"I'm standing on the bridge, I'm waiting in the dark"—purposely wandering off-key.

Linny perked up. "So you'll do it?"

"Um."

"Darren can set up the sound," Mei offered. "He's wiring the stage for my . . . Harvard party a week from today." She buried her face in the crook of her elbow, laying her whole head on the table. "What am I going to do?"

Linny curved her arm around Mei's shoulders, and we sat quietly for a moment. Mrs. Liu had installed mirrors along one wall to make the room look bigger, and I could see our reflection—three black heads bent together. I'd dyed my reddish brown hair black a few weeks ago, which made it resemble a giant ball of yarn, but still, sentimental feelings rose up in me. Soon everything would change.

Linny's phone buzzed yet again.

Mei lifted her head at last. "I'll figure it out."

Linny tucked away her phone without reading the new text. "Why don't you ask Miss Fortune Cookie? She's funny and insightful. I bet she totally understands about Chinese mothers."

I sat on my hands, which tend to float upward when I'm nervous. A serving cart crashed into a wall, rattling all the plates. "I don't know. Maybe."

"Think about it." Linny winked at me when Mei looked away. "Call Darren right now about the sound system. We've only got the weekend and Monday to get this all together."

Mei took out her cell but, before making the call, pointed it toward a couple of tourists at a table nearby. "Watch," she whispered. The woman held the soy sauce bottle upside down over her plate, drowning her rice in a dark ocean. "What's the right word, Erin?"

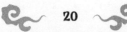

"Tragic?"

"I was thinking *bai tou*." Mei let out an inane hyena giggle.

I froze. Erin=ice sculpture. *Bai tou* literally means *white head*—a non-Chinese barbarian with white skin. It was true that drenching Mrs. Liu's jasmine-scented rice in soy sauce counted as a travesty. But the proper use of Chinese condiments can be learned by anyone, regardless of their DNA. I stood to leave.

Linny slapped Mei on the arm. "Oblivious Comment Alert!"

Panic flashed in Mei's eyes. "I didn't mean *you*, Erin! You're not like that."

"I have to go anyway."

Mei yanked on my arm to make me stay. "I'm so sorry. Sit down, sit down."

"It's okay. Really."

Linny understood I wouldn't give in and stood up to kiss me good-bye. "Come to my house tomorrow, X. We can make signs for the protest and pick a song for you." She squeezed my hand and smiled. "Should we invite Mei?"

Mei looked stricken. "I really didn't mean it."

I sighed. "I know. You should come tomorrow so we can open your email from Harvard all together."

Which made it seem like I forgave her.

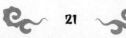

CHAPTER

4

Fate will come looking for you.
Don't bother hiding.

Outside Hay Fat, the gray cold seeped through my clothes, vacuuming away the warmth I'd collected inside. My coat was still in the kitchen, meaning I would have to go get it. My toes have a special talent for whining, and it's ten against one, so they always win. I decided to circle around to the alley entrance to avoid Mei. The odor from her *bai tou* comment still clung to me, like when you eat crab and forget to scrub under your fingernails afterward.

It had history.

When I dyed my hair black, Mei stopped short the first time she saw me, kind of squinting while she gave me the once-over. "You look cute that way." Her eye would've twitched if she were prone to that sort of thing.

"Thanks," I said anyway.

"Are you trying to look Chinese?"

Maybe a little. But was it so terrible to want my hair to match my Chinese heart?

Besides, the *bai tou* comment had even more history. History all the way back to eighth grade, when she dumped me. My stomach started hurting, thinking about it.

When I reached the alley, I heard yelling inside the kitchen. The door banged into the Dumpster, and smoke billowed from the opening. Burying my face in my shirt, I made my way inside. Luckily, the fire had been put out, and as the smoke cleared, I saw the waiter with the PhD clutching a small extinguisher.

Mrs. Liu stood calmly amidst the commotion. "All is hunky-dory."

The waiter yelled in Cantonese and shook the extinguisher at her.

"What he say?" Mrs. Liu asked the chef.

Some people laugh at how first-generation Chinese-Americans speak. The laughers are ignorant of the profound simplicity and elegance of the Chinese language. The Chinese do not conjugate verbs, for example. *Shi* = is. The words *are*, *was*, *were*, and *has been* do not exist in Mandarin.

"You must buy a new stove," the chef told her.

"But they want highway-robbery prices. Throw away stove is big waste."

According to Mom, Mrs. Liu sends more than half her income back to China, which is really generous of her. Still, I think she should use some of the profits to upgrade the restaurant equipment. The situation called for a clever solution, like writing her a threatening letter and signing it The Fire Marshal.

She handed me a greasy paper bag. "Turnip cakes."

*"Xie xie." Thank you.*

I found my coat and headed to Donatello's, where I could be alone for a while. I thought Mei had changed in high

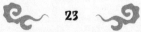

school, that she'd stopped viewing me as outside the community, a friend who wasn't quite Chinese enough. But all these years I'd been fooling myself. Nothing had changed.

The stroll through Chinatown calmed me. Large red and gold signs decorated the entrances to every shop. Boxes of plastic snakes, electronic gadgets, and cloisonné meditation balls spilled onto the sidewalk. While passing the apothecary, I breathed in the scent of dried herbs. So healing.

Just where Chinatown turns into North Beach, a woman lay sleeping in a doorway. A long time ago, I bumped into a box that housed a homeless man, and he grabbed my ankle. I never recovered from that. But when I swerved to avoid this new woman, I noticed a sign scrawled on a paper bag: I'M HUNGRY. So I turned around and set the bag of turnip cakes next to her.

After two long, steep blocks of dragging my heavy school-bag uphill, I arrived at my favorite café, with its gleaming wood counters and delicious coffee smells. The doughnuts sang to me from under the glass, and I pretended ignorance about trans fats and processed sugar. "One chocolate-glazed and a double latte." Except I didn't have enough money. "Change that to a regular coffee. For here."

While the barista brewed a new pot, I read the *Chronicle* at a nearby table. The same instant that I noticed an oily mega splotch on my shirt, probably from cooking at Hay Fat, a group of cute Asian-American boys came in. I recognized one from Recycling Club at school. Practically no one from Lowell lives in Chinatown or North Beach, so it caught me off guard. I lifted the newspaper to hide behind.

"Coffee up!" the barista called out.

Temptation moment—I could abandon my order and sneak away. Unfortunately, the barista knew me by name. "Erin?"

With the bravery of a rodent in the presence of felines, I

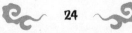

darted forward to grab the mug from her. As I wheeled around, I smacked into one of the boys, launching the croissant off his plate and to the floor.

*Erin + cute boys = Inevitable + disaster*

"Sorry. I'll pay for that." Some time in the future, since I just spent all my money on a cup of coffee.

He seemed to read my mind. "I accept credit cards." His full lips curved upward in a mischievous smile, and his eyes shone. "Candy, too. Twizzlers. Kisses. Hershey's Kisses."

Perhaps his roundish face would've looked more at home on a package of noodles than on the cover of *Rolling Stone*, but my heart pounded anyway. He was exactly the kind of boy who made me blush and stammer—in other words, *my type*, if a girl who's never had a boyfriend can have a type.

"Hey. Hi. Do I know you?" I bit my tongue. Dumb, dumb, dumb. Except that I could blame my lack of eloquence on his amazing dark eyes. They seemed to take in the whole me, inside and out.

"I'm Weyland."

Weyland had nicely shaped earlobes, too. "Hi." I tried to cover the oil splotch on my shirt with my coffee mug, and stepped backward onto his croissant. "Hell on toast. Sorry."

The boy from Recycling Club peeled it from the bottom of my shoe. Before I could thank him, he said to Weyland, "She's Erin."

Had I forgotten to say my name? Clearly, my brain had evaporated, leaving just two pathetic neurons to muddle through. "I go to Lowell. Do you go to Lowell?" I asked.

Weyland's eyebrows slanted upward from the center like the ones on the more attractive anime characters. "I used to go there. My little brother still does." He pointed to the boy

holding the flat croissant, and then ran his fingers through his thick black hair.

It curled up like a wave rising from a moonlit sea. My hand yearned to touch it, and drifted upward by itself, in fact. As I pulled back, blood rushed to my face, and the whites of my eyes felt hot. "I think we've met. I've met your brother, I mean. At Lowell." My coffee was in imminent danger of spilling. "I'm here to . . ." Make a fool of myself. ". . . use the computers. Bye."

"Nice to meet you, Erin," he said, still smiling.

I scampered away to the farthest computer, sat down, and pretended to search something. But Weyland kept looking over at me, distracting me with his attention. Had he really suggested kisses for payment? I blushed, letting my hair fall over my face like a curtain. A patch of light danced along the computer table, and after a moment, I realized that it came from his cell phone. He was catching sunlight from the window and reflecting it toward me. Deliberately. Flirting. But, by the time I gathered the courage to smile back at him, he'd turned away.

Boys can be fickle like that.

So I signed in to my blog and counted the letters in my queue. Four years ago, not long after Mei dumped me, my uncle briefly ghostwrote a celebrity advice column for a gossip magazine. Though I already loved advice columns in general, and worshipped Carolyn Hax in particular, it only occurred to me then that I could create my own. That's how Miss Fortune Cookie was born.

In the beginning, things were slow. I mostly wrote the questions *and* answers myself. By *mostly*, I mean one hundred percent of the time. My first *real* letter didn't arrive until Day 67 of the blog, and contained several grammatical and spelling errors. Still, it shot me over the moon with happiness.

Then, a year and a half ago, my project really took off when a reporter from our student paper—the *Lowell*—wrote an article about it. After that, the *Lowell* began reposting my entries. Last summer, the *San Francisco Chronicle* picked up the story, and I started getting so many letters I could barely answer them all.

Dear Miss Fortune Cookie,

Did you know that fortune cookies aren't Chinese?

Jillian

I could've written this back:

Dear J,

**Miss Fortune Cookie says: If you travel on the road paved by your intelligence, you will not go far.**

Don't act like a smarty-pants when you're an idiot.

Miss Fortune Cookie

Of course I didn't. Instead I sent *Jillian* a polite note pointing her to my tab titled A Short History of the Fortune Cookie. Controversy surrounds the cookie's origin. One faction claims they were first introduced at the Japanese Tea Garden in San Francisco, while a competing faction insists that the owner of the Hong Kong Noodle Co. in Los Angeles invented them to provide encouraging words for unemployed workers.

The next letter made me laugh out loud, but not loud enough to attract Weyland's attention. Darn it.

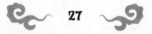

Dear Miss Fortune Cookie,

My best friend stole my boyfriend. Now she's going to the prom with him. Is it wrong to give her mono by drinking from her soda can at lunch?

Tempted

Too funny, but *Tempted* still needed to reconsider her priorities—friend versus boyfriend. Last year, when I had a crush on a certain trombone player, he happened to ask Linny out. Without even consulting me, she turned him down. Between sips of coffee, I searched through my binder of fortunes, looking for something appropriate. My other uncle is always sending me the weirdest ones. I love them all—the ones that predict the future, the ones that give you a compliment, and the ones that remind you of a profound truth.

Dear Tempted,

Can you really give someone mono by drinking from her soda can? I wish they taught us useful things like that in bio.

Seriously, though, **Confucius said: Before embarking on a path of revenge, first dig two graves.** Are you still friends with her? If so, tell her how you feel. If you are no longer friends, revenge won't make anything better.

Miss Fortune Cookie

I wondered if Carolyn Hax would agree with my reply. She's nationally syndicated and hugely talented. In fourth

grade, I would print her letters off the computer and then run up to Mei's apartment to read them with her on the couch. It was our tradition. When Mei dumped me, I quit reading Carolyn's column for a whole year. Rejection can make a person do incomprehensible things.

The air stirred. A thirty-something man in an expensive suit took the computer next to mine. His short blond hair was plastered to his scalp, making his head shine like a glazed lotus bun. A red stamp in the middle would've completed the effect. Immediately I got an icky-stomach feeling, what Mom calls a bad vibe. When *Teen People* came up on his screen, I propped my roller bag between us.

Dear Miss Fortune Cookie,

I can't imagine life without my best friend! So we applied to all the same engineering programs at major universities!!

Now I'm scared because we just had a huge fight! I really, really, really want to go to Cal Tech!! It's number four in engineering!!! She wants to go to Northwestern! But it's only number fourteen! What should I do?

Natalie

Several San Francisco high school newspapers run Miss Fortune Cookie now, so the letter could've come from anywhere. But the question was oh-so-honors-track-Lowell. Since September, most seniors I knew were obsessed with applications, personal essays, recommendations, scholarships, early decisions, et cetera. This letter particularly annoyed me because of Natalie's apparent obliviousness to her good

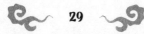

fortune. It's like when the prettiest girl in the class complains that her eyelashes are too thin. Lots of San Francisco high school students wouldn't be going to college at all. It made me want to smash a decorated cupcake.

Dear Natalie,

Stop using so many exclamation points!!!!!!!!!!

I deleted and started over.

Dear Natalie,

**Miss Fortune Cookie says: Always choose opportunity over friendship.**

You will make new friends at college.

Also, you should consider the weather. It snows at Northwestern. Would you really deny yourself sun and warmth for a friend?

Miss Fortune Cookie

I stared at the screen. Would *Natalie* understand the sarcasm? Maybe I should write about my own experience somehow—that Linny and I planned to go to UC Berkeley together. When I agreed to the plan before hearing back from Harvard, Princeton, or Brown, Linny got so excited that she filled out our joint application for student co-op housing the next day. She even bought some furniture for our room-to-be.

Then again, the probability of Harvard, Princeton, or

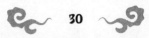

Brown admitting me was so minuscule, a person would need a microscope to see it.

The man in the suit cleared his throat. "Excuse me." He pushed aside my bag. "Can I ask you something?"

There is too much rudeness in the world, which explains why I try to be polite. "Sure."

He loosened his tie. "What's your name?"

Meg Cabot? Except he may have heard of her before. "Erin."

"If I were to buy you a present, Erin, what would you like?"

The ick-feeling worsened. I looked across the café for Weyland, but he had left with his friends. I tried not to fix my eyes on the man's slicked-back hairdo, because it's wrong to judge people by their appearance. "I don't know...." A phone, a computer, a new wardrobe.

"Do you like lingerie?"

"*Pang zhu,*" I said. *Fat pig.* It just slipped out.

His eyes widened. "Gesundheit. Do you have a page on Facebook?"

If I could choose a superpower, it would be the ability to vanish in a shower of sparks. Unfortunately, I didn't have a superpower at all, except for moving fast. Before you could say Nebuchadnezzar, I thrust my binder into my bag, hit the publish button, and left the café. The lotus-bun perv didn't follow me, and after a block of speed-walking away, I felt safe again. And by safe I mean elated. I'd called a man a pig to his face. In Mandarin, but still.

I can be wild like that.

# CHAPTER

# 5

Today your liver will catch fire.

After my escape from the lotus-bun perv and the brisk walk home to our apartment, I pushed open the door to the tiny atrium we call the lobby, catching a whiff of something familiar. Mei was hovering by the wall of mailboxes, a dragon fruit in each hand. We were alone together, and my stomach promptly tied itself into a granny knot. A whistling came from between my teeth. Note to self: Stop doing that.

"Our mail carrier is late," Mei said, offering me a fruit.

I took it from her. Back in our ghost-girl days, we believed that dragon fruit warded off evil spirits. Real dragons would've been more effective, of course, but we didn't have any. "Did you order something online?" I asked.

Her eyes looked a little crazy. "What if Harvard sends a hard copy of the letter before the email tomorrow?"

"You're going to hide the letter from Shoe Fang?"

"Just for a few days." She grabbed my arm, hugging it like

she used to when we scared ourselves silly for fun. "Erin. Promise me you won't tell Ma."

I leaned against her shoulder to give her a sideways hug. For the moment, I let myself forget she called that tourist a white head. "Of course I won't."

She let go of me. "Thanks."

"But—" I interrupted myself because a person should never follow a promise with words of doubt.

A crease appeared between her eyes. "But what?"

"The email from Harvard. Does your mom know it comes tomorrow?"

"I'll delete it before she can see it."

"Won't she just call Harvard admissions?"

Mei squeezed the dragon fruit until it bled onto the floor. "I told Ma that their website announced a delay on decisions."

Um. Though Mrs. Liu distrusted electronics—did her taxes with an abacus, in fact—one of her web-savvy friends would check before long. "Does this have something to do with the plan you mentioned earlier?"

All at once, tears flooded Mei's eyes, which somewhat startled me. The last time she cried in front of me was in sixth grade. We had dressed up as crow spirits, all in black. When she jumped off her bed to fly to her warrior lover's fortress, she landed badly, twisting her ankle so it swelled to twice its normal size.

Mei never fell apart these days. I hurriedly extracted some tissues from my bag. While she buried her face in them, I took the damaged dragon fruit from her, ran it to the trash, and wiped the juice up from the floor.

"I don't want to be apart from Darren," she said, muffled by mucus and paper. "He feels the same way." She lifted her head. "Pearl—you know, my friend from Key Club—keeps

reminding me that long-distance relationships are hard. She seems happy about it."

Pearl, in my opinion, was noisy on the outside and empty on the inside, like how some people revel in the downfall of celebrities, acting jubilant every time Lindsay Lohan gets arrested and sent to rehab. "Pearl's just jealous."

"You think so?" she asked.

"Yes."

Harvard and Darren had so thoroughly consumed her that she forgot to mention anything about Harvard and *me*. Maybe she no longer remembered that I'd applied too. Or maybe she wanted to spare me the embarrassment. Tomorrow, when the emails arrived, our conversation *would* be egregiously awkward.

Me: *Sorry you got in.*

Her: *Sorry you didn't get in.*

Who needed that?

Mei dried her face. "Thanks, Erin." Though her eyes stayed red, the familiar barrier had gone up as if she'd shrugged on her coat and zipped it to her chin. Which made me feel kind of nonexistent. In a bad way. "You look cold. You should go up and take a hot bath," she said, casual now, like we'd been discussing American Lit homework.

"Well, okay." Bringing up the past could wait until *after* she'd heard from Harvard.

"See you later." She pushed the elevator button for me.

"Bye."

Our elevator had gotten stuck between floors at least twice in recent history. Do-it-yourself adventures don't appeal to me, especially ones that involve weaving a rope from your clothes and constructing a grappling hook using only pens and rubber bands. I headed for the stairs.

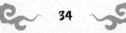

The incident—the event that drove Mei and me apart in eighth grade—unfolded on an ordinary Friday after school in Mei's apartment. She'd made new friends that year, Chinese-American girls she met in a tutoring program, and that afternoon they called to invite her to sleep over. Though I'd never met them, I wanted to go too. Mei said I could.

So I went to my apartment to pack and was happily stuffing my blanket into a garbage bag and deciding between my Raichu and Domo T-shirts for sleeping when Mei came barging into my room. "Tonight's not going to work out." She shielded her eyes with her hand as if I'd transformed into the sun on a cloudless day.

That should've clued me in, but I assumed the best. "They canceled?" I fell onto my bed, inflatable Erin punctured by disappointment.

I can be naïve like that.

The silence lasted a long time. When I finally sat up and looked at Mei, she had backed up against my door. "Listen, Erin. You won't have a good time."

"You're still going?"

"You won't fit in, that's all." She vanished before I fully understood.

Though I already knew that I wasn't Chinese, that afternoon was the first time I considered myself as different and apart from my community. After that, I spent too many weekends staring into a hand mirror at my Irish nose, freckles, and annoyingly bright hair, until I threw the loathsome thing out the window. Luckily, I didn't believe in seven years' bad luck.

Pretty much.

Mei never called to say sorry or invite me over or ask me to see a movie, or anything. And I stopped calling her too. If I came into the kitchen at Hay Fat when she happened to be

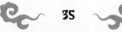

there, she'd walk out. At the apartment, she started taking the elevator to avoid meeting me on the stairs. At least we lived on different floors. It might've been the end of our friendship forever if Linny hadn't invited us both to hang out with her freshman year. We didn't bring up the past, though. At first Mei brushed off my attempts to talk about it, and later it seemed less important because we'd become friends again.

Not like before, though.

Now that I thought about it, letting go of the incident and moving on had been a mistake. We lost something. Next year we'd go to different schools, make new friends, and drift further apart. I didn't want that. I still missed the giddy happiness Mei and I used to feel in each other's company. She had to see how Chinese I was on the inside. My favorite poet was Li Bo.

*I was born in China and lived there until my dad died.*
*I live in Chinatown.*
*I can pick up a single grain of rice with chopsticks.*

And it wasn't like Mei had zero faults. She can be insensitive.

*She talks too much.*
*She often ignores my ideas.*
*And she eats more than her share of the food.*

So there.

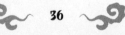

CHAPTER

6

Don't kiss an elephant on the lips today.

When I got to our apartment, I found Mom on her hands and knees, ripping up the floor in the kitchen. I don't know a lot about the proper use of tools, but she had an enormous crowbar jammed under the edge of a linoleum tile, which struck me as excessive. Strands of her ginger-colored hair stuck out as if a strong wind had swept through the room. "Friggin' frig," she said. "Oh hi, Erin."

I went over to smooth her hair and kiss her on the cheek. The scene disoriented me—Mom wearing work gloves, the exposed plywood, and worn tiles strewn about. Though translating documents from Chinese to English didn't pay a ton, she had so much work that home maintenance rarely fit in to her busy schedule. She always hired someone to do little repairs. Or not. When the paint in the living room started peeling, she just covered the worst spots with Art Show posters.

"Can you help me with this?" she asked.

"What are you doing, exactly?"

She lifted the crowbar from below while I pulled on it from above. Just as the linoleum tile flew upward, the metal tool crunched into the wood underneath and Mom fell over. She started laughing. "What do you think I'm doing?"

"Digging for treasure?"

She wiped her forehead with her sleeve. "I thought our apartment could use a little makeover. We deserve a nice place. Check this out." She handed me a stack of samples. "How do you like the Whispering Blue?"

"It's pretty."

She touched the dent she'd made. "I might get Peter to help me tomorrow." Peter was her semiboyfriend who doubled as her tax accountant. They didn't seem that serious, which suited me fine.

*Peter's sense of humor$= \sqrt{-1} = a$ thing that does not exist*

Then again, Mom needed someone so she wouldn't be alone when I left for college. I worried about her rattling around in this empty nest. Not that people rattle.

She arranged the loose tiles over the rough plywood, the perfect setup for tripping the unwary. "I'm hungry. Shufang called to say you made turnip cakes. Can I have one?"

"Sorry," I said. "I gave mine to a homeless woman."

"A Chinese homeless woman?"

"What do you mean?"

Mom snort-laughed. "Most people don't recognize turnip cakes as a comestible item."

But they're buttery soft, savory, and delicious. Just thinking about them made my mouth water. "I'll cook dinner tonight after homework. I need your computer for a bit."

"That's fine. But the Internet is down right now." We tap

into the neighbor's Wi-Fi for free. "Can you do your homework without it?"

I explained about Westboro Baptist Church and Linny's counterprotest. "I'm going to email all my choir friends to see if anyone wants to sing on Tuesday."

"I still have minutes on my cell," Mom said. "Why don't you call them?"

Because email rejections hurt less?

"Thanks." I took her phone and retreated to my sanctuary, my bedroom-that-used-to-be-a-laundry-room. Cozy suits me. I'd painted the walls yellow and strung up dozens of tiny Chinese lanterns for extra cheeriness. My donkey collection occupies a wide shelf beneath the tiny window. I have a thing for donkeys. Butterflies made from bird feathers flutter overhead. They were a gift from Mei in seventh grade. A large black-and-white mounted photograph hangs over my bed— Linny, Mei, and me in the rain by Lake Merced, our bodies blurring together. Darren took it.

My old choir list was rife with divas. I considered them all, and even the possibility of singing something myself, like "Imagine" by John Lennon. I have a better-than-decent voice. I know this because my choir teacher told me so. She complained that I sing too softly, though, and since I couldn't find my volume-control button, I dropped out last year.

I left a bunch of voice messages until the rumbling in my stomach drove me to the kitchen to start dinner. A quick assessment suggested Dragon Phoenix soup, which sounds grander than it is. I heated some broth, threw in leftover meat and veggies, stirred in a few eggs for excitement, and poof: dinner. While Mrs. Liu's shumai defrosted in the microwave, I set the table without taking a single step—one of the many advantages of a nanosized apartment.

"*Chi fan*," I announced. *Come eat.* The direct translation is *eat*, actually.

Mom came out of her room. "This looks lovely, Erin. Thank you." She sat down and slurped from her spoon the way she learned in Shanghai. Traditional Chinese eat with gusto because it makes food taste better. "The Internet came back up while you were in your room. I Googled Westboro Church. They're horrible."

"I know. Linny can't stop talking about them." I chased a dumpling across my plate. The slippery skin and odd shape added to the challenge. Still, I prefer the elegance of chopsticks to the barbarity of a fork.

Mom put both hands flat on the table. "Can you believe their URL is godhatesfags.com? They picketed the funeral of a young man killed in the Iraq War and claimed he died because God hates gays in the military."

"I thought God favors Don't Ask, Don't Tell."

"That's not funny, Erin. Besides, DADT was repealed."

I closed my eyes. "I know."

If I allow myself to think about hate, really think about it, my mind goes to a dark place. Haters have lizards where their hearts should be. Except that's unfair to lizards. Haters are less than human. I hate hate.

Mom touched my arm. "Erin? I didn't mean . . ."

"I'm okay." I opened my eyes.

Mom's cell went off in my jeans pocket, and I got it out. "It's Mrs. Liu."

Mom grabbed it from me. "*Wei.*" *Hello.* Pause. "Did they say for how long?" Slurp. "*Hen qiguai!*" *Very strange.* Slurp. "I'll ask Erin." She covered the mouthpiece with her hand. "Did you hear that Harvard delayed sending out decisions?"

Since I'd finished eating, I stood to clear my bowl, turning

my back toward her before answering. "Yes." Technically speaking. Then I added a second lie to increase believability. "There's a rumor going around that a girl fainted in AP German when she heard the news." I ran the faucet to cover the thumping in my chest.

"Erin says it's true," Mom said to Mrs. Liu.

After a sincere lie goes bad, it keeps growing like some kind of mutant foot yeast. Blerg.

Mom hung up. "Poor Shufang," she said. "I hope Harvard sends the emails before the party next Friday. Aren't you dying to find out if you got in?"

I put the eggs back in the fridge. "Kind of. It doesn't really matter, because I want to go to Berkeley. Don't forget about my scholarship. Besides, Linny and I have already picked our first-semester classes."

Mom rinsed her bowl in the sink. "You should really wait to make up your mind until you've heard from everywhere you applied to. I thought you liked Brown."

I happened to be pouring rice from a plastic bag into a metal tin right then and lost control of the operation, creating an avalanche across the counter. "I won't get in, you know."

Mom clapped me on the back with her wet hand. "That's the spirit."

"Can we change the subject, please?" I stooped to get the dustpan and broom.

Mom sighed. "Sure. May I go with you to Linny's counter-protest?"

My anxiety shifted into some new emotion that involved cringing. Lately Mom wanted to participate in all my activities, and though I liked her company, it made me awkward around my friends. I didn't want to push her away, either. "Of course. Linny will give you a job to do."

"I'm going to dress up as a hippie and dance for peace."

Ack. "Coolio," I said. "Can I borrow your computer now?"

Her smile looked a little thin. Think skim milk. "Go ahead."

After closing the door to my room behind me, I flung myself onto my bed face-first. My friends envied me for having a mom with few rules. She never grounded me or withheld privileges. She knew about Darren but kept the secret from her best friend, Shufang. I tried to feel grateful. Except . . .

*lonely mom = worry to the* nth

Next I did my calculus homework, which totally relaxed me. A little too much, even. I couldn't stop yawning, in fact. After that, I signed into Miss Fortune Cookie and read the first letter in my inbox.

Dear Miss Fortune Cookie,

Thank you for the advice! I'm sending in my acceptance to Cal Tech tomorrow!!! I'm scared to tell my friend, though! Can I do it by email?

Natalie

Oops. In the midst of my freaky encounter with the lotus-bun perv, I'd actually posted my sarcastic reply to *Natalie of the exclamation points.* Luckily, my bad advice actually suited her personality. If she'd attended Northwestern just to be with her friend, she probably would've resented it later, anyway.

But giving her friend the news by email? Abhorrent. Heinous. Shuddersome.

Dear Natalie,

**Miss Fortune Cookie says:** ~~A closed mouth gathers no feet. Just don't tell her.~~ Bad joke!

Tell your friend about your decision when the two of you have time together alone. And bring her favorite treat to sweeten the bitter news. ☺

Miss Fortune Cookie

Two more letters were queued up in my inbox.

Dear Miss Fortune Cookie,

My dad is driving me crazy. Whenever I bring a boy over, he asks a ton of embarrassing questions. Can you do your own laundry? When was the last time you changed the oil in your car? What's your gpa? How fast can you run a mile? And if he doesn't like the answers, he says we can't go out. What should I do to keep myself from strangling him?

Sneaking Around

After a nano-moment, I started writing.

Dear Sneaking Around,

**Miss Fortune Cookie says: Don't force gratitude to live under a rock.**

Seriously, you don't know how lucky you are to even

I stopped and deleted what I wrote. Sometimes it's hard to come up with a good answer, because my heart gets in the

way. Like in this case it upset me that *Sneaking Around* didn't appreciate her dad. Mom met *my* dad in China during an internship after college, when she still hoped to become a translator for the UN. He was Irish-from-Ireland, a businessman, and loved all things Chinese.

Just before my third birthday, while we were still living in Shanghai, he died from a ruptured appendix. Mom says he used to call me Banana and pretend to eat my head. This, apparently, sent me into hysterics. When I gaze at my favorite photograph of us together—on top of the Great Wall of China, my face half-hidden by a gigantic Mongol hat—time stops. Like, I might glance at the clock a minute later, except a whole hour has passed. I wished I had a dad like *Sneaking Around*.

A good columnist has to be objective, though. So I read the letter again, trying to picture *Mom* grilling my imaginary boyfriend that way, and a better reply came to me.

Dear Sneaking Around,

**Miss Fortune Cookie says: A girl with one chopstick will go hungry.**

Think of you and your dad as a team. He's looking out for you, making sure you don't end up with a loser—a slob who will expect you to do his laundry.

Start a conversation with your dad about what to look for in a partner. And—if you don't care about how fast your boyfriend can run—share your feelings on the matter.

Good luck!

Miss Fortune Cookie

Dads are more qualified than anyone else to recognize the hazards of dating. If my dad were alive, I'd ask him for advice about boys. Hypothetically speaking. I had no plans in that department until I'd settled into college. But daydreaming was another matter. I thought about Weyland, editing the memory so I acted suave instead of dorky and he asked me out. When I got to the end of our fantasy date, I considered kissing my pillow, except experience told me it wouldn't be satisfying.

So I kissed my hand instead.

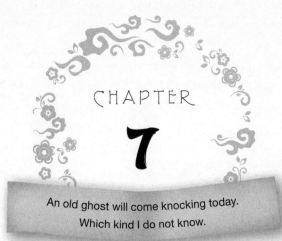

CHAPTER

7

An old ghost will come knocking today.
Which kind I do not know.

I spent Saturday morning—Ivy League acceptance/rejection day—writing a paper for AP World History about the Hmong during the Vietnam War, trying not to think about the zillions of emails set to go out in a few hours. When I finished, Mom offered to drive me to Linny's house. I worried she might decide to stay, so I took Muni instead, bracing myself to face the craziness. One time, an intoxicated medical student on Muni gave Mei a lecture about the dangers of breast implants, as if she, a 34C, were considering them.

"Call me the moment you get the news," Mom said before I left. "And smile!"

I spent the first two stops crammed between shoulder blades and armpits—a frequent fate for those of us suffering from extreme lack of height. Then I spotted an empty seat next to a sleeping man with profuse facial hair that looked like a baby tarsier clinging to his chin. Before I mustered the nerve to check his pulse, he sat up and started rapping a Weird Al song. He had an amazing voice, actually.

When we reached the Sunset, I pulled my hood up against the drizzly fog and walked the block to Linny's stucco two-story. Linny's mom, Adele, greeted me at the door, insisting on throwing my wet sweatshirt into her dryer right away. My freezing hands worried her, as did desertification in Africa, nuclear power plants, and the bee blight.

We got along.

"You look nice," I said, taking in her silk blouse and pretty necklace.

The *San Francisco Chronicle* was spread across the couch, the single untidy thing in her orderly living room. "I'm going out with Benjamin. Can I fix you an afternoon snack before I leave?"

"I just had breakfast. But thanks." When I went into Linny's room, I found her kneeling among cardboard, scissors, tape, and markers. She stood to hug me.

Adele peeked in through the half-open door. "What's all this?"

"Protest posters."

"You know how I feel about protests, Linny. No more, okay? Tear gas causes permanent brain damage." I understood Adele perfectly. Except she drove Linny crazy, which was why I kept my opinions about protests and bee blight to myself.

Linny looked her mom in the eye. "Don't worry. The protest will be at Lowell on school grounds. Even Erin will be there."

"Be careful, then, for me." Adele looked at her watch. "I could make you some ramen."

"We'll cook lunch ourselves and clean up afterward." The moment she shut the door, Linny grinned at me. "By cooking,

I mean opening a jar of Nutella, and by cleaning up, I mean putting the lid back on." Nutella is a chocolate-hazelnut spread from Europe that Linny smears on everything. Even tortilla chips.

I somewhat shared her enthusiasm for it. "Yum."

"Check it out." She grabbed a leather jacket from the floor and put it on. "Tell me I look Italian."

I blew her a kiss. *"Bellissima!"* Her yen to be Italian made me feel better about my desire to be Chinese. "You should be re-created in marble and displayed at the Uffizi. You're so Italian, you use olive oil for perfume."

She laughed. *"Grazie.* I think. Dub found it in the Castro and bought it for me."

I wondered if she'd thought more about . . . the big event she had planned with Dub. She didn't bring it up, though, so I didn't either. "My mom says she wants to come to your protest and dance like a hippie."

Linny glowed. "What a fab idea. We should invite all the parents."

"Good point." If a lot of parents came, that would dilute Mom's presence.

"We could get a dozen dance parties going all at once." Linny's eyes blazed, and she started texting. "I'm asking Kevin to put out a call for boom boxes. Have you decided on your song yet? I'm thinking something with *love* in it to counteract the hate."

I'd never actually been to a protest before and considered it unfair that Linny wanted me to sing in front of everyone my first time. Luckily, a choir friend of mine had called this morning to volunteer. "Mischa wants to do it."

Linny bit her lip. "I don't know about Mischa. She's hella crazy. I heard from Pearl that Gabby got drunk at this party

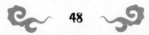

and kissed Mischa's boyfriend, and Mischa threw up in Gabby's shoes for revenge. After that, Mischa posted a picture of Gabby's shoes on Facebook, and then Gabby took a picture—"

I interrupted. "You only have mascara on one side."

"I'm not saying Mischa's bad," Linny said. "I'm just saying she's not exactly the poster child for world peace."

"It's hard to take anyone with asymmetrical eyelashes seriously."

Linny rubbed her eyes impatiently. "Anyway, you sing way better than her."

"I don't want to get arrested." If I got a police record, my scholarship to Berkeley could be revoked, forcing my mom to become a streetwalker to cover tuition. Not that I wanted to let Linny down.

"You need a little excitement in your life."

"Mom couldn't afford to post bail for me right now."

"We won't get arrested, X!"

Instead of arguing further, I studied the collage Mei made after she and Linny did a service trip to Panama last summer. It showed the two of them having a raucous time in dozens of locations. Which made me wistful. Wistful being a euphemism for jealous. A brochure tacked to a corner of the board caught my eye. "Volunteer Partnerships for West Africa." "What's this?"

Linny dug through her bottom drawer, flinging socks every which way. "That reminds me about your computer situation."

"This brochure on your board?"

"Huh? Oh. An organization that interviews women applying for microloans." She moved onto another drawer, this time tossing out scarves. "So they can buy goats and things. I might volunteer with them someday."

"Oooh. I want to buy a goat. Can I get one with curly horns?"

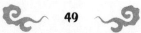

"Ha ha." Linny straightened up, handing me her slightly aged but adorable mini laptop. "I know it's been hard to share a computer with your mom, so I want you to have this."

"Wow, really? Thank you, thank you, thank you!" I said, swimming in happiness. Gratitude really *does* gush.

"I've barely used it since Mom got me my iPhone. Don't mention it to her, though, 'kay? She totally flipped when I gave away my formal dresses to Goodwill. You'd think I'd donated my body to science."

"It probably has something to do with empty-nest syndrome," I said.

"That's true. Thank God for Benjamin. Mom's almost half-sane when he's around."

Whereas my mom had no boyfriend to distract her. I didn't count Peter, because he yelled at the TV during bowling championships, and I knew Mom wouldn't tolerate that for long.

"The computer won't solve your phone problem," Linny said, "but it has Wi-Fi capability. The battery is kind of marginal."

I opened the screen. "It's perfect. Thank you."

"You're welcome. Hey, so . . . Mei decided to come today."

I forced my face to stay cheerful. "Supergreat."

Linny sighed. "Is it the *bai tou* thing? Because Mei totally forgot you weren't Chinese yesterday when she said that. She doesn't care that you're not."

"I guess."

There was a knock on the door. "Hide the computer," Linny whispered. I shoved the laptop up my shirt, which made me look like I might be pregnant with a rectangular alien. Linny threw me a pillow to hide behind. "Come in," she said the second I caught it.

Adele opened the door. "Mei, Darren, and Benjamin are

here. I could make him wait a minute and whip up some real lunch for you."

Linny shook her head. "Just go and have fun."

I wished I'd let Adele make me a snack earlier. "We'll be fine."

Darren had a portfolio tucked under his arm. He is as tall as Mei, lean and golden skinned, with a broad forehead and nice cheekbones. I think of him as a Filipino-American Legolas from the *Lord of the Rings* movies, except with spiky black hair. In a word, *hot*. Mei had brought her violin.

"You came!" I said to Mei, squeezing the pillow to my chest and trying to feel glad.

Mei swooped down to kiss my cheek. "It's because of what you said, Erin. You were right. I need to be with friends today."

She looked all nonleathery and open when she said it. I dropped the pillow and slid the laptop from under my shirt. "Don't ask. It's a long and complicated story."

Darren made a funny face at me. "What are you doing with that?"

"I told you not to ask."

"A science-fair project?"

"That's right," I said, hiding it under my shirt again. "First you incubate a laptop until it hatches. After that, you water it every day with Diet Coke to see what happens."

Everyone but Mei laughed at my nerd humor. Was she mad at me for goofing with her boyfriend? It's just that Darren happened to be the only boy I could talk to without stumbling over my tongue. Not that she had anything to worry about, since Darren truly loved her.

Then the strangest thing happened. Mei handed me a present wrapped in orange tissue paper and vast amounts of tape. "I have something for you." I tore through all the layers

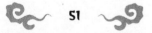

to the photo album underneath. When I opened it up, my breath stopped. The pictures had been stuck in somewhat at random, but that didn't matter.

I squinted at an image of myself with mung-bean sprouts arranged in my mouth to mimic the scraggly teeth of a vengeful ghost. It was taken ten years ago. "I totally remember that day. Where did you find these?"

"Mom has a drawerful. I went through them last night because—" Mei looked at the floor.

To bribe me? To keep me from tattling on her to Shoe Fang?

"To make up for yesterday at the restaurant," she said.

"Thanks." My throat constricted. The gift was more than an apology. It was a declaration. *Those good times we had together are still important to me.* For the first time in a long while, I thought maybe, just maybe, Mei and I could go back to how things were before, back to the kind of friendship with no secrets and lots of trust.

Linny shot me a significant glance. *See?*

I paged through the rest of the album, lingering over a photo of me dressed as a peony spirit. Mei looked over my shoulder and, for the second time that day, kissed me on the cheek.

CHAPTER

8

A mouse dropping will fall into your porridge.

Mei prowled Linny's bedroom, picking things up, putting them down, and checking the clock on her cell phone every minute or less. Darren followed her with his eyes. Linny worked on a protest sign, ignoring them both. I tried to lighten the mood with a joke. "It's one o'clock," I chirped. "Just 360,000 milliseconds until Harvard sends out their emails." No one laughed. Really, a person had to wonder why the Ivy Leagues and other major universities chose to send the news on April 1.

High school senior: *Mom! Dad! I got into Columbia!!!*

Mom and Dad: *Congratulations, princess! This is our proudest day ever.*

High school senior: *April fools.*

Darren patted the edge of Linny's bed. Mei went over, and they sat down at the same time. He put his arm around her. "Whatever happens, we'll be okay," he said. She relaxed into his shoulder.

Linny finished lettering a poster board—SF IS A HATE-FREE ZONE. "You know what I found out?" she said. Without waiting for a reply, she started talking at approximately one hundred kilometers per hour. "Westboro has a ton of stops in SF besides Lowell—Twitter headquarters, the Jewish Community Center, the Golden Gate Theater. They'll run themselves ragged."

"Why the Golden Gate Theater?" Darren asked.

"They're staging a production of *Fiddler on the Roof*."

Gah! Targeting a theater for putting on a Jewish musical? Lovely people. What if they decided to go beyond shouting hateful slogans on Tuesday? The large signs they carried weren't exactly harmless. With their long handles, they made convenient weapons, if you thought about it. "Are you sure we know what we're getting into?"

"The police will set up a barricade. That's what Kevin told me," Linny said.

Mei dropped to the floor next to Linny, all dark and broody. "If I could go back in time, I would sabotage my application to Harvard somehow. I know it sounds crazy."

It *did* sound severely insane, actually. "You could've spelled it H-a-r-v-*e*-r-d on the envelope," I joked.

Linny capped her Sharpie with unnecessary violence. "Can't you see I need a little help here? No more college talk until the emails come, 'kay?"

I wondered if her grouchiness stemmed from more than Mei's extravagantly obsessive behavior. Linny didn't have an email waiting for her—good or bad—because she hadn't applied to anywhere but the UCs. Mei ran her thumbnail across her bottom incisors, struggling not to bite down. I picked up an orange neon marker and started coloring in the letters on Linny's poster.

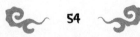

"I brought sheet music for 'Hava Nagila,'" Mei said. "I could do a run-through."

"That's what I'm talking about," Linny said.

While Mei tuned her violin, Darren opened his portfolio. "I went through my photos. One of these would work for a flyer to advertise the protest." He spread out some poster prints—a close-up of hands entwined; a man in a yarmulke embracing a woman in a bright blue sari; a toddler with a halo of wispy blond hair wearing a peace-sign shirt.

"Wow," I said. "I haven't seen these before. No wonder you won that prize." Recently, a San Francisco company had awarded him first place in their photography contest.

Darren smiled modestly.

"They're amazing," I said. "You should show them to Mei's mom. They would totally win her over."

He cleaned his glasses and puffed out his chest with mock supergeek pride. "I am Locutus of Borg. Resistance is futile."

*Geeks > (Dudes)$^2$*

Mei lifted her violin and started to play, each note strong and fluid. Darren got up to dance along, crossing his arms Cossack style and flinging his legs forward. When Mei made a mistake, he froze in place with the toes on one foot pointing upward, which was kind of funny. I laughed, in fact, until Mei tried again and missed the note a second time. Her roar of frustration wiped the smile from my lips.

In a nanosecond, Darren transformed from clown to supportive boyfriend. "You'll get it, Mei." That counts as a superpower, I think.

Mei *did* get it on the next attempt, nailed it to the wall without seeming to try, then played it through three more times

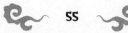

before putting her violin away. The final version bordered on distressingly flawless to my mortal ears. She exchanged a sweet smile with Darren.

"God you're good," Linny said.

Mei sucked her lips into her mouth. She dislikes it when one of us says *God* casually. She's okay with Linny saying *hella* though. I love my friends, but they could be less complicated.

Linny noticed Mei's disapproving look as well. "*Gosh* you're good. Your turn, Erin."

"No, thank you."

"Just a few verses, 'kay? It's not that hard," Linny said.

I could sing just fine. I just didn't want to. So I channeled the worst songbird ever, the macaw, smoothed my feathers, opened my beak, and squawked the words to "Imagine" until Linny threw a pillow at me. "Be that way. You can make signs while I set up a Facebook page. The talented duo can make the flyers."

After taking a moment to revel in my victory, I thought about what to write on a sign.

GAY RIGHTS NOW! Except that was boring.

LET FAIRIES MARRY! Cute. Except intolerant people used *fairy* as an insult. Besides, it might upset Mei, who didn't care one way or the other about sexual orientation but believed gay marriage went against the church.

From what I'd seen on the Internet, Westboro pickets always included the sign GOD HATES FAGS! How about the exact opposite? GOD LOVES FAGS! Which made me positively bubble with laughter. Unfortunately, it fell into the category of politically incorrect.

So I changed it to GOD LOVES GAYS! Then again, God was a touchy subject for a lot of people, not just Mei, though I felt certain that He/She would approve of any sign I made.

I looked around the room. Mei was busy spreading glue on the back of one of Darren's poster prints while he held it flat. Linny tapped away on the computer keyboard. No one could hear my inappropriate thoughts. Thank Gosh.

Finally a safer idea came to me. "All you need is love," I said aloud. "What do you think?"

Linny swiveled in her chair. "That's not bad, X. Go for it." She stretched her arms over her head. "I'm going to blow off my AP tests in May."

Mei jumped up off the floor. "What? Why?"

"What difference do they make?"

I drew an Art Deco heart in the upper corner of my board and added a tail blowing in the wind. Mei put her hands on her hips. "Earth to orbit-Linny. If you pass the APs, you get to skip all the lame intro classes in college."

"I need to do *something* out of the ordinary to wake myself up," Linny said, sliding off the band that held her ponytail together and shaking her hair at Mei.

My neurons clicked sharply, like when you snap your fingers, only quietly because it happened inside my head. This might explain Linny's impulse to have a less-than-meaningful intimate experience with Dub.

Both Darren and Mei spoke up at the same time. "Dye your hair pink," Mei said. "Dye your hair blue," Darren said. They looked at each other and cracked up.

"Or both," I said.

Linny stuck out her tongue. "Pink *and* blue?"

Glancing first at Darren, Mei opened her mouth to say something. A nuance in his expression stopped her, though. Then he raised his eyebrows at her and lifted his chin. Mei must've understood what that meant, because they both headed for the door.

"I'm hungry," she said over her shoulder. "And we brought a treat." So we gathered in the kitchen, where Mei opened a box of iced Mickey Mouse cookies. "Darren bought them, actually."

Our benefactor hopped onto the counter, holding a cookie next to his head. "Any resemblance?"

"Your ears stick out more," I teased.

Linny reached into the cupboard. "You know what would make these even better? Nutella." She spread the brown goo right over the icing. "Now I can die happy."

Darren took a bite of cookie, bugged his eyes out, and lifted his hand to his throat. "Cookie. In. Esophagus," he gasped. "No. Air." He fell onto his side.

Mei slapped him. "Stop that. Joking about death is bad luck."

He sprang to life, then scooped her up and kissed her. For a very long time. With his tongue. I couldn't stop myself from noticing, and by noticing, I mean gawking. Sometimes it seemed as though they'd invented their own category beyond boyfriend-girlfriend, glomming into a single boygirlfriend.

When they stopped, Mei smirked at me. "Erin needs some romance in her life."

Behind his glasses, Darren's eyes glittered with mischief. "Should we set her up? You're into dark and handsome, right?"

My eyes rested on his face too long. When Mei swatted me, I blushed and drifted out of the kitchen. "I don't want Darren. I mean, you're supercute and all. . . . I mean I would . . ." Kiss you. ". . . except I wouldn't. . . ." I collapsed into the mound of Panda accent pillows on the couch.

Everyone followed me to the living room. "We can find someone for a pretty girl like you," Darren said, "not that I've ever noticed your looks, since I only have eyes for Mei. It's just this rumor I've heard."

Linny sat down next to me. "Maybe you'll meet someone at the protest. Like I did."

Except a boyfriend would mess everything up right now. I had my future to consider—AP tests, final exams, graduation, moving to college.

And most important, kissing lessons.

Mei sat down on the other side of Linny. "Did you tell your mom about the protest?"

"Of course I did," Linny said. "She made me swear up and down I wouldn't accept candy from strangers or run with scissors. Otherwise she was fine with it."

Mei's eyes narrowed. "I don't believe you."

"I could've hid it from her, because she's leaving on a business trip Monday afternoon. But I didn't lie about it. Not like some people."

Darren cleared his throat and shook his head at Linny. I studied the painting of a teapot on the opposite wall. Mei flushed. "My situation is different from yours. If I tell Ma the truth, she'll ground me until I leave for Harvard." Suddenly her eyes widened, and she slapped her forehead. "This is perfect! We can have a party at your house on Monday."

Had I missed something?

"A party? I'll be crazy busy Monday," Linny said.

"Come on. Not really a party. Just the three of us—you, me, and Erin. I'll tell Ma that we have a group project for school. Please, please, please?"

"I'll think about it," Linny muttered. Tepid soup would've sounded more enthusiastic.

But Mei high-fived Linny anyway and followed it with a complicated handshake closely resembling patty-cake with elbows. While Darren taught them the proper dude shake, I had the misfortune of noticing a sliver of fabric between the

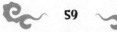

cushions, and foolishly yanked on it. A pair of men's plaid boxer shorts popped out. I threw them across the room with a minishriek.

Linny howled with laughter. "Benjamin's. He's always leaving his stuff where it doesn't belong. You wouldn't believe the things I find. Like the time I came across his—"

"Too much information!"

"—bottle of hair-growth promoter. He doesn't have a bald spot, so I had to wonder."

Mom never let her boyfriends stay over at the apartment. At this particular moment in time, I considered it a boon.

Mei looked at her phone and sprang up from the couch. "It's two-oh-two!" she yelled. We all raced to Linny's computer. While Darren opened her account, Mei's face changed from excited to scared to excited, like the oscillator we once observed in physics. "There's an email from Harvard," she squeaked. "I might throw up." She plucked at her sleeves and bit her knuckle. "I'm shaking like a . . . What am I shaking like, Erin?"

"You're shaking like a girl about to be rejected."

Not that I believed it. Mei had more than just academic smarts. She excelled in music, sports, and organizing events. Her interpersonal skills with certain girlfriends could possibly be better, but that kind of thing didn't show up on college applications. Admissions committees might even favor self-centeredness.

Darren stood up to fold Mei into his arms. "Breathe," he said.

The air in the room stopped moving altogether, except for a few molecules of carbon dioxide that escaped my mouth when I randomly gasped for no reason. When we all moved closer to the screen in unison, readying ourselves for the moment, Linny and I clunked heads. "Ow!"

Darren finally clicked on the email. "I am delighted to inform you . . ."

Silence reigned. At this very moment across the globe, approximately eighteen hundred applicants to Harvard were absolutely ecstatic, dancing with glee in front of their computers, whooping and throwing things. Mei was ghostly pale.

Darren smiled first. "You got in. I knew you were a genius."

The bright-side approach seemed wise, so I followed Darren's lead. "Your mom was wrong. Having a boyfriend didn't drag you down." Mei had to feel a little excitement about getting accepted. Who in their sane mind wouldn't?

Mei shifted out of Darren's arms and looked up at him. "I know I'm really lucky, but I don't want to move that far away from you."

He looked into her eyes. "I know."

"What if you get into Stanford?" Linny said. "Your mom would be thrilled."

Which proved that Linny didn't understand Mrs. Liu at all. Last time I checked, *U.S. News & World Report* had ranked Harvard as the number one university in the country. Stanford came in at number four. To make it worse, Chinese people consider four an unlucky number because in Mandarin the word for *four* sounds the same as the word for *death*.

Mei wrinkled her nose. "I know what Ma will say. What medal do they give when you come in fourth at the Olympics? No medal."

Darren stretched his mouth into a copy of a smile. "I beat up a dragon with nunchucks yesterday. I can deal with her."

"Ma's not some video-game dragon," Mei snapped.

He sobered up immediately. "I'm sorry. I didn't mean that."

Mei softened too. "No, I'm sorry. You were just trying to

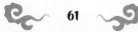

make me laugh. I'm so upset right now, I don't know what I'm saying."

Linny and I went to the living room to give them privacy. "Do you want to check your email?" she asked me.

I imagined it for a moment. Sympathy would ease the pain when Harvard, Princeton, and Brown rejected me, but it might feel even better after I'd recovered somewhat from the first cold shock of disappointment. Like when you drag yourself out of a freezing ocean and there's a person waiting on shore with a warm towel. That's nicer than if a person throws a towel at you while you're still in the water.

"Maybe later," I said.

# CHAPTER 9

An unpleasant delight awaits you.

I sat in the back of Darren's van on the ride home from Linny's, leaning against the raw metal door, looking out the window. Last year, Mei had sewn fuzzy leopard seat covers to brighten the interior. Outside, the fog had burned off, and steam rose from the shiny street. Inside, a gloom emanated from Mei that pressed down on the three of us. I turned sideways and tried not to eavesdrop.

Unsuccessfully.

Darren remained calm, almost cheerful. "Let's talk to your mom. Let me meet her, at least. I might be able to change her mind."

"She doesn't care about anything except Harvard," Mei said, sounding more vulnerable than angry. She never wore her second skin with him, a fact that somewhat bothered me. Bones really *can* be jealous.

Darren kept talking in a relaxed voice. "Stanford is a top-end school. It's just as good as Harvard." While Linny and

I were in the living room, Mei had gotten an acceptance letter from Stanford, a second life-changing email zinging through the cable lines just minutes after the first one—a miracle of modern communication.

Mei sighed. "I wish Ma could see it that way. Then we could be together on the weekends."

"I'm glad I robbed that bank and used the loot to bribe the dean of admissions," Darren joked. "It turned out to be my smartest move ever."

Mei kind of laughed. "I thought you were up to something."

"Your ma will let you go to Stanford when she sees how much I love you."

Mei shook her head sharply, like a fly had buzzed her ear. "She doesn't believe in love."

"What if Stanford gives you a better scholarship?"

Mei shook her head again.

Inside my personal globe of silence, I worried that Darren might say the wrong thing. *Your ma has no right to dictate our lives*, for example. Something Linny might come up with. I cranked open a window—the van was that old—and stuck my head into the sun-kissed air, hoping for a long run of green lights. Darren never did say anything wrong though. He understood about loyalty to family. Instead he said, "Harvard *is* an incredible opportunity."

"I know." Mei sounded almost meek now.

"I'm here for you," Darren said. "Whatever you decide, we'll be fine."

That melted me despite the cool air pouring in through the open window.

After Darren dropped us by the apartment, Mei sat down on the low wall near the lobby door. The unstable mood from the van persisted, as if a mini storm cloud had taken up

residence above her head. "How do I choose between the two things I care about most?" she asked, her eyes haunted.

She wanted advice from me, the lesser third? What could I say that would possibly help? I sat down next to her. "It's not really choosing between them. You won't break up with Darren if you go to Harvard."

Her eyebrows came together. "But it *is*. I'm so happy when we're together. Before I met him, I was just grinding through the days. He makes me into a better person than I am by myself—happy and funny. Without him I'm so . . . I feel like a . . . lump. What's the word for that, Erin?"

Incredibly romantic? He breathes life into you. "Love?"

She looked at me, almost begging. "I'm asking as a true friend. Don't be nice. Just imagine yourself in my situation."

One of my smaller organs flopped inside me—my gallbladder, maybe, or my pancreas. "How can I imagine it? I've never even had a boyfriend. We're too different."

"We're not so different. We're both ghost-girls, right?"

*But you said I wouldn't fit in.*

I scooted toward her, took one of her hands from her lap, and squeezed her fingers. They were long and beautiful except for the single callus on her pinkie knuckle. I decided to start with the basics. "If you and Darren had never fallen in love, which would you choose? Harvard or Stanford?"

She made a familiar face at me—eyes half-closed in disbelief, cheeks stiff—looking exactly like an annoyed donkey, in fact. "Hello? Who wouldn't pick Harvard?"

Um. "So you're willing to give up Harvard for Darren?"

Her knuckle went into her mouth. "You don't understand. I wouldn't give up Harvard to be near just *any* boy. But I'll never love someone like I love Darren." She jumped up and crisscrossed the sidewalk like a dog on a very short leash.

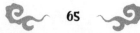

My freshman science teacher at Lowell used to roam the aisles the same haunted way, until one day he leapt out the window without warning. Fortunately, the window happened to be open and the classroom happened to be on the first floor. Still, he didn't come back the following semester.

"Do you think I should do something...drastic?" Mei asked.

"Drastic?" I echoed, standing too.

Her eyes pleaded with me until I had to close my own to protect myself. Then she exhaled slowly. "It's not your problem, Erin. I don't mean to lay this on you. You're a good friend."

Her gaze was almost sweet now, which made me want to forget that the past had ever happened. Yet it remained the elephant in the room, a weighty African pachyderm with dusty skin and long, pointy tusks. Or in this case, the elephant in the alley. I marshaled my courage. "Do you remember that time in eighth grade? That sleepover you got invited to?"

Her body went rigid for a second, as if I'd jabbed her unexpectedly. Then, all at once—zip, zip, zip—she turned smooth except for a concerned furrow down the middle of her forehead. Maybe I'd imagined the first part. "Sort of. Did we have a big fight at the sleepover?"

"No. You really don't remember? You made new friends in that tutoring program. Then you said I couldn't go to their party because I wasn't Chinese."

Mei's eyebrows flew up. "I did? But you practically *are* Chinese."

Which sounded pretty great coming from her. "That's how I remember it."

She put her arm all the way around me. "I'm so sorry if I hurt your feelings. Are you sure I said that?" Her phone went

off. *"Wei."* Pause. "I'll be right up." She brushed off the back of her pants. "That was Ma wanting me home."

"Are you going to tell her about Harvard?"

"I don't know. I'll call you." She went into the lobby and then came back out halfway, her head and shoulders protruding through the crack in the door. "I'm so sorry about that sleepover thing."

"Forget about it. Thank you for the photo album." I put my hand over my heart. "It meant a lot to me." I tried to gauge her reaction, but her face didn't tell me anything.

"Don't say anything to Linny, okay?" she said. "About me . . . doing something drastic. I didn't mean it. Erase it from your mind."

"Erased."

After she left the second time, I stayed outside to soak up the sun, imagining the photons bouncing against me, imparting infrared energy to my skin. Mei had gotten all absorbed into her own crisis and ruined the moment. True, she *had* apologized about eighth grade like I'd always wanted her to. Except . . .

*I'm sorry* if *I hurt you* ≠ *I'm sorry* that *I hurt you*

Plus, the part about not remembering struck me as weird and not entirely honest. Sincere lies protect people's feelings, but this felt like the other kind—a self-serving lie.

Something moved, and I looked up to see Armageddon Guy lurching toward me from across the street, all six-and-a-half feet of him, his lank black hair streaming down his face. I scrambled up from the wall, escaped into the lobby, and ran up the stairs. One time, he mesmerized me with the intensity of his eyes and then yelled into my face, "The end is near! Brush your teeth!" Which made me laugh (afterward) because he had horrible breath. Still, I preferred to avoid him.

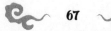

Inside the apartment, Mom stood near the top of a ladder in our living room, scraping at the peeling paint with a putty knife. She had covered the furniture with plastic sheeting, at least. I shut the door behind me. "I'm home."

She pointed at me. "Well? Did you get in? You didn't call me!"

"I haven't checked my email yet. It was kind of crazy at Linny's." I changed the subject. "What's going on in here?"

"I lost the Hubei Chop Suey account, and now I have the afternoon off."

I set down my bag. "Oh."

"Don't scowl at me, Erin, we'll be fine. This room could use some fresh paint anyway, don't you think? I've seen dungeons in BBC miniseries with cheerier walls. I can't believe you didn't check your email. You must be dying to know."

Pretty much. "I can guess."

She stepped down from the ladder. "Don't be a pessimist. Let's go look right now."

My stomach clenched. "In a little while." I really, really, really wanted to open my emails in private, freak out on my own, and *then* face all the disappointed looks and sympathetic pats when I felt stronger.

Mom looked so surprised, you'd think I'd signed up to become a skydiving instructor. Fortunately, she backed off. "Help me pick a color for the walls. You should have a vote, since there's still a chance you might live here and commute to Berkeley."

I studied the color charts she handed me. "I might move in with Linny."

"Or move to Rhode Island to go to Brown." She pointed to one of the little squares. "I'm partial to the Van Alen Green."

"It's nice."

After that, I dug out the supplies I'd used to repaint my room from under my bed. Among the brushes and rags, I found two scrapers. Mom fetched a second step stool, and we worked side-by-side for a while, chips of dusty ecru paint accumulating below us. "What would I do without you?" she said.

I enjoyed doing projects with her, actually. She asked me about my day at Linny's, and I filled her in on the sign making and violin playing and cookie eating. Finally, I admitted that Mei had gotten in to Harvard. "The rumor about delayed decisions wasn't true," I added, covering for my earlier lie. "They sent the emails today."

"That means you have an email from Harvard too," she said.

"Maybe they lost my application."

Mom snorted. "Mei must be so happy."

No! "Kind of. But she got into Stanford, too. She wants to go there because Darren is going to UC Berkeley, and then they wouldn't be two-and-a-half-thousand miles apart."

"Stanford. Wow, that's great."

Arrgh! We were like two novice Urdu speakers trying to discuss the theory of relativity. "Mrs. Liu won't like it. Mei hasn't told her any of this yet. Promise you won't mention it to her."

Mom took a break and plopped onto the plastic-covered couch, getting paint dust all over her clothes. "My lips are sealed. But Shufang will have to find out eventually."

I noticed a sort of exhausted pastiness to her complexion. "Mom. Is there something you're not telling me? Are you ... nesting?"

She sat up straight and guffawed at me. "I'm not pregnant, if that's what you mean. One crazy daughter is enough for me. I don't even have a boyfriend."

She didn't consider Pete-the-accountant her boyfriend? A

minifiesta started up in my heart, complete with a little mariachi band. His hostile goatee got on my nerves.

"I haven't been sleeping well. Maybe it's the full moon." She stood up. "I'm going to take a quick nap and clean this up later. Wake me if you decide to open your emails."

As soon as she left, I powered up Linny's laptop in my bedroom with the door closed. When I joined the network, all three messages zipped into my inbox, sitting there patiently—one from Brown, one from Princeton, and one from Harvard. Though I expected three rejections, little bits of excitement fizzed through me of their own accord. I flung myself onto my bed and tried to talk sense to myself.

*hubris = future retribution from the Greek gods*

My lecture didn't work, so I clicked on the message from Brown anyway, the pixels on the screen vibrating with anticipation. A nano-moment later, the universe collapsed around me. Brown—a mecca for intellectuals—didn't want me. The weight of the neutrons spiraling inward shrunk me to the size of a bug. Disappointment really does *crush* a person. I barely had the strength to slide the cursor to the email from Princeton.

Click. Another rejection.

This time a few tears leaked out and my lungs got all sticky. Since I felt intensely horrible already, I decided to get the last rejection over with. I opened the message from Harvard and read the words beneath the crimson shield wreathed in oak. *Veritas.* Truth.

The tears froze in my ducts.

$O(h)^2$

$M(y)^5$

$G(\text{osh})(od)^{nth}$

How had this happened?

CHAPTER

# 10

You will fall into a ditch.
Don't stay there.

Harvard wanted me. I screamed with shock and happiness—quietly though, to avoid disturbing the neighbors. The man in the apartment to our left sometimes called the police if we turned up the volume on the TV too high. Then I threw every last one of my donkeys into the air, not even bothering to catch them as they came raining down. Why is there never real confetti handy when you need it?

After that, I stood on my head for an entire minute, using my beanbag as a cushion and the wall to balance against. Chinese medicine doctors recommend headstands to boost alertness. I mainly do it to see the world upside down. It gives me a fresh angle on things. A new perspective. Like realizing that Harvard probably sent me the wrong letter by mistake. Brown and Princeton had sent rejections, after all. I flipped to upright again to check. The email from Harvard had my full name on top and appeared authentic.

When I crossed the apartment to deliver the news, I found

Mom in bed, reading. "Are you feeling okay?" she asked. "Your face is flushed."

I told her what had happened in two long words. "BrownandPrincetonsaidno butHarvardsaidyes!"

She sprang up and muffled me in a hug. "Erin! That's fantastic. You got in. It's incredible. You're going away to Harvard." She let go and looked at me with sad, shining eyes. "How will I live without you?"

Which pretty much doused my fever with a giant bucket of cold water. Mom would die of loneliness if I left.

I backed up to the doorway. "I didn't say I would go."

Her face dropped. "Oh."

"It's horribly expensive. We can't even afford minutes for my phone."

The lines around her eyes softened. "Is that all? My low income bracket will be an advantage when it comes to aid packages. And we'll buy you minutes next week, I promise. You'll survive until then, right?"

I lowered my gaze. "I don't want to go to Harvard," I said. "Linny and I have already planned to be at Berkeley together."

Mom rested her hands on my shoulders, staring me straight in the eyes. "This is your future here, not a slumber party. You should give it some real thought."

I wanted to pull away, but I kept my limbs perfectly motionless. Still, my insides wiggled a little. "I *have* thought about it." Linny was like my favorite comfort food—sesame balls, the Chinese version of cinnamon-sugar toast—warm and sweet with an edge of tang and crunch. The weird things she said made me feel okay about the weird things I said. I couldn't let her down. Besides, my decision made life better for Mom, too. Without me close by, she would end up completely alone. "Can we talk about something else?"

Mom straightened her bedside rug with her foot. "What else should we talk about?"

"Celebrities in rehab?"

Dinner was an awkward meal. Mom didn't bring up Harvard but kept gazing at me till I wished I could disappear. The long silences didn't help, either. I considered raising the core issue—how she'd fall apart without me—but didn't. Why make her feel bad unnecessarily? While we cleaned up the kitchen together, I finally mentioned a related topic. "Do you mind not telling Mrs. Liu that I got in, you know, to Harvard?"

Mom needled me with a look. "Why not?"

Could it be more obvious? "Mei hasn't told Mrs. Liu the news yet. Plus, when Mei finally does come clean, the fact that I got in could make it more awkward for her."

Mom scrunched her face together. "I don't understand."

I retreated to the living room. "It just would. I'm going out with Lok."

A neighbor had hired me as a dog sitter for Lok, a zippy Pekingese, every Saturday evening. On the downside, walking a dog is a euphemism for letting him do his business in the Great Toilet Outdoors. And the owner paid me in dimes. But Lok's tragic face and jaunty stride had stolen my heart. He had floppy orange ears and a green tail dyed to match the chrysanthemums on his collar. And dimes add up.

The moist air bit through my clothes as I hurried down the deserted alley. When we reached the busy street, where we could linger safely, I stopped to let Lok sniff the dirt under a eucalyptus tree, and to think. Though I'd decided not to go to Harvard, the acceptance letter still made me dizzy. Had Miss Fortune Cookie tipped the scales in my favor? Though I took the blog seriously, I assumed others wouldn't because of

my sometimes-silly answers. I almost hadn't shown it to my Harvard interviewer.

I bent over to clean up Lok's little gift, and when I straightened up, a white shape swirled across the unlit window next to me. Then I heard a loud thump, like a ghost beating someone up. Without waiting to verify the precise details, I scooped Lok into my arms and sprinted toward home, only daring to look back once.

Which was enough excitement for me on a Saturday night.

Mom had two cups of ginger tea waiting. Since I still didn't feel like talking about Harvard, we discussed the implications of Linny's counterprotest until I thought my ears would fall off. After tea, I hid out in my room to do my calc homework in bed. *Determine the maximum volume of a right circular cone inscribed in a sphere, where* $r = 3$. I sighed. Just because I have a math brain doesn't mean I find each problem equally fascinating.

To make things more interesting, I lay down and considered it in a different context. Did Mei, Linny, and I form a triangle or a cone? Linny would be the apex in either case, the highest point. Now that Linny had a secret from Mei, and Mei had a secret from Linny, though, I no longer felt so much like the lesser third. Our friendship had become equilateral.

I must've fallen asleep, because the next thing I knew, a crash in the living room startled me, revving my heart to maximum. I sat up and looked at my clock. It was 2:00 a.m. If that ghost from earlier followed me home, I hoped it wasn't the headless kind that lived in the ceiling and fed on a person's soul with its long tongue.

I listened carefully for clues. There was soft bumping, rustling, and occasional footsteps outside my room. After a minute, I tiptoed to my door and pressed my eye to the crack. Mom sat

cross-legged on the plastic sheeting, sorting through cardboard boxes. My heart rate decelerated, and I went to join her. "Mom? What's going on?"

She looked a bit dazed. "Did I wake you?"

I dropped down next to her, pulling my T-shirt over my knees. "Sort of."

"Sorry. I'm cleaning out my closet. Moths have gotten into my papers."

"Do you want some help?"

She squeezed me in a sideways hug. "I'm fine. Go back to bed."

I did, except my eyes refused to close on their own. The middle of the night was my time for action. Mom wanted me to sleep regular hours, say 9:00 p.m. to 6:00 a.m., a wholesome, sedate, and entirely laughable ambition. If I did, when would I complete the mountains of homework assigned by my teachers, comment on my friends' blogs, and write Miss Fortune Cookie letters?

Leaving my light off so as not to worry Mom, I opened Linny's laptop. The emails from Brown, Princeton, and Harvard were still there. I signed in to Miss Fortune Cookie.

Dear Miss Fortune Cookie,

My friend likes to go out for lunch all the time. I don't have much money, so I order cheaply. My friend always eats way more than I do, and then she wants to split the bill. When I try to pay for my share, she says, "I hate people who make a fuss over a few dollars." What should I do?

Mad

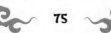

I had a friend like that freshman year. Whenever we passed the vending machine, she happened to be broke and hungry. She never offered to pay me back. When I finally mentioned how much she owed me, she couldn't afford it. Then, two days later, she had the nerve to show off a pair of boots she'd just bought at Nine West, and I thought about asking for them in exchange for funding a year's supply of cheese crackers for her. Not that I ever would.

Dear Mad,

**Miss Fortune Cookie says: The richer your friends, the more they will cost you.**

Then again, the Beatles said money can't buy you love.

Maybe they mean the same thing.

Here's a little practical advice. Whenever you go out with your friend, tell her you're not hungry. Don't order anything, and see what happens.

Miss Fortune Cookie

Fixing *other* people's problems was somewhat simple. When it came to my own issues, I had Linny to guide me—like helping me decide what to wear in the morning when the weatherman predicted that the fog would burn off by noon. But sometimes a hard letter landed in my queue.

Dear Miss Fortune Cookie,

Lowell ruined my life. I was happy when I got in. Now that it's senior year, I'm disillusioned.

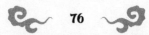

Every UC I applied to rejected me. I'm going to City College next year.

If I'd stuck with my local high school, I would've been at the top of my class. My best friend avoided Lowell. Now he's going to UC San Diego, and I'm smarter than he is.

Middle school nerds, take heed. Don't come to Lowell!!!!!

Matt

Ack. A lot of Lowellites feel this way. The high brainiac ratio makes ordinarily smart people suffer. Even so-called *gifted* students like me get lost in the craziness. My GPA could be better, for example. And I'm one of the lucky ones, because I enjoy learning and don't mind studying for a zillion hours straight. I think it's fun, even.

I thought about how to respond to *Matt*. Whenever I get too lavishly pleased with myself about an A on an assignment, Mom reminds me that success takes more than good grades. She says there are many ways of being smart. Some people can communicate at a higher level or think more deeply or move their bodies with split-second precision. Life isn't just about acing a multiple-choice test.

I know Mom's right, because when I do activities that require coordination, my body has a low IQ. Since academics come easily, I get impatient with how long it takes me to learn things like dribbling a soccer ball. Fortunately, my SAT scores weren't linked to my ability to mingle at parties, either. I understood *Matt*, got how much it sucked to wallow in the bottom third. Still, *Matt* didn't have to know the specifics of my deficiencies. I'm a giver of advice, not a model citizen.

Also, I loved Lowell and wanted to defend it.

Dear Matt,

**Miss Fortune Cookie says: The water that ~~floats~~ sinks your boat will also ~~sink~~ float it.**

Don't you have good memories from Lowell along with the bad? Maybe you learned some cool things, made true friends, or did an amazing project. Maybe one teacher really inspired you.

I'm an optimist. Sorry! ☺

Since Lowell prepared you well, you'll ace your classes and transfer to the university of your choice. Did you know that O. J. Simpson went to City College before attending USC?

It's not about what you know, but what you do with it.

Miss Fortune Cookie

Before posting my answer, I deleted the reference to O. J. Simpson. He was the only person I recognized from a list of notable alumni I found on the Internet, but including him might not cheer *Matt* up.

The next letter turned my blood to cold paste.

Dear Miss Fortune Cookie,

I'm in love with a boy. We've been together for a long time, and I know we're meant for each other. We both got into Dartmouth, but I can't go because my parents insist I attend Princeton.

My parents emigrated from China. They have worked very hard to provide me with a good life. Getting in to Princeton is a huge honor for my family. I have never disobeyed them.

How do I choose between the two things I care about most?

Desperate

Though the details were different—the college, the number of parents—the final line matched word for word the question Mei had asked me this afternoon. She wrote this letter. Ack. What should I say? If I said love supersedes achievement, Mei would probably follow my advice. And if I said honor your parents, she would probably follow *that* advice. After all, Miss Fortune Cookie had credibility.

But which answer was correct?

Maybe Mrs. Liu had it right. A girl couldn't know true love at eighteen.

Then again, what if Mei and Darren couldn't manage to stay together because long-distance love was just too hard on the spirit? And what if Mei never found true love after Darren? I could be responsible for destroying the greatest romance of all time, like breaking up Elizabeth Bennet and Mr. Darcy.

Then again, *again,* Mrs. Liu cared about Mei more than anything in the world. I could feel the love concealed behind her grouchy demeanor. She wanted the best for her daughter. That kind of love, a mother's love, should be trusted above all else.

Dear Desperate,

**Miss Fortune Cookie says: Trust the pan that gave you life.**

Which came from an old proverb, but it still sounded crazy, so I rephrased it.

Dear Desperate,

**Miss Fortune Cookie says: Trust the well-seasoned pan most of all.**

Tell your parents about your boyfriend. Since they have guided you well this far, you should involve them in the most important decision regarding your future. Your parents have your best interests at heart.

Miss Fortune Cookie

I hoped so, anyway. After sending the letter, I shut down the computer and tried to power down my brain with its pointy thoughts and useless doubts while the rustling from the living room continued. It was well past four in the morning when I finally fell asleep.

CHAPTER

**11**

Disregard all previous good fortunes.

Mom kneaded my shoulder a little too roughly. "Wake up, Erin. We leave in three minutes." Every Sunday morning, we volunteered at the hospital together. I still had on my clothes from last night, a T-shirt and sweatpants. Since we would change into uniforms there, it didn't really matter. Mom had heated our breakfast *dousha bao*, steamed buns filled with red bean paste, and set one on my dresser.

"And we're off," she said when I'd made it upright and slipped into my shoes.

Our living room resembled a very small warehouse. Stacks of tile and papers and boxes covered the floor, which was already carpeted with plastic sheeting and paint scrapings. Mom acted as though this could possibly be normal. At the bottom of the stairs, we ran into Mei. Oh, right. She'd sent me a Miss Fortune Cookie letter last night. What had I advised her to do, exactly? I wished my brain would wake up faster.

"Good morning," Mom said, hurrying toward the exit. "We're late."

Mei didn't stop pacing when she saw us, too deep in her thoughts even to register my disheveled appearance. Now I remembered my advice—tell Mrs. Liu about Darren.

"Are you okay?" I whispered. Mei didn't seem to hear me.

By now, Mom had already made it outside the building. Was Mei considering telling Mrs. Liu the truth—a course of action that seemed sage in the middle of the night but in the retina-piercing light of day might be less so? Before I could get Mei's attention, though, Mom came charging back in, snagged me by the elbow, and pulled me out. "But I have to talk to Mei," I said.

"You can talk to her later." She hustled me down the sidewalk, keeping her hand between my shoulder blades until I buckled myself into the ancient Corolla.

When she settled into the driver's seat, I asked to use her phone.

"I left it in the apartment," she said.

Why were parents so maddening? I hoped Mei wouldn't do anything rash before I got to the hospital. Not that I considered my advice overtly heinous, but I preferred that she make the decision knowing all the facts—like Miss Fortune Cookie's true identity.

Now that I thought about it, Mrs. Liu could get somewhat extreme when provoked. She'd grounded Mei for three months sophomore year after catching her in a lie. No cell phone, no Internet, no friends, no fun of any kind. Who knew what she'd do when she found out that Mei had told hundreds of lies to cover for her relationship with Darren over the past thirteen months?

A chopstick peeked out from behind Mom's right ear. As

she reversed from our parking spot, I removed it. "Put it through my bun, will you?" she said. Just then, she accelerated, followed by a tap on the brakes that sent me flying. The chopstick missed impaling her neck by a nanometer.

I would've offered to take the wheel, except for several sturdy and inarguable reasons. Thinking about Mei's situation had frazzled me. Besides that, I didn't have a license and my learner's permit had expired. The time Linny gave me driving lessons, I accidentally backed into a newspaper vending machine—reverse-mode fail. Fortunately, the ramming occurred below the fender, so that only people less than three feet tall could see the dent.

"Mei seemed out of sorts this morning," Mom said.

Exactly. But you wouldn't let me talk to her. "Yep." I smacked my lips a little on the *p*.

"The decision about Harvard versus Stanford must be hard."

"Yep."

A Ford Excessive passed us on the right, nearly clipping our side-view mirror. "Stay in your lane, Mr. SUV man," Mom said. "Have you given Harvard any more thought?"

"Nope." Except:

*Going to college with my amazing friend = nirvana*

And if I went to Harvard, I'd become like *Matt*, the boy whose life was ruined by Lowell. Hanging out in the bottom percentiles at Harvard could be depressing. Mom turned on the radio. After two songs, the guilt over ignoring her attempts at communication got under my skin. Guilt really *does* rack a person. I gave in. "It's weird, you know," I said loudly, to be heard over the music. "Part of me is so done with high school, I can't wait for it to end."

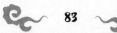

Mom turned off the radio. "That doesn't surprise me. You work so hard all the time."

"I guess. But another part of me wants it to last forever."

Mom patted my arm. "Me too. I treasure every moment we have together." Which proved my point about how much she needed me.

The Corolla glided into a parking space in the Med Center parking lot. We went inside and changed into our pale blue scrubs, and then we parted ways. Mom likes to work reception. I like to switch jobs all the time. This month, I'd been assigned to create "meaningful one-on-one interactions with patients through helping with menu selections." Mostly I listened to people complain about the food.

When I got to the nursing station, I asked to use the phone. Luckily, the person in charge liked me, which meant I didn't need to come up with a good reason to make a call. Shoe Fang answered on the first ring.

"*Ni hao ma*," I said. *How are you?* "Can I speak to Mei?"

"No talk today. She lose chitchat privilege." A metallic edge sharpened Mrs. Liu's voice. My kidneys—the organ where anxiety resides—kicked in.

"What did she do?"

"Too much homework. No time. Good-bye. *Zaijian!*"

"Wait." I guessed that Mei had told Shoe Fang about Darren. And Stanford. And Harvard. "Can I ask you something? I need your opinion, actually."

"Ah." Her assent sounded brisk.

"I have this friend? A senior like me. She ... her ..." Her mom. "... her dad wants her to ..." To go to Harvard. "... do something, but her heart is telling her to do something else. Nothing bad. But if she obeys her dad, it will make her deeply unhappy. Should she follow her heart?"

My kidneys tensed while I waited for the reply.

"Follow heart is always good."

Yes! My kidneys did a happy dance. Mrs. Liu understood that parents and children sometimes disagree, that a daughter might have to go against her parents' desires.

Misfortunately, she had more to say. "Always follow heart. But whose heart to follow? Girl's heart or father's heart?"

Crap in a blender. She wasn't going to budge.

Before I recovered, Mom appeared out of thin air in the hallway. "Thank you, Mrs. Liu," I said. "Bye."

"*There* you are," Mom said when she spotted me. "They have too many volunteers in reception today. Why don't I tag along with you?"

Um. "That would be great."

After I introduced Mom to the supervisor, we started our rounds. Since the conversation with Mrs. Liu had freaked me out, I had trouble concentrating. Luckily, the first patient got my attention. She had hepatitis A, a viral infection of the liver, and the whites of her eyes were so yellow that they could've been mistaken for egg yolks wearing blue contact lenses. After we chatted, I got down to business. "No alcohol until you're better. Red meat can cause iron buildup in your liver. Coffee, chocolate, and refined sugar should be avoided, too."

"What's left? Dandelion leaves?" she joked.

"Actually, those are good for you."

Before I got through my list of liver-healing foods—parsley, chicory, and kumquats—she opened her cell to show Mom and me pictures of her grandkids. I liked that part of the job. The photos were okay; the kids had fuzzy heads, pouty lips, and cute teeth like Chiclets. But watching the change come over someone was the best part. Love does that to a person.

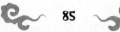

As I crossed the room to put the complete menu in the holder, another patient stopped me. "Excuse me, are you the doctor?"

"No. I'm just a volunteer," I said, startled. "Do you need a nurse?"

She started laughing loudly. "What a relief!"

I laughed too. "I'm almost eighteen. My birthday is next week."

"Erin didn't get her period until she was a sophomore," Mom said.

Which would've been the perfect moment to disappear in a shower of sparks. Superpower fail. I handed Mom the menu for the next patient. "Why don't you give it a try?" I asked.

After she got the hang of it, I went to hide in the break room. For the first minute, I just stared at the poster that hung over the microwave outlining the steps involved in cleft-palate surgery. But then I got an idea, brushed the crumbs off the seat in front of the computer, and logged into Miss Fortune Cookie.

My uncle—the one who ghostwrote a celebrity advice column for a while—taught me a useful trick. Most people seeking help already know what to do, he said. Often, he would just chop off the second paragraph of the letter and change it to his own words to get the answer. I read Mei's entry again with that in mind.

Paragraph 1 is the conflict: *I know he's the one. But my parents insist I go to Princeton.*

Paragraph 2 is the answer: *I've never disobeyed my parents.*

The knot between my shoulder blades loosened. Miss Fortune Cookie had not completely bungled things.

Probably.

Maybe.

Actually, I wished I hadn't answered Mei's letter last night at all. But the universe didn't offer do-overs, so I opened the next letter to distract myself from imagining Mei locked in the apartment with Shoe Fang.

Dear Miss Fortune Cookie,

My friend and I don't agree on something. She likes this boy but won't talk to him. They, btw, are meant for each other.

I've come up with a hundred and one ways to get her to talk to him, but she won't listen. She says that if it's meant to be, *he* will approach *her*.

Eros

I thought about that. Two summers ago, I was somewhat obsessed with this boy Fermin from trig. Linny happened to know his best friend. Instead of doing the usual go-between routine, though, she set up a beach party on a hot day and invited us both to come. She even lent me her prettiest bathing suit. Unfortunately, Fermin didn't share my Feelings of Swoon. On the upside, I didn't waste any more time pining for him. Mostly.

Dear Eros,

Tell your friend that **Miss Fortune Cookie says: A man stands for a long time with his mouth open before a roast duck flies in.**

It's true that if they're meant for each other, they'll find each other . . . eventually. But she might be wrinkly by then.

Give fate a hand. Invite them both to a party, maybe?

Miss Fortune Cookie

The next letter made me think even harder.

Dear Miss Fortune Cookie,

I have this talented friend who doesn't believe in herself. She is smoking hot on cello but won't stay in orchestra unless I do.

I would rather sign up for drama next year.

If the situation were reversed, she would stay in orchestra for me. We are going to be friends forever, so I don't want to mess that up.

Codependent

Freshman year, I attempted the viola and learned twenty-three versions of the same song, "The Sea Lion's Lament" in C minor. So I dropped out. Apropos of nothing. More to the point, I would've stayed in orchestra if a good friend had begged me to.

Dear Codependent,

~~Just sign up for orchestra with her, and then drop out after the first two weeks.~~ Bad joke.

~~Miss Fortune Cookie says: Cloning is the sincerest form of flattery.~~ Second bad joke.

Friendship is give and take, but more giving than taking.

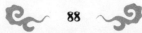

No. No. No. While I was tinkering with the answer, Mom entered the break room. I managed to hit blog view just in time. "What are you reading?" she asked.

"A blog." I hadn't told her about Miss Fortune Cookie because she would've asked to help me with it. Though she had more experience with the world, I'd wanted the column to be mine.

"Can I see?" she asked.

I tilted the screen toward her. Mom scrolled through my Miss Fortune Cookie letters, laughing as she read. I thought about telling her the truth, but the setting seemed wrong, a break room with grotesque posters on the wall. I'd confess later. Like when I'd moved away from home.

The next hour passed quickly, with one highlight—a glimpse of someone-who-looked-like-Weyland in the hallway, though he disappeared before I could catch up with him. Maybe I should rejoin Recycling Club and get to know his brother. Eventually I could bring Weyland up in a casual conversation, right?

On the drive home, I asked Mom for permission to go to Linny's get-together tomorrow night. Her answering smile was strangely smirky. "You can go. But I'll have to give you a quick refresher on *the talk* first."

I shifted in my seat. "What the what?"

"A boy at the party could proposition you. You should have an idea of how to handle that. Boys have changed a lot since the last time you went to a party."

Embarrassment precluded direct eye contact, so I stared at the dashboard. "It's not a party, Mom. It's just Linny and Mei. No boys." Blood flowed up my neck. "Besides, I still have that condom you gave me in my bag, in case of an emergency."

Mom laughed. "Have you checked the expiration date? I should buy you a new one."

Condoms have expiration dates?

When we got back to the apartment, I retreated to my room and just breathed. Everyone should inhale eight cups of air a day. Nine out of ten doctors say so. Then I went back out to grab Mom's phone to call Linny.

"Thank God it's you," she said. "I'm like one second away from losing my mind. Mom is oppressing me again."

Linny actually gets a charge out of rebelling against her mom, unlike Mei and me. Questioning authority is her superpower. "Poor thing," I said.

"Don't be sarcastic. I *am* a poor thing." She sounded more cheerful already. "You know what she wants from me now? To declare a major by the end of first semester."

While she ranted, I changed into clean clothes, which is pretty hard to do with a phone stuck to your ear, and only one free arm.

"Nothing will stop my mom," she continued. "She's relentless. God. She's yelling at me right now to get off the phone. I promised to look at the catalog with her after lunch. Talk to you later."

"Bye."

"Wait. Don't hang up. Will you call Mei? She's not answering my texts."

Because of me.

"I will."

# CHAPTER

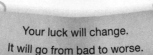

## 12

Your luck will change.
It will go from bad to worse.

Last December, Mom started driving me to Lowell every day when a certain morning commuter on Muni wouldn't leave me alone. He looked pretty normal, except for his SpongeBob pajama pants, but his vibe creeped me out. And that was *before* he told me a dragon warlord had threatened to kill everyone in his family.

On Monday morning, Mei came to our apartment to catch a ride to school with us. Which meant that Shoe Fang had released her from the dungeon to attend classes. I happened to be in the midst of a scarf crisis when she knocked, and hoped that Mom would let her in. Scarf on. The cloth felt soft against my neck, but it made me look middle-aged. Scarf off. Or was that Bohemian? Scarf on.

Actually, I was terrified to see Mei face-to-face.

"Can you get it?" Mom yelled. "I'm in the bathroom." When you live in seven hundred square feet, every personal detail of your morning routine becomes public information.

I hurried to the door, talking as I opened it. "Sorry for making you wait!"

Shoe Fang stood there bursting with excitement, her face aglow like a thousand golden suns. Mei stood behind her, demure. Uh-oh. The toilet flushed, the sink ran, and Mom came out into the living room.

Shoe Fang charged toward her. "I deliver good news. Harvard say yes! They send announcement late last night. Can you believe, ah? I go to school for illiterate restaurant workers. Now my daughter go to number one school in America. She forget how to make kung pao chicken."

Mom hugged Mrs. Liu and knuckle bumped Mei. "Wonderful news. Erin got—" I drowned her out with a hideous bout of fake coughing, and mercifully she changed course. "Congratulations, Mei."

Mei smiled shyly at my mom, the essence of the modest and compliant daughter. "Thank you. I'm so lucky to get in."

Then again, maybe she actually chose to go to Harvard.

Mrs. Liu fanned herself with a piece of paper. "Here is acceptance form. I check with horoscope. Today is auspicious day send mail." She beamed at us.

Mom snapped a picture, and then a second one because I'd accidentally crossed my eyes the first time. The drive to school was strangely normal—I got seasick in the back seat; Mom had one-way conversations with bad drivers; Mei organized papers into color-coded folders. As if I'd imagined all the drama from before.

At a red light, Mom put her hand on Mei's shoulder. "I understand that Darren won't be going to Harvard. How did he take the news?"

Mei smiled sweetly. "He's happy for me. Of course he's

disappointed that we can't be together as much. We've talked a lot about how to make the distance thing work."

"Brave girl. Smart, too."

Mei laughed. "Being apart will let me concentrate on my studies. They say the first year at Harvard is really difficult."

I'd read that, too, while perusing various college blogs and such last night. Just for fun. Brown University's website encouraged their freshmen to create an independent major across departments, which would've been hell on a stick for a decisiveness-challenged person like me. I also learned that Harvard had a wickedly successful women's fencing team.

When we arrived at Lowell, Mom missed sideswiping the LOADING ONLY sign by an inch. She shouted *I love you* to me through the open window. An ordinary day.

Since Mei and I both had AP English mod 1/2 (first period to non-Lowellites), we walked to class together. Lowell has over two thousand students, so we weren't alone. Mei kept bumping me with her bag by accident and then apologizing. I noticed the miniplush donkey I'd given her clipped to the zipper.

I should've confessed to her about my Miss Fortune Cookie letter, except now it was too late to change anything. Besides, she needed a friend to lean on, so why make her mad unnecessarily? "I'm glad Darren took it well," I said.

Mei gave me a funny look. "Uh-huh. Speaking of boyfriends, what's the deal with Linny and Dub? It's weird that she won't talk about him, don't you think?"

Obvious subject change. Getting Mei to open up about her feelings wouldn't be easy. "I know. She's so mysterious, you'd think Dub works as a spy, and she has to protect his identity."

Mei smiled. "That's so true. I want details—his favorite ice cream, what he looks like."

"His name," I added.

That cracked her up, and I felt like we were on the same team again. When we took our seats near the front of the classroom, I finally dared to ask, "Are you really okay?"

She pressed her pinkie knuckle against her front teeth. "Yesterday was . . . Remember that ghost story we used to act out? The scholar whose first wife died, and then each time he remarried, a terrible accident would befall his new wife. Yesterday was like that."

"Insidiously horrible?"

"No! His new wives kept dying because he'd neglected his first wife's grave. Remember?"

"Oh. You mean inevitable."

She leaned over to open her bag. "Yesterday was inevitable."

"What happened, exactly?"

She straightened up and smiled. "Nothing happened. I have a present for you."

More evasion. The tiny package had been wrapped tightly in green tissue paper and, of course, lots of tape, Mei style. It hurt my nails to scrape it open. After a long struggle, a shiny plastic card popped out, an Arizona driver's license with my picture on the front and my name somewhat altered, from Erin Kavanagh to Erin McFerrin.

"Um?" I asked like a baby mouse with a too-tight bib. A couple of girls turned their heads to look at me. You could say a lot of things about my friends, but they were never boring.

Mei leaned in. "Shhh. It's a fake ID. The guy at the place made me one, too. Linny already has one. We're going out tonight. Don't argue."

My idea for the get-together at Linny's tonight had been a little different—Linny and me pouring sympathy over Mei while she cried about giving up Harvard to be closer to

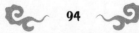

Darren, or cried about moving far away from Darren to go to Harvard. Maybe we'd bake cookies and eat them while watching funny YouTube videos, getting crumbs all over the keyboard. Then we'd turn out the lights and talk in the dark.

"You're coming with us," Mei said.

The whole idea seemed incongruent.

$$tragic\ (situation) \neq going\ out + fake\ ID \pm alcohol$$

A tall man dressed in black strode into the classroom—presumably a substitute—and dropped a stack of books onto a chair. When that failed to quiet us, he stood on his desk with a small urn tucked under his arm. "These are the ashes of my former students." Which got everyone's attention.

While he outlined the four types of irony, some of the less-motivated students in class didn't take notes. Less motivated being a euphemism for totally indifferent, which sometimes happens to seniors about to graduate, even at an academic institution like ours. Besides, we covered irony sophomore year.

The sub noticed. "You will write a paper incorporating irony into a mock debate by the end of the week. Five pages, minimum, twelve-point font, one-inch margins."

Gabby, all *Gossip Girl*–y in a plaid mini, spoke up. "But, Your Honor, we have AP tests coming up."

"Make that ten pages."

Mei passed me a note:

What's the word for him?

I wrote back:

Misanthrope, mutant, troglodyte?

Mei giggled.

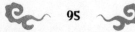

"You in the scarf," the sub bellowed at me, and I froze. "What color is that, anyway?"

I looked down. "Umber?" More like Chinese mustard actually, my favorite shade of yellow, and a lucky color too.

"You in the umber scarf. Give me an example of dramatic irony."

I appreciate irony, so an answer came easily. "In *Romeo and Juliet*, Romeo kills himself because he thinks Juliet is dead. Except she isn't dead."

"Good," he said. "You in the plaid skirt. An example of situational irony."

Gabby looked flustered. "But we're supposed to be discussing the rhetorical strategies used by Orwell in his novel *Nineteen Eighty-four*."

I felt for Gabby. She'd probably prepared a list of rhetorical strategies last night from the Internet. She didn't like English, but her parents wanted her in this class. Gabby thought for a second. "You fall madly in love with someone, but then you find out that he's actually your fraternal twin brother, who got kidnapped as a baby and your parents never told you."

Mei snorted.

"Not bad. *Soap Opera Digest* needs you. You in the bow tie, another example."

I turned around in my seat to pass a note to Mei, except she was crying. Before I could say a word, she shot from her seat and bolted from the room.

"May I? It's kind of an emergency?" Without waiting for actual permission, I gathered our things and ran after her. She'd already made it to the end of the hall, looking like the silhouette of an exclamation point against the glass door. "Mei!" I yelled.

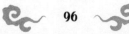

She stopped to let me catch up. Red lines bisected her cheeks as if she'd tried to scratch off her tears. "I couldn't breathe in there."

I waited.

She closed her eyes. "Yesterday, Darren came over to the apartment. I told Ma how much I loved him and that I wanted to go to Stanford instead."

"Crazy. What did she say?"

Mei stared at her hands. "She said that family comes first. She didn't leave her home in China and come all this way so I could throw it away on some boy."

I shook my head. "Stanford isn't exactly a garbage can. And Darren isn't exactly some boy."

Mei's shoulders, neck, and elbows all slumped at once. "Ma already told every relative we have in China that I got in to Harvard."

"So you're going."

"Harvard *is* the best school in the country." Her crazy hyena laugh startled me. "Did I tell you? I forged a rejection email from Harvard when I got home from Linny's on Saturday. Lots of people had posted real ones on the Web, so it wasn't hard. I didn't show it to Ma, though. Then yesterday I told her the truth."

Because of me. My veins iced up. The timing made sense. She told the truth *after* reading Miss Fortune Cookie's advice.

"Erin." She mangled my name like it had been caught on teeth inside her throat. Her agony showed through, as if covered by a single piece of paper held up to the light. "Do *you* think I should tell Harvard to kiss my ass?"

I dropped her mega-heavy backpack right on my foot, which hurt. Linny would tell her to go for it. But what did I truly think? Harvard was a huge deal.

Mei took it from me. "Stanford offered me a scholarship. I could enroll on my own, without Ma's help."

Confucius touted filial piety above all else, reverence of one's elders. Though some considered him antiquated, he still held sway in modern China. Then again, when I'd written Miss Fortune Cookie's advice to *Desperate* last night, I thought that Shoe Fang would come around to Mei's point of view. Now that didn't seem likely.

"You should do what's right for you," I said.

"Thank you. You're the best friend ever." The heat from her eyes sautéed my face, singed my bangs. "By the way..." She looked down. "I kind of remembered that sleepover in eighth grade. You were right, I said you couldn't come. I'm really, really sorry." She threw open the door and headed down the steps.

I remained in the entranceway, half in and half out, letting the moist morning air cool me off.

She stopped running and turned to face me. "You forgive me, right?"

"Of course." Pretty much. Kind of. "Where are you going?" I asked.

"I'm doing what you told me to," she said, giggling again. "I'm running away!"

CHAPTER

**13**

An interesting sports disaster is in your future.

A t first I thought Mei was joking, but after she disappeared from view, I wondered. And by wondered, I mean panicked. In retrospect, I should've chased after her, asked her exactly what she meant by "running away." Cutting her morning mods? Or hitchhiking to LA with Darren to get jobs as characters at Disneyland? And I should've told her she'd misunderstood my advice. Then again, before English started she'd insisted that we were going out tonight to a place requiring fake IDs.

I was confused.

After English ended, I borrowed someone's phone to call Mei's cell and then Darren's. Both of them were turned off. At lunch, when Linny didn't show up at our usual table in the courtyard, I checked the arcade, wove through the craziness in the cafeteria, and went outside again, looking for her. She'd know what to do. Students were strewn all over the lawn on this warm spring day. Some shirtless boys tossed a Frisbee, and I paused a moment to admire them.

After failing to find Linny, I curled up on a swath of unmowed grass—the softest kind—too exhausted to brush away the ant or whatever that crawled on my leg. My eyes closed by themselves, and I basked in the red glow through my eyelids. I have this bad habit of drifting off when I shouldn't. And—in that hypnotic state before falling asleep—Weyland's brother's name came to me. Winston.

Loud talking nearby woke me. I blinked into the sun. The lawn was empty, except for two girls laughing hysterically, which meant that class had already started. I didn't mean to eavesdrop, but what can you expect if you gossip at two thousand hertz—soprano gerbil—and above a certain decibel level?

"Do you know Linny?"

"I don't *know her* know her."

"I don't know her either, but she sits in front of me in Khmer. She asked me what I was going to do after graduation, and I said it depends on where I get in. Then guess what she said."

"Go to Vassar and get straight A's?" Clearly the girl didn't know Linny at all.

"Not even close."

I closed my eyes again so they wouldn't notice me.

"She said"—dramatic pause—"'you know what I'm going to do? Buy some silk lingerie and seduce a rich old man. Then I'll marry him and give him a heart attack on his wedding night.'"

Ack.

"No way! Was she like April fooling you?"

"This was last week."

When they moved on to shred someone else's reputation, I hauled my sleepy body off the ground. I didn't believe them, exactly, but the story seemed like another sign that Linny might be unraveling.

She had badminton after lunch. When I reached the gym, I spotted her on a middle court. You're not allowed to wear street clothes inside, and I couldn't get her attention from the doorway.

Five minutes later, I'd changed into my gym gear from last semester. I was a Person of Mildew. The moment the coach seemed inattentive, I snatched a racket and ran over to Linny's court. She shrieked when she saw me.

"Act normal," I said. "Where were you at lunch today?"

"At a meeting." The birdie made a pleasing *thwock* as she served it.

Linny's opponent, a girl named Sarah, smashed it back toward me. It hit me in the chest and tumbled to my feet. "Six–four, my serve," she yelled.

I stooped to get the birdie. Since I'd never played badminton before, I tried to throw it across the net, and it plopped onto the floor on our side. Sarah ran forward to grab it, her ponytail flipping with annoyance. "Use your racket. That's what it's for." An excellent example of verbal irony, by the way.

"Sorry," I said.

Linny bumped me with her elbow. "It's so insane. Some of the administrators wanted us to ignore the Westboro picket— like pretend it wasn't happening. It took all morning to convince them to let us do the counterprotest."

The birdie came sailing over the net toward me again. This time I had the sense to step backward. Linny lunged sideways and managed to return it. "No fair," Sarah said. "Two against one."

"I didn't touch it," I said.

Linny fetched the birdie and served it. "What are you doing here, anyway?" she asked me.

"I need to talk to you." *Mrs. Liu came barging into our apartment this morning. Mei apologized about eighth grade. Some girls were gossiping about you.* "Mei told her mom about Harvard. Mrs. Liu is sending in the acceptance form today." I danced around the court, trying to dodge Linny's racket, which kept whistling dangerously close to my face.

"No big surprise there," Linny said.

I stood by the net to be out of the way. "Can we talk this afternoon?"

Air from Linny's racked fanned my neck. "I have hella work to do for the protest."

"Give me a list, and I'll stay up all night."

"Thanks." Linny sent the birdie flying into the bleachers on the other side. While Sarah went to find it, we managed to exchange a few more sentences. "I'm going to the JCC after school to ask them to organize Jewish folk dancing for when Mei plays 'Hava Nagila.'"

Uh-oh. "What if Mei doesn't show up to play the violin tomorrow?" I asked.

Linny's eyebrows came together. "Why wouldn't she?"

I lowered my voice. "Remember how Mei said something about a crazy plan before? And you pestered her, but she wouldn't tell us what it was?"

"She doesn't have a plan," Linny said, positioning herself for the next serve.

"She got me a fake ID for some reason," I said. *And she mentioned doing something drastic.*

"Really? That's weird."

The coach eyed me lurking by the net. "I should really go," I said.

Linny rushed forward to nail another shot. When Sarah missed, Linny turned to smirk at me. "Call me later. And be prepared to tell me all about your new boyfriend." She poked my arm a few times and wiggled her eyebrows significantly, as if she'd found out about my IM romance with Zac Efron.

While I tried to understand what she meant, Linny served too high and Sarah smashed the birdie down with all her strength. It whacked me hard in the eye. I sat down, burying my face in my hands, blinking fast, and trying not to cry.

Linny put her arm around me. "Are you okay?"

"I'm great," I said. "If I ignore the pain." The first thing I saw when I lifted my head was the blurry form of my attacker with her hands on her hips. She didn't even say sorry. "Does my eye look bad?" I asked Linny.

Linny moved in closer and squinted. "Which one?"

The coach came over to look too. "You'll live."

I touched the skin around my eye carefully. "It feels puffy."

In the end, the coach sent me to the health center, just in case. Back in my regular clothes, I started trekking in that direction. But then I wavered. The nurse would just chart my injury as an NBW—No Big Whoop—give me some ice, and send me back to class looking like the victim of a mugging. So I changed direction and walked toward the gap in the back fence.

CHAPTER

14

You will meet a crane among a flock of chickens.

After leaving campus, I tromped down the wooded path to Stonestown Galleria, a regular hangout for Lowell students. The sun-warmed eucalyptus pods smelled delicious. I was cutting all my afternoon mods for the first time in history, and it felt pretty good. JD almost. But when I got to the mall itself, the surreptitious looks people gave me reminded me about my freshly minted black eye.

So I boarded the first Muni home, finding an empty seat behind two men talking in Mandarin. From their conversation, I gleaned that the one in the blue shirt had just emigrated from China. When his friend disembarked, I spoke to him. *"Xihuan Meiguo ma?"* Do you like America? His head whipped around, and he stared.

*"Ni hao ma?"* I asked when he didn't answer. *How are you?*

He laid his arm across the backrest, propped his chin on his elbow, and gazed at me as if I were a fascinating ghost. Though I told him my name in Chinese, Eren (*graceful/benevolent*), and asked him his, he said nothing. He remained completely motionless, in fact, as if blinking might make me disappear. Seconds turned into minutes, minutes into decades, and all that stress made me need to pee.

When we pulled in to my stop, I hurried to a sandwich place to use the facilities. The bathroom door was locked, so I asked for the key at the counter.

"It's for customers only."

"Can I have a veggie on rye with olive oil to go?"

The sandwich maker worked at top speed. "Are you going on a picnic?"

Um. "No."

"Too bad. It's the perfect day for it," she said, handing me the bag. "Have fun."

"Can I have the restroom key now?"

"Sorry, it's out of order."

Hell in wax paper. Luckily my bladder situation had abated somewhat.

As I waited for the bus into Chinatown, a familiar street person sat down near me, Cigarette Willie. With his short bangs and shoulder-length brown hair, he resembled an older Prince Valiant, except for the beard, the grime, and an unlit cigarette between his lips.

People said that he went carousing one night and forgot to put out the cigarette he'd been smoking in the kitchen of his restaurant before he left. His wife and daughter were asleep in the rear apartment, and they both perished in the fire. In my mind's eye, I could see the tragedy unfolding, the flames shooting upward into the night sky, the firefighters holding him by the shoulders as he tried to hurl himself into the burning building.

A bicycle messenger whizzed by me. I stepped backward,

tripped on someone's bags, and fell onto the sidewalk. Cigarette Willie stood in a flash, offering me a hand up. "Are you all right, miss?" he asked in a British accent. His voice startled me because I'd never heard him speak before.

"I'm fine."

The cigarette stuck to his lower lip when he talked. "Were you in a dustup?"

I touched my eye, which felt increasingly bulbous. "What's a dustup?"

"A brawl." His stomach gurgled so loudly, it could be heard over traffic.

"I have a sandwich. Do you want it?"

He sat down again and swept the cigarette from his mouth, an elegant gesture involving his middle and index fingers. "Now that you mention it, I am a bit peckish. Can you tell me what's in it?"

I thought of Katharine Hepburn. His voice was gravelly like hers. "Roasted peppers, kalamata olives, and spinach."

"Any mayonnaise? I'm vegan."

"None." When I leaned over to give him the bag, blood rushed into my head, which made me wobble.

"Are you sure you're all right, miss? Let me escort you home."

"I'll be fine."

The set to his chin implied stubbornness. "I insist."

What was the harm in it? Hannibal Lecter was not a vegan, after all. "Thank you." So we waited together under the tangled spiderweb of overhead wires, with him munching the sandwich and me pondering various conversation starters:

*Where do you sleep at night?*

*How old would your daughter be if she had lived?*

*Don't those olives give an otherwise bland sandwich a certain piquancy?*

Since I'd never talked to a homeless man before, I didn't exactly know the etiquette. He seemed comfortable with the silence between us, giving me space to practice insouciance until the bus came. This particular bus line had two claims to fame: (1) Passengers sometimes smuggled aboard live waterfowl, and (2) One time, a fistfight broke out between a Chinese-American woman and an African-American woman over a seat. Fortunately, the only fight today occurred between a man and his invisible gorilla.

After we disembarked in Chinatown, Cigarette Willie followed me all the way to the landing in front of our apartment. "Thanks for seeing me home," I said, inserting the key in the lock. Before I'd successfully jiggled it to the sweet spot, Mom opened the door from the inside.

"What happened to *you*?" she asked when she saw me.

"An accident in badminton. This is Cigarette Willie. Cigarette Willie, this is my mom."

Mom swung the door open wide. "Hi. Nice to see you again. Would you like some tea?"

Unusual occurrences will follow you
wherever you go.

Cigarette Willie stepped over a stack of tiles and sat down on the plastic sheeting that draped the couch. He took the cigarette from his mouth, holding it between his fingers.

"No smoking inside," Mom said.

Which kind of cracked me up, considering the condition of our living room.

He crossed his legs. "I don't smoke, miss."

I ran to the bathroom, leaving the two of them alone. While I washed my hands in the sink, I studied myself in the mirror. The skin around my eye looked smooth and reddish like a nectarine. Luckily, we didn't keep any fruit-eating bats in the apartment. When I came out, Mom and Cigarette Willie were chatting away.

"Will and I met . . . before. At the grand opening of his restaurant, isn't that right?"

He laughed. "That night was a fair-sized disaster. There

were spots on the cutlery, and I mistakenly used sweet dough for the calzones."

"Everything else tasted fabulous, if I remember correctly," Mom said.

I dropped down into the plastic-covered armchair just as Mom went into the kitchen. A loose tile slid under her, and she caught herself on the counter. "Milk or sugar?"

"No, thank you. Do you have chamomile?"

"Sure thing." She filled the kettle with water from the tap, which meant she hadn't dismantled the kitchen sink, at least, in a quest to change out our plastic pipes for copper ones.

Yet.

"You're renovating, I see," Cigarette Willie said to me. He took up a lot of room, and by that, I mean he smelled strongly. Not that it was his fault. "Mom thought it looked like a dungeon in here."

"How does that eye feel?" Mom asked me. "Did the school nurse give you ibuprofen?"

"I came straight home without seeing the nurse."

"She fell on her bum for no reason, miss. She may have a concussion."

"Erin! Why didn't you tell me?"

"I don't have a concussion. I tripped, that's all. Anyway, if I do have a concussion, I should lie down and rest. Thank you for bringing me home." I stood to go.

Cigarette Willie took off his hat. "My pleasure."

After that, I grabbed some snacks from the kitchen, took Mom's phone, closed myself into my bedroom, and listened to them laugh together. They got so rowdy, I had to resort to earplugs just to think. I'm accustomed to a quiet home with just the two of us. When the sound of scraping paint started up through my wall, I put my pillow over my head.

My concern over Mei's announcement about running away had grown since this morning. Worry really *does* gnaw at a person. I took out the earplugs and called her again, but her phone jumped directly to voice mail. I didn't leave a message, because what if Mrs. Liu had confiscated her phone?

I opened the laptop and checked Facebook. Mei wasn't online. No new messages from *Desperate* at Miss Fortune Cookie, either. The question from the girl and her cellist friend still languished in my inbox. Since there was nothing more I could do about Mei, I decided to answer *Codependent*'s letter, poring over Confucian sayings for something appropriate, like, "The superior man is modest in speech but exceeds in his actions." Except that was too serious. I finally settled on a poignant Chinese proverb.

Dear Codependent,

**Miss Fortune Cookie says: True friendship is as rare as twin lotuses on a single stalk.**

Still, you should never martyr yourself for anyone. Honesty is the only foundation for a long-lasting friendship. An open conversation will make your friendship stronger.

Miss Fortune Cookie

After posting, I felt much better, and ready to tackle the next one.

Dear Miss Fortune Cookie,

This noob in photography won't leave me alone. He keeps asking me dumb stuff like how to view his pictures.

I keep telling him to ask the teacher, but he ignores me. How do I get rid of him?

Annoyed

Noob meaning *newbie*. I dug through a mess of unsorted fortunes on my desk that had just arrived in the mail from my uncle. They were wickedly funny, and a little nasty—just what this letter called for.

Dear Annoying,

**Miss Fortune Cookie says: Someone is speaking well of you. Because they don't really know you.**

Don't be a jerk. The hallmark of noob behavior? Calling someone else a noob.

In other words, it takes one to know one.

I'm rubber, you're glue. Everything you say bounces off me and sticks to you.

Miss Fortune Cookie

I didn't post this reply, of course. I may be petty, but Miss Fortune Cookie is not. Instead I wrote a new letter.

Dear Annoyed,

**Miss Fortune Cookie says: Open your heart. You can always close it again later.**

Be nice. Everyone is a noob sometime in their life.

 **111**

Besides, maybe this noob knows how to view his pictures but is looking for friendship or romance. Anything is possible.

Miss Fortune Cookie

After that, I checked my email, because ever since my phone ran out of minutes, I couldn't get texts. The only interesting one came from Linny. And by interesting, I mean somewhat irritating.

Hi, X! How's your eye? I forgot to tell you that the badminton coach collects nail clippers. She has 20 in her office. Weird, huh? ha ha. Makes me laugh when I think about it. I have another meeting, so can't talk this afternoon. It's crazy. SORRY!!!!!! ~lin

The counterprotest had so consumed her that she couldn't even reschedule our phone date? Which put me in a bad enough mood to take on my backlog of chemistry homework. I didn't love chem, but it was a building block for any degree in science. Mei and I had spent hours debating different career tracks. Jobs in science pay better and give you more prestige, but I enjoy my humanities classes more.

After finishing, I rewarded myself with a little goofing-off time, looking through Harvard's course catalog online for fun. Along with the usual, they offered classes like Melodrama in East Asian Cinema and Forensic Archeology, plus many obscure languages I'd never heard of. I don't mean Aramaic and Manchu. I'm talking Gikuyu, Yoruba, and Twi. Not that I wanted to learn Twi, exactly, but still.

Princeton's catalog included Topics in Anthropology:

Revisiting Sacrifice and Philosophy of Randomness and Risk. But no Twi. Which definitely counted as a strike against them. I added that to the strike they already had for not letting me in.

I removed my earplugs momentarily. Mom and Cigarette Willie were still in the living room talking loudly. I looked for a video on YouTube about laying linoleum tiles and watched it twice so that I could help her finish the kitchen floor. Then, after a little scrounging under my bed, I came across something to use for a protest sign, a red plastic saucer sled.

While I wrote LOVE KNOWS NO GENDER on it with a black Sharpie, an even better idea came to me. I turned it over and wrote on the back DO THE MATH! ♡ + ♡ = ♡. Just as I finished, the laptop beeped at me, and a chat box popped onto the screen.

> **Mei:** hi
> **Erin:** where r u?
> **Mei:** at d's
> **Mei:** meet me @ 647 valencia 9pm
> **Erin:** ?
> **Mei:** 911
> **Mei:** bring linny & id
> **Erin:** ?????????
> **Mei:** ma's got a thing tonite. ttyl

My heart sped up. Mei hadn't run away to LA, at least. Still, I wasn't going to meet her on some street corner by myself. Which meant I'd have to go to Linny's house first and convince her to come with me. My stomach growled viciously, mainly from hunger. It demanded food at the most inconvenient times, except that the apartment was finally silent, which made it the perfect time. I cracked open my door. Empty living room. So I went into the kitchen to find something to eat.

Water ran through the bathroom pipes. While I revived a bowl of rice and mapo tofu in the microwave, I sang "Nrrrd Grrrl" by MC Chris. The video was hilarious, especially when Nrrd Grrl's Princess Leia figurine kisses her Chewbacca figurine. "'I'm like elixir when I'm with her, 'cause I think I like her type ... eeeeee!'"

Cigarette Willie appeared out of nowhere with wet, combed-back hair, wearing sweatpants and one of Mom's oversized button-down shirts, the tip of his cigarette poking out from the breast pocket. "Don't stop. You have a smashing voice."

"Thanks." I opened the microwave and crammed a bite of dinner into my mouth.

Mom came out of her room. "I smell food."

"I made myself a snack before going to Linny's. Can you drive me?"

"Sure. Will offered to lay the tiles in the kitchen next, and I have to pick up some adhesive at the hardware store, anyway. What are you doing tonight, exactly?"

"Nothing special. Going out to get facial tattoos. What's your opinion on prison teardrops?"

Mom laughed and grabbed her long coat.

I ate a few more bites of food and then got my protest sign from my room. While I was in there, I organized a purse for the evening, my giant boho because it had room for everything, including the laptop. Then I dug out the fake ID Mei had made for me. Just in case.

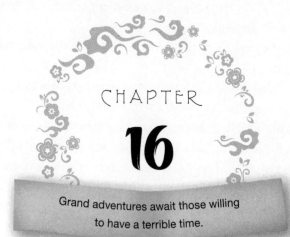

CHAPTER

# 16

Grand adventures await those willing
to have a terrible time.

Mom drove me to Linny's, leaving Cigarette Willie alone in the apartment, which somewhat surprised me. Not that we had diamonds and gold bullion strewn around. Even our DVD player verged on neolithic. Still, she usually treated our home like a Buddhist monastery for two, going *out* to see friends or the occasional boyfriend. Then again, Cigarette Willie had nowhere else to go.

On Stockton, the car ahead of us stopped to make a tight turn. Mom hit the brakes. "Use your blinker, you bozo." Strands of her hair stuck out this way and that. I flattened the worst of it with my palms.

"I'd like to spend the night at Linny's, if that's okay."

"On a school night?" she said.

"Mei's pretty miserable right now, actually, and we'd like to take her out for dinner to cheer her up, and that could take a while." Which sounded more wholesome than chasing Mei down at some place on Valencia.

"Mei seemed okay this morning on the drive to school," Mom said.

"It was kind of an act. She introduced Darren to her mom yesterday, and Mrs. Liu wasn't happy about it."

Headlights bore down on us as a truck neared our rear bumper. Mom slowed to a crawl, and the driver honked. "Back off, mister. Mei *has* kept Darren a secret for a long time."

I held on to my seat in case the truck rammed us. "That's not what I meant. Mrs. Liu thinks Harvard is the most important thing in the world. She's forcing Mei to go."

The truck turned down a side street. "Shufang wouldn't make her go against her will. I bet there's something else going on. Smart girls like Mei don't usually throw away the opportunity to go to Harvard, even to stay close to their amazing boyfriends. Mei is probably using her mom as an excuse to let him down easy."

I considered this. Mei *had* said she would go to Harvard if Darren didn't exist. After perusing Harvard's website at length—its history, its location, its students coming from over a hundred countries, the number of scholarly professors per square foot—the allure of it had expanded in my mind. Except Mom didn't see Mei and Darren together very often, so she didn't realize how much they differed from usual couples. And she didn't know that Mei had threatened to run away this morning.

I thought about confiding in her, except I wanted to handle the situation on my own.

With Linny's help, of course.

When we arrived, Mom popped the trunk. Before I got out, she put a restraining hand on my shoulder. "Hold on a

116

sec," she said, digging through her pockets. "Do you have any money?"

Um. "Five dollars, I think." Things must be bad if she needed to borrow from me.

She opened her wallet. "Take twenty. So you can treat Mei."

I extracted a bill. "Thanks."

Then she took another thing from her voluminous pocket, a small and very battered blank book with an egg on the cover. "I've been meaning to show you this. When I was cleaning out my closet, I found one of your dad's old journals. He scribbled in it all the time when you were a baby." As she set it carefully in my open hands, I noticed that the egg had legs and feet.

I opened it and took a long moment to absorb the handwriting on the first page without reading a word. My dad wrote this. He sat down at a table or a desk with a pen in his hand and wrote this. The paper itself almost gleamed with amazement and wonder. He wrote about me.

When Mom reached to take it back, I swiveled in my seat away from her, tightening my grip on the journal. "Let me have it."

"It's yours. But you'll be busy tonight. I can keep it safe for you."

I pressed it against my heart. "Please. I promise I won't lose it. I swear."

When she saw my face, she relented.

"Thank you." I tucked the precious thing into the inner pocket of my boho, got my protest sign from the trunk, and climbed the steps to the house, turning to blow Mom a kiss before she drove off. Linny had left the front door unlocked, so I went straight to her room. She was sitting in front of the

computer. *"Buona notte."* My insides shimmered. I was effervescent.

She turned toward me. "Erin! What are you doing here?"

I couldn't quite remember. I wanted to waltz her around the room, tell her about the journal my dad wrote, read it from cover to cover, sharing the passages with her that should be shared. And keeping the private bits to myself.

Linny hugged me. "Answering Mei's 911, perhaps?"

Oh, right. Dad's journal would have to wait for a better time. "Mei called you?"

"She texted me some address we're supposed to meet her at."

A Google search of 647 Valencia led us to the Elbo Room—a trendy live-music venue in the Mission, according to SFGate. Having been to only three school dances in my entire life, I knew less than nothing about nightlife and clubs. Except that the Elbo Room probably didn't serve soft drinks or employ teacher chaperones or have a fog machine.

Linny scowled at the screen, an aggravated cat with flat ears and a twitchy tail. "Clubbing on a Monday night? What *is* Mei up to? I've only been to a club once. *Me*, with an older boyfriend."

"I know, right?" I slapped down my fake ID. "She went to a lot of trouble."

Linny squinted at my new birth date. "I don't see how this constitutes an emergency. Did her mom even give her permission to spend the night at my house?"

"She IMed me that Shoe Fang had plans tonight. Her mahjongg group, maybe?"

"Well, I have a headache and piles of work to do. I'm not going to some club."

"Not even for an hour? But . . . ?" Air whistled through my teeth.

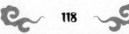

118

"No way."

I swallowed. Thrice. Going to the Elbo Room by myself was inconceivable. Navigating safely between school and home posed enough of a challenge, and that happened during the light of day before the real crazies came out. I had to change Linny's mind. "Actually, it *is* an emergency. Because I kind of told Mei to run away."

Her jaw dropped, and she shook me by the shoulders. Gently, of course. "You *told* Mei to run away?" Her eyes sparkled. "Wow, Erin. That's amazing."

"Well, sort of. I don't know what got into me. Confucius is all about respecting our elders, and I totally respect Mrs. Liu. It's just that Mei seemed so unhappy in class this morning." Like a ghost with no family altar to visit on feast days, forced to wander from village to village begging for scraps of food, to be precise.

"I'm sure Confucius is a font of wisdom," Linny teased, smiling with dimples, "but he's a little boring, don't you think? You, on the other hand, are totally wild. You have opinions and act on them." She took my hand and twirled me under her arm.

I hoped she felt the same way when I put the kibosh on her plan to marry a gullible and elderly man for his money. "I guess."

"Not I guess. You're like Erin 2.0. Erin-Xtreme. Okay. I'll go to the Elbo Room with you for an hour. Don't stand there with your mouth open. Go raid my closet for something to wear."

Like special fungus, your love
will grow in strange places.

inny had agreed to go to the Elbo Room with me, except
we didn't have a car, and I refused to consider Muni
after dark. I followed her to the bathroom, where she took
something for her headache. "How are we going to get there?"
I asked.

"I'll call someone if I can find my iPhone."

"It turns itself invisible just to thwart you," I joked. "It's
like a Hogwarts phone."

While she looked for it, I sifted through her closet. Since
there's nothing more frustrating than taking ages to choose an
outfit only to find that no shoes exist to match it, I worked from
the ground up, starting with a pair of boots because they're
better for fending off random assailants. As if I knew how to
karate kick someone. Then a clumpy pair of platform sandals
caught my eye, and I was stuck having to make a decision.

Until Linny came back in and put on the boots. "I found
us a ride," she said mysteriously.

I cleaned my feet before slipping on the sandals. Why does toe sweat have to smell so bad? Actually, it's a known fact, butyric acid. Still, I could see no evolutionary advantage to stinky feet. "Who with?"

"I'm not saying. Unless *you* have something to tell *me*, something about last Friday?"

"Um. No."

That's when I noticed how electrified she'd become, as if her drained batteries had gotten a serious recharge. Or else she'd just downed a double espresso.

I wiggled into the swishy skirt and tank top she threw at me and tied a scarf through my long hair like a headband. Not satisfied, I braided two long strands near the front. After concealing my black eye with makeup, I tried to blend it with my natural skin tone. By the time I'd finished, Linny had burned three hundred calories fidgeting with impatience, and another hundred yawning. "I've been so distracted, I forgot to ask. Did you get in anywhere else?"

Ack. I wasn't ready for this conversation. "Sort of."

Linny laughed. "What do you mean *sort of*? Princeton said maybe, and put you in some kind of Ivy League purgatory?"

Which totally cracked me up because I lived in a kind of purgatory *every day.*

"Brown and Princeton said no, actually. But Harvard let me in. Crazy, huh?" I smoothed the tank top and twirled the skirt. "Does this top work?"

Instead of looking at me, she collapsed onto the bed in high drama mode, with her arms out to her sides. "Harvard! I bet the admissions committee swooned over your Miss Fortune Cookie letters. They really show off your talent."

"Thanks." Except she didn't ask me if I wanted to go there.

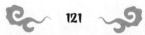

"Anyway—Harvard's so far away and expensive and overly academic," I said.

"And pretentious."

She truly believed it, I think, but I wasn't so sure. She also might've been slightly anxious that I'd bail on her and Berkeley. "I'm not going. Can you see my black eye?"

"For the millionth time, no." She's sweet like that. "I'm getting sleepy again. Let me nap on the way there, 'kay?" She rolled off the bed and jammed her favorite knit beanie over her hair. "What do you think?"

The hat changed her head into a snow cone. I took it off and put it back on as if I were really considering it. "No. You don't want to hide that amazing hair of yours." I loosened her ponytail and added volume with my fingers.

When a horn beeped, Linny ran to the living room and pulled back the curtain. A car flashed its lights at us. Not just any car, either, but a shiny green Mini Cooper. She shoved a sparkly pair of earrings into one of my hands and a hoodie into the other. "Don't look so grim. We're not on a mission to buy crack behind a warehouse on Potrero. Let's have some fun." She locked the front door behind us.

The earrings were hard to thread on. "I don't know anyone with a Mini Cooper."

"Yes, you do." She opened the passenger-side door and whispered something to the driver, who shoved the seat toward the dashboard. Linny climbed into the back. "Weyland, Erin, Erin, Weyland. Talk among yourselves, and don't forget to wake me up when we get there."

"Winston's brother," I said. "We met at Donatello's." You're the boy who flirted with me and turned me into a gooey something. There had to be a word for it.

His gorgeous dark eyes smiled at me. "You still owe me a croissant."

Linny leaned forward between the seats and spoke in an eerie voice. "What a strange coincidence. Weyland and I met at a gay-marriage rally in Berkeley."

Oh. Linny met *Dub* at a gay-marriage rally in Berkeley. And the name Weyland started with a *W*.

$$Ergo\ Weyland = Dub$$

They say if you sink a Styrofoam cup a mile or two into the ocean, it shrinks to the size of a thimble. That's what happened to my heart when I realized I'd succumbed to yet another crush on a friend's boyfriend.

Weyland melted me with a look. "Erin?" His full lips curved upward.

My foam expanded a little. "Huh?"

"Can you close the door?"

I slammed it shut right onto my enormous boho. I'm not a clumsy person, except when something or someone overwhelms my nervous system. Which Weyland emphatically did. Still, I managed to secure the door the second time around. He backed out into the street without a moment's hesitation, so different from how Mom drives. I barely managed to suppress my gasp of admiration.

Linny leaned forward again, her head between ours. "At the rally, Weyland had on this curly rainbow wig. He looked so awesome that everyone totally mobbed him."

"They just wanted my tutu," Weyland said with a modest shake of his head.

Linny had won him over that day, and I had no business—not a single shred of business—minding, but I decided there was

nothing wrong with wanting him to think of me as Linny's attractive friend. My hand rose up to cover my eye.

Weyland turned toward me. "Are you all right?"

"I'm fine." I peeked around the seatback at Linny. She had snuggled up to a huge, round canvas bag. "Did Linny tell you about my badminton accident this morning? My eye doesn't always look like a baseball."

"Twenty-five cents, X. You're up to $2.25 today."

Had I really put myself down nine times? Damn her sharp hearing and digital piggy-bank ways. Fortunately, I had Mom's twenty with me.

Weyland studied my face. "It looks cute, like you're a tiny prizefighter."

He called me cute.

His outfit—a silky button-down shirt, a cutaway coat, and well-fitting pants—qualified as one hundred percent club. I tried to imagine him in a wig and tutu. He kept giving me sidelong glances, which made me realize I'd been ogling. I needed to start a conversation. "Have you ever been to the Elbo Room?" So far, so good.

"Only once. I'm taking a lot of classes this semester, and I don't get out much." The skin at the corner of his eye crinkled when he smiled, dissolving me like sugar in water. "Do you dance?" His eyes rested on me while he waited for my answer. But sugar water can't talk.

"She loves to dance," Linny murmured.

Weyland ran his fingers through his thick hair. "Me too. Can I have the first one?"

Which sounded pretty flirty, if you thought about it. Then I reminded myself that Darren flirted with me all the time without harmful side effects. He enjoys indulging my

minicrush, even, and since Mei didn't see me as competition, why would Linny?

She appeared to be asleep, anyway.

"I'd like that." The car smelled agreeably of ginger. "Did Linny tell you about what's going on with Mei?"

"A little. You're worried that she might run away with her boyfriend. She also said you're crazy for thinking that."

I bit my lower lip. "I guess."

Weyland turned his dangerous eyes on me. "I think it's nice you want to help her. It's good to take care of your friends. Going off to college is a tough time, all the good-byes you have to say."

Which somewhat choked me up. A four-leaf clover dangled from his rearview mirror, and I twirled it to change the subject. "What? No fortune cat? How very Irish of you."

He answered me in an accent. "My parents brought this shamrock from the old country when I was but a wee bairn." His accent was atrocious, and Scottish instead of Irish, with an emphasis on the ish. I laughed.

He pulled into a parking space, and before I could get out, he jogged to my side of the car to offer me his hand. As we stood together on the sidewalk, I happened to notice that his height made him the perfect slow-dance partner. For me.

And for Linny, naturally. I shivered from the fog.

"Are ye sufficiently dressed for the cold, lassie?" Without warning, he peeled off his jacket, half hugging me as he wrapped me up in it. My body caught fire, and my head floated off its neck. After reassembling myself, uniting my two halves again, I chanted to myself: He's Linny's boyfriend he's Linny's boyfriend he's Linny's boyfriend he's Linny's boyfriend. The one she planned to give her virginity to.

Until Weyland undermined my resolve. "You look beautiful tonight."

Gah! Had I led him on? Guilt swept over me like a forest fire.

I woke Linny, and she rubbed her eyes before climbing out. The faint smell of ginger in the air tickled my nose as I unwrapped myself from his coat and draped it around her shoulders.

Weyland frowned. "I regret that I have but one jacket to give to my country."

I ignored him. "You fell asleep, Lin."

She yawned. "Did I miss it? Is it over? Can we go home now?"

"Ha ha."

CHAPTER

18

Bad luck will infest your pathetic soul for eternity.
(Just kidding.)

I checked Linny's appearance in the yellow light outside the Elbo Room. Though her mascara had survived napping in the back seat, Weyland's coat slid off her shoulder, exposing three sets of messy straps. "We need to fix this when we get inside."

She yawned. "What are you talking about?"

"I'll explain later."

Weyland looked at the poster near the door. "The Giant Wicks are playing."

A huge man blocked the entrance. In the movies when pretty girls arrive at a club, they get ushered in past a long line of people. Reality was quite different. For one, no line. For another, this particular bouncer didn't believe in ushering. "IDs," he said.

Generally speaking, I have a rule against deceiving men with axes tattooed on their necks. Not that he did, but he could have had. Except his face seemed somewhat friendly, and I hoped he was the kind of guy who watched *Beverly Hills 90210* on his night off. When he squinted at my ID, I crossed my fingers behind my back. Unexpectedly, he nodded, and I zipped into the packed room before he could change his mind.

In Mandarin, *re* means *hot*, and *nao* means *noisy*. You put the two words together to make the Chinese word for *fun*. The Elbo Room was definitely fun, lavishly hot, and thumpingly noisy. Linny and Weyland joined me at the edge of the crowd, and the three of us gaped like tourists airdropped into a foreign land. A very loud foreign land.

The club had an eclectic decor with padded barstools, booths, glass-tile walls, and festive lanterns hanging from the ceiling. The Giant Wicks shook the walls with their throbbing bass, and as the dancers went crazy, the guitar player took off his shirt. Sweat dripped down his chest. I looked away, and by looked away, I mean I stared until it became necessary for me to avert my eyes.

When the song ended, the dancers moved off the floor. I caught a glimpse of Mei with Darren near the stage, which reminded me that I hadn't prepared what to say to her. I ducked behind the nearest potted plant, a tall and bushy ficus. When Linny and Weyland followed me, I pretended nonchalance.

"What are you doing?" Linny asked.

"Crouching." Which couldn't last forever, so I pushed through the crowd, away from the stage, leading us to a quiet spot near the bathroom. "Can you excuse us?" I asked Weyland. Linny followed me in, sat down on the counter by the sink, and raised her eyebrows.

"Have you ever thought about the word *bathroom*?" I asked. "It's not like we're going to take a bath." I checked myself in the mirror. No goombas between my teeth. "But no one would

dare ask for directions to the urinationroom. Or even the gossiproom."

"What do you think of Weyland?"

Ack. "He's"—I struggled for the correct degree of gush— "great."

"He's more than great. He's hella adorable! Don't be so restrained, X."

"I brought you here to fix your bra, actually. Have you noticed how dingy the straps are? You might want to take it off."

"Don't you love how his hair curls around his ears?"

"Yep," I said. For those unfamiliar with bra geometry, there's a little-known method of removing one without taking off one's top. I leaned against the door while she wiggled out of it—a lace thing made from two square inches of fabric.

She handed it to me to deal with because of her useless nano-purse. "And he's got one of those chin dimples."

"Uh-huh." The bra disappeared into my bag, between the laptop and my mascara. I thought about showing her my dad's journal, but we had business to take care of. "We might as well strategize while we're in here. Plan what to say to Mei."

Linny dropped her head to one side. "There's nothing to plan, X. I don't think Mei will run away from home. If she really wants to, though, we won't be able to change her mind. You know how she is."

Donkey-ish. Which was one of the things I liked about her. "I guess I'm more hopeful."

She frowned. "It's awesome that you're hopeful."

*awesome + hopeful = idiotic?*

"What's wrong with that?" I asked.

She almost rubbed her eyes with her fingertips, but I stopped her in time. "I'm tired from working so hard on the counterprotest, that's all." She looked like she wanted to say more but thought she shouldn't.

I hid dread behind fake enthusiasm. "No, really, what is it?"

She lowered her eyes. "It's just that you've sort of kept your distance from Mei for a long time, and now you're so . . . involved with her."

I looked down too. "Well, she gave me that album of old photos, and then she apologized for dumping me in eighth grade. But the main reason is, I feel she really needs me right now." I swallowed a few times to get the last part out. "Does it bother you?"

In answer, Linny slung an arm around me and kissed my cheek. "Not at all, X! I'm the one that begged you to give her another chance, remember? Okay, just a little, but I'm over it now. Let's go dance."

So we went out and rejoined Weyland, who was waiting for us by the glass-tile wall near the bathroom. All felt fine in the world again, until I saw Mei and Darren together in a booth, holding hands and talking quietly. Judging from the squared angle of her shoulders and the pinched intensity of her mouth, they were discussing something big. Plan D, maybe.

In first grade, Mei and I did a bad thing. Mom would sometimes take us to a place that sold elongated doughnuts and warm soymilk for dipping, a specialty in southern China. One day, we decided to go by ourselves and snuck out of the apartment. Our stolen nickels and pennies came up short, but the shopkeeper fed us anyway. Afterward—with full stomachs and happy hearts—we skipped home, weaving between the people cramming the sidewalk. Except we made a wrong turn, and suddenly, unfamiliar signs and stores surrounded us on all sides.

Petrified with fear, I clung to a lamppost and refused to let go.

Mei assured me she knew the way home. When I remained frozen, she commanded me to close my eyes and hold on to her. I obeyed, and she led me up a hill and down another and up again. While we walked, I concentrated entirely on her voice guiding me, and the feeling of my hand in hers. Finally, we made it home.

I wanted to repay her for that day tonight, do for her what she did for me—lead her to safety somehow.

Mei lit up when she saw us, sprang from her seat and wrapped us in big hugs. "Let's go dance." Before I could say anything, she pulled Darren toward the stage, where the sheer immensity of the sound made conversation impossible. Though her ballet shoes clashed with her flapper costume, she whirled like a dervish unself-consciously, the fringes of her dress flying upward, all the time holding hands with Darren. Note to self: True love comes just as sweetly to those who fail to accessorize.

The hot and sweaty stylings of the Giant Wicks tattooed my eardrums, moved my body to the beat. Every now and then, I let myself watch Weyland, his arms, legs, and hips going in all directions. He looked at me often. Since he belonged to Linny, I could enjoy his flirty smile without worrying about what came next, a perfect equation for a romance-challenged girl like me, if you thought about it.

When the Wicks transitioned to a slow song, Darren swept Mei into waltz mode, rocking her across the shiny floor. Blue strobe lights flashed. She smiled hugely at having to rescue his glasses as they almost fell off his face, her troubles forgotten in the joy of dancing. Weyland stepped toward me, but I turned away from him. After that, he took Linny into his arms and twirled her around while I swayed at the edge of the crowd, thinking how to corner Mei.

As the set ended, Linny cupped her hand over my ear. "I want to go home."

"I'm thirsty," I shouted. Which was part of my plan.

Mei led us back to their booth and slid in next to Darren. In the confusion of the moment, I ended up sandwiched between Linny and Weyland on the other bench. Our thighs touched, making it harder for me to maintain the correct level of detachment toward my friend's boyfriend.

"We haven't met," Darren said to Weyland.

"I'm Weyland."

"Nice to meet you."

A waiter came to our table, and Mei immediately ordered a Manhattan, which sounded sophisticated for someone who'd never been to a club before. Or drunk alcohol. She'd probably researched bar drinks on the Internet in advance so as not to make a fool of herself tonight. I wished I had thought of that.

Taking their roles as designated drivers seriously, Darren and Weyland both ordered a club soda with lime. "What am I having?" I whispered to Linny.

"A martini."

Up till that point, I'd been contemplating a Shirley Temple. Though a martini sounded more mature, I didn't want anything strong. Mom sometimes served me a small glass of rice wine with dinner, and the alcohol made my head muzzy. Besides, if my ID came into question, I could get into trouble.

While I hesitated, Linny ordered a virgin piña colada, and that gave me an idea. "I'll have a virgin martini. Shaken, not stirred."

A strange look came over the waiter's face. Did he loathe James Bond movies or just James Bond imitators? "Are you sure?" he asked.

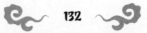

Hot blood filled the capillaries beneath my concealer—Rudolph meets CoverGirl. "Of course." The instant he left, I asked, "What did I say?"

Mei smiled sympathetically. "A martini is made with gin and vermouth."

I'd never even heard of vermouth. "So?"

"They both contain alcohol. If you leave them out, all you have left is . . . nothing."

"You mean I just ordered a glass of air?"

Mei understood the pain of wasting good money. "With an olive. You could call him back."

"No, thanks."

Weyland spoke up. "This round is on me." Which was very considerate of him.

Then Darren changed the subject to a less embarrassing topic than drinks—the band. Linny poked me in the ribs. *Keep it moving.* So I started with an innocuous question that didn't assume anything. "Does your mom think you're at Linny's tonight?" I asked Mei.

She looked at Darren, uncertain whether to confide in me, maybe. His eyes encouraged her to tell me. I loved watching them communicate like that, in their own secret code. "I left Ma a note."

The waiter returned with our drinks. Mine came in a classic cone-shaped glass with an olive speared on a toothpick bathed in clear liquid. "A virgin martini," he said, setting it in front of me with a flourish, his chin quivering a little. I took a sip. At least he'd had the decency to fill the glass with water before serving me.

After he left, I pressed on. "Do you think you'll get in trouble for sneaking out?"

Mei brought her pinkie knuckle to her teeth. "I should . . ."

She took a sip of the Manhattan, wincing as if she'd swallowed a paper clip, and then looked at Darren with that same question in her eyes. I swirled my olive in its crystalline bath. Linny and Weyland sipped their drinks.

Darren cuddled Mei's hand against his cheek. "We can trust them."

Mei's eyes shone. "I wanted you, my best friends in the whole world, to be with me tonight for a special occasion."

Darren dropped Mei's hand, and together they raised their glasses to us. "We're getting married," they said in unison.

"We're eloping," Mei added.

"Tomorrow," Darren said.

They laughed.

Silence fell on our side of the table—think of a cartoon where an anvil drops from a third-story window onto the person below. *Thump.*

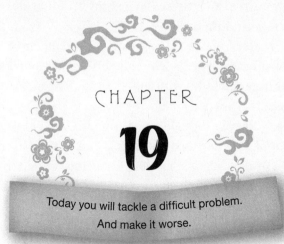

Today you will tackle a difficult problem.
And make it worse.

My mouth turned into a vast and arid wasteland so sandy I could taste the camels. Shock really does paralyze a person. Still, I managed to lift my glass to drain my virgin martini, aka water, in a single draft. "Hmm," I said. Nothing else came out. Mei and Darren seemed to be following in Romeo and Juliet's footsteps—a young couple deeply in love, defying familial obligations by eloping. Except the comparison did not please me, considering the double-suicide angle.

Linny ruffled her hair with her fingertips, which made it look more electrocuted than usual. "You're getting married?"

Mei smiled bravely at her scowling face. "Ma won't insist that I go to Harvard and live apart from my *husband*. Family first, you know."

Husbandy, husbandy, husband. A Fog of Fluster descended over my brain processes, muffling them in misty white. I wished I could discreetly stand on my head somewhere to help me think.

Darren gazed sweetly at Mei. "My beautiful bride."

Brididy, brididy, bride.

"We'd talked about getting married sooner or later, anyway, like after college," Mei said, setting her hand on the table. Darren covered it with his.

Except that sooner ≠ later.

"Have you even thought this through?" Linny asked.

Mei took another sip of her drink, and by sip, I mean gulp. "How about I'm so happy for you, Mei. Congratulations, Mei," she said. "You told me to stand up to Ma, Lin, so I'm standing up to her in the only way I know how."

Darren gently removed the Manhattan from Mei's grip.

I could feel the heat rising off Linny's skin. "I meant you should insist on doing what you want no matter what *she* wants," Linny said.

Mei picked up her drink again. "You know I can't go against Ma. It's like a piece of gravel trying to stand up to a mountain."

Weyland's hand sought mine under the table, and squeezed. I didn't know what to make of this, so I kept perfectly still.

"You've made up your mind, then. Congratulations," Linny said.

Tears pooled in Mei's eyes. "Don't be . . . What's the word, Erin?"

*Sarcastic? Mean?* With Weyland's hand cupping my hand under the table, it was hard to concentrate. "Perfunctory?"

Darren kept trying to catch Mei's eye. When she finally looked at him, she calmed down. Abruptly, Linny half stood and, leaning across the table, kissed Mei on the cheek. "I'm such a jerk sometimes. Don't cry. I'm sorry. I know you're in love."

Everyone around the table relaxed an inch or two.

Except me. I still needed to figure out a subtle way to raise a few issues. Like how getting married at eighteen was

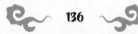

somewhat deranged. And a secret marriage would shred Mrs. Liu's heart into ribbons. The blame for this turn of events pretty much rested on my shoulders. If I hadn't written a Miss Fortune Cookie letter to Mei, she would've forged a rejection letter from Harvard, and this insane elopement never would've seen the light of day. Or night.

Postulate A: The probability that one mistake will change someone's life is small.

Postulate B: Never confuse low probability with impossibility.

Before an opening to speak up came along, Linny grinned at Mei. "I have this cousin who got married at eighteen," she said. "He had a fling with his dentist after the wedding, and separated from his new wife. She slept around some too. But they got back together a year later and just celebrated their twelfth wedding anniversary."

"Great story, Linny," Darren said, laughing hard.

Mei leaned into Darren's side. "We'll be different."

After that, the conversation turned to the dress Mei would wear tomorrow, et cetera. Ignoring Weyland's hand around mine, I considered objection after objection. If only I could conjure a fortune cookie with just the right message inside:

1. The worst luck comes to those who elope on a Tuesday.
2. Beware of judges.
3. Your mistake will lead to a lifetime of pimples.

While I stewed in silence, Linny went beyond acceptance to a state of near giddiness. "Well, my lovebirds, where do you plan to do the deed?"

Mei gasped. "Linny!"

"Not that! I meant where are you going to tie the knot?"

Mei laughed. "I'd like to get married at my church, but we can't, so we made an appointment at the courthouse."

"Where will you stay tonight?"

"At the Sleepy—" Darren said.

Mei interrupted him with an affectionate swat. "No we won't, remember? I got us that room at Stanford Court."

I found my voice at last. "Boys who marry before the age of twenty are four times as likely to go bald, you know." Unfortunately, it was my joke-a-minute voice, which no one takes seriously.

Case in point—Mei giggled and Darren shook his hair at me. "Not in my family."

So I had to stop the Car of Craziness another way, stomp on the brakes, so to speak, blurt out the truth. "I think it's a bad idea. Eloping, I mean." That brought the happy times around the table to a screeching halt, engulfing us in rubbery smoke. Mei covered her ears.

"Just listen to me for a second," I said. "My mom said that your mom would never force you to go to Harvard." Not that I had entirely believed her. Yet Mei and Darren's plan was so warped, it called for a little dishonesty. Running away to Los Angeles to work for Disneyland seemed reasonable by comparison. Seriously.

Mei uncovered her ears, her whole body shaking now. "She *will* force me. In her own way."

"Your mom loves you more than anything," I said. "She wants the best for you."

"I'm her trophy daughter to display on a lacquered shelf," Mei said bitterly. "But I don't want to be number one anymore. I just want to be happy."

"It's okay, Mei," Darren said. "Just hear Erin out."

Mei wheeled on him, looking hurt. "Oh. Now you don't want to marry me anymore?"

Darren returned her gaze with melting earnestness. "Of course I do. You're the love of my life."

Mei's eyes softened. When she faced me again, though, she adopted her more familiar in-control facade. "What did your mom say, exactly?" she asked.

Eeep. "We talked about you tonight during the drive to Linny's. I hope you don't mind. Mom asked about you, so I said you were conflicted about going to Harvard. I told her your mother was forcing you to go. Then *my* mom said your ma would never do that."

Darren and Mei exchanged a long glance. I held my breath and waited patiently. And by patiently, I mean I managed not to dive across the table, take her by the shoulders, and shake some sense into her. "You're right, Erin," Mei said, at last. "We shouldn't elope." Darren smiled. Somehow they'd agreed to call it off without using words. They could be amazing like that.

"That's great," I said, flinging my arms in the air. Unfortunately, my elbow grazed Linny's piña colada, and the glass tipped on its side, emptying a waterfall of freezing slush into my lap. I yelped from the cold.

Weyland stood to let me slide out of the booth. My new vertical position encouraged additional clumps of ice to slide down my legs into my borrowed sandals, not a pleasant sensation. "Be right back," I said. I made a dash for the bathroom with Linny right on my heels. When we got inside, I wiped at my skirt with a handful of paper towels.

"That went well," Linny said, pausing dramatically, like if she gave me enough time, I might find the evening hilarious. But she could wait forever. She could wait for Godot, and

Godot would never come. "Well, James," she added in a sultry Russian accent. "At least we defeated SPECTRE."

Which made me laugh despite my best intentions not to. "The name is Bond, Lame Bond. Bring me an olive in water. Shaken, not stirred." I wadded the sludgy paper towels into the trash bin.

"Take off the skirt and give it to me."

I obeyed. While she labored over the sink, I cleaned off my legs with more damp paper towels. "Their plan was so messed up," I said. "No wonder Mei wouldn't tell us about it before."

Linny squirted soap from the dispenser. "The thing is, she's an adult now. She can live her life however she wants to."

I leaned against the door. "Thank God I talked her out of it."

After wringing out the skirt, Linny held it under the hand dryer in a futile attempt to make it somewhat less wet. "I don't want to think about it anymore. I need to go home and sleep for a hundred years."

"You were the one who got so mad at Mei. At first."

Linny rotated the skirt under the hot air. "That was revenge. She got really pissy with me when I told her how old Dub is." She changed her voice to Mei's. *"What do you think you're doing dating an older man?"*

"Dub's not that old. He said twenty-one, right?"

Linny froze, stopped moving the skirt under the blower, in fact. Her face grew pink and her tired eyes began to shine. Then she shrieked and threw the skirt up into the air. After catching it, she cracked up, and by cracked up, I mean laughed to the point of hysteria. The more she howled, the more I felt like the big, round butt of some absurd joke.

"What the . . . ?"

She gasped for air. "You think Weyland is Dub!"

Um.

She made a funny face. "You misunderstood when I said we met at that gay-marriage rally in Berkeley. You see, I met a ton of people that day—Dub, Weyland, and a bunch of others. We all went to a party together afterward."

I opened my mouth.

Linny interrupted. "Just listen. I'll tell you everything I know. Friday, after you left Hay Fat in a huff, you hung out at Donatello's. Weyland happened to be there, and he totally fell for you."

"He was just being friendly because I stepped on his croissant."

She started drying the skirt again. "Let me finish. So Weyland's brother, Winston, told him you were this brilliant senior at Lowell that hung out with Linny and Mei. Weyland made the connection and called me Sunday to get your number. By the way, why didn't you tell me all this? Anyway, I called him tonight on a whim, and he happened to be free. It's like a fairy tale come true."

"Really?" I squeaked.

Linny beamed at me. "I take it you like him back."

Weyland had fallen for me? The light in the little bathroom changed so that everything went goldeny and wavy, even the bathroom stall. The sink shrank to dollhouse size, cute and weird looking. My insides heated up and flipped around like they were stir-frying. In a good way. I wondered if my dad would have approved of Weyland. Weyland was older. Would my amateur kisses and inexperience frustrate him? Would my European ancestry bother him after a while?

"Erin?"

The bathroom door flew open, nearly knocking me over, and Weyland himself came running through. When he saw me

in my skimpy underwear, he covered his eyes with his hands. "Sorry! I just thought you'd want to know that Darren and Mei are leaving. I think they decided to elope after all."

Linny sort of pushed him out the door. "Hurry up and get dressed," she whispered to me. "Your boyfriend's waiting."

You will become a crispy noodle in the salad of life.

When I stepped into my skirt, some sections of it were almost dry. But as I tried to slide it up my legs, the damp waistband caught on my skin. I never should've trusted Mei. "We have to stop them."

Linny didn't answer.

I struggled with the zipper. "Don't you care?"

"Of course I care. If Mei runs away, who will play 'Hava Nagila' at my protest tomorrow?"

The lining got all twisted around my thighs. "Ha. Ha. Are you forgetting the utter madness and mayhem of eloping while still in high school?"

Linny bumped me with her shoulder. "I was joking. I'll call Mei right now." She dug around in her tiny purse. "But I can't find my phone."

Fortunately, Weyland had waited for us outside the bathroom door and owned a working phone with minutes on it and everything. Misfortunately, Mei had turned off *her* cell.

After I left a message, my brain whirred until I had a new idea. A half-baked idea, but still. "We're going after them."

Linny rested her head on my shoulder. "Everything has a rainbow aura around it." New purplish smudges had bloomed under her eyes.

"I'll take a cab," I said with bravado. Having never actually taken a cab before, I wondered if twenty dollars would cover the fare. "Can I borrow your phone, Weyland, just for tonight?"

"I suppose you want to borrow my *car*, too. How well do you drive?"

"Um," Linny said. "Erin is . . . a good driver."

"Except I don't have a license. And I'm pretty terrible, actually." Then I mentally added twenty-five cents to the Linny Entertainment Fund.

Weyland laughed. "Sorry. It wasn't a serious offer anyway. You don't want to know how much I care about my car."

"Um."

"But I can drive you to Stanford Court. We'll take Linny home first."

Linny smeared her mascara down her cheeks with her palms. "The Sunset is a long detour. Why don't *I* take a cab home." She gave me a squeeze to show she meant it. "Now go."

I obeyed her, semirunning toward the exit, except that running turned out to be impossible inside a crowded club. So I banged into a lot of people until Weyland caught me by the hand and threaded me through the last of the throng.

"Good night," the bouncer said as we zipped by him. He was humming the theme to *90210*.

Not really.

This had to be the zaniest moment of my life—rushing into the night with a dangerously cute college boy who actually

liked me, to stop my friend from eloping. We're talking near–spy-thriller material, except without the electronic gadgets, secret codes, and exploding helicopters, of course. Usually nothing happened to me—my daily routine ran more like an artistic French film where everyone just sits around and talks. Well, except I don't drink a lot of coffee or chain-smoke cigarettes.

As we hurried down the sidewalk toward his car, Weyland kept a grip on me. I left my hand in his, savoring the size of it and his calluses and even the dampness of his skin. Breathing was hard because of the buzzing in my chest, and yet each breath felt incredible, like I'd been hooked up to pure oxygen. The last boy with a crush on me invited me over to play video games at his house, *Bloody Battlefield* or something. This felt entirely different.

We passed a row of blocky three-story apartment buildings with shops underneath, finding the Mini Cooper dwarfed by a Ford X-Large. It looked like a kid's toy, in fact. Weyland unlocked the doors and jumped in. By the time I'd fastened my seat belt, he'd started the engine and released the hand brake. "I know the way to Stanford Court, more or less. It's on California, right?" he asked.

A van pulled out ahead of us. "There they are! Mei and Darren." In the excitement of the moment, I grabbed Weyland's arm, and the feeling of it against my palm—the warmth and firmness—sent a current through me. As if I needed any more zapping. "They're in the big white van. You can cut them off."

Weyland revved the engine, dropped the clutch, and accelerated into the street just two cars behind them. "You're nothing like I expected."

"What were you expecting?"

He zoomed forward and grinned at me. "Linny said you're . . . the opposite of an adrenaline junkie."

I pretended to be all relaxed. "I'm having a great time." One of the cars that separated us from the van made a right turn. "Did Linny say anything else about me?" When the traffic light ahead turned yellow and Weyland punched the gas, I consciously kept my hands loose and in my lap. The van turned at the next corner, losing the other car between us.

"That's weird," Weyland said. "They're going the wrong way." His phone went off somewhere inside his clothing. "Can you get that?"

I hesitated.

"It's in my shirt pocket."

I pushed aside his coat and extracted the phone with delicate precision.

*Weyland's chest = hot toaster*

"It's Linny," I said.

"Aren't you going to pick up?"

Um, right. "Linny. You found your phone!"

"It was inside my boot the whole time. Thank God, because Mom would've killed me if I'd lost another one. I'm on my way home now in a cab. Thanks for understanding."

"No, thank *you*."

"No, thank *you*," she teased. "And kiss Weyland for me."

I ignored her. "We're right behind Darren's van on Sixteenth. They're heading east, away from Stanford Court."

"Hah! I knew it. Darren said the name of another hotel first, remember? Before Mei interrupted him. Sleepy something."

"Sleepy Inn!"

After we hung up, I studied Weyland's phone. "Can you access the Internet on this?"

"Sorry, no G4. I'm just a poor student."

Which made him doubly sweet for treating us to drinks. Careful to keep my hand from shaking, I slid the phone back into his shirt pocket. The phlebotomist at PacMed once commented on my steadiness. That's how phlebotomists flirt, I think.

Darren whipped around another corner without signaling, and Weyland sped after him. The large cloth bag slid across the back seat. Near the entrance to the Bay Bridge, Darren hurtled through another yellow light, leaving us stuck behind the red.

"Hell in a blanket," I said.

Weyland gunned the engine. "I can run it."

"Don't." I put my hand over his on the gearshift, lifting it when it broke out in a profusion of sweat. "That car behind us? It's probably a policeman in an unmarked vehicle. After he hauls you off to the station and leaves me alone in this forsaken neighborhood, some wereghost will come along and tear me to bits."

He inched the car forward. "You have an interesting imagination." His smile was positively wicked as he rolled under the red light.

"*Ni feng le!*" I yelled. *You're crazy.*

He accelerated to the speed limit and beyond. "What did you call me?"

"Mildly insane. You don't speak Chinese?"

"Just a little. Like five words."

"They're getting onto the Bay Bridge," I said.

He accelerated even more. "Don't worry, I'll catch up with them. Teach me something in Chinese." Like we were chatting over a steaming cup of oolong tea rather than involved in a car chase wherein numerous laws had already been broken.

He changed lanes into a narrow gap, and a red truck blinked its lights at us.

I watched him drive, the calm grip he had on the wheel, his lips curved up in a half smile, memorized him for future daydreaming purposes, actually. "Repeat after me. *Ni de zui-chun hen hao kan.*" *Your lips are very beautiful.*

"Knee duh sway . . . What are you making me say?" he asked with mock fear.

"*Your car is nice.* Do you see the van?"

"We'll find them again at the end of the bridge. How did you learn to speak Chinese?"

"I was born in China, then we moved to San Francisco after my dad died, and I did Chinese school after regular school. I'm not exactly fluent, like when I read a story, I have to look up a lot of words in the dictionary."

"I've read a little Confucius, but it was translated into English."

He'd read the Analects? Be still my heart.

When we arrived at the end of the bridge, we both looked around. "We've lost them," he said.

"I have a laptop on me."

He smiled and raised his eyebrows at me. "I've always wondered what girls keep in those huge purses."

"We nerd girls are always prepared. I have Kleenex and a calculator, too," I said with an indignant toss of my head. "If you know a place with Wi-Fi, I can look up the Sleepy Inn."

"My cousin Joel lives nearby. We can use his Wi-Fi."

We glided past tall buildings of glass and steel. "It's past eleven. Won't he mind?"

"Not unless we wake him. Linny told me you're going to Berkeley. That's where I go."

A swoosh of hair half covered his forehead. I used to think

that the heaving emotions portrayed in romance novels couldn't possibly happen in real life. How could a lock of hair make your heart pound? Except it just had. My lips felt dry, and I rummaged through a side pocket in my boho for an emergency tube of lip balm. "What's your major?"

"The most popular one. Undeclared."

I laughed. A few loose fortunes escaped from my bag and fluttered onto Weyland's immaculate floor mats.

"What are those?" he asked.

"Fortune cookie fortunes. I sort of collect them. Just for fun. I know they're not really Chinese, but . . ." I stopped myself, not wanting to come off as a ditz.

"What? I'm curious."

"When you slide a fortune from a cookie, it makes a little hissing noise—a little warning that anything could happen. Mostly good things."

He didn't laugh at me. He gazed at me intently, in fact. "Tell me my fortune."

I pretended to read one. "The man who keeps his eyes on the road will live another day."

We entered a semi-industrial neighborhood with warehouses and auto-repair places. Weyland slowed down. When I least expected it, he whipped his hand out and tried to snatch the fortune from my fingers. "You're lying," he said.

I held it to the far side of the car, where he couldn't reach it.

"We're almost out of gas," he said, pointing to the gauge.

When I leaned over to see, he struck again and captured the fortune this time. "Hmm," he said, reading between glances out the windshield. "You will gain admiration from your pears. Pears. Does that make me a pear too?"

"More like a tangerine, actually." Gah!

Weyland pulled into a scruffy parking lot. As I turned to

unbuckle my seat belt, he did the same, bringing our heads close together for a moment. "A tangerine, huh? Why's that? Is my skin orange?" His eyes held mine like he might kiss me, and my cells hummed, resonating at the nearness of his.

Can electrons flowing through a person's lips generate a magnetic field?

Probably not, because he didn't kiss me. Disappointed, I sat up straighter, looked out the window, and somewhat changed the subject. "I love the mistakes made in translations. Like this restaurant in my neighborhood serves corrugated iron beef. I ordered it once just to see what it could be. The meat really *was* thin and wavy."

"We should go in." He came around to my side and opened the door for me. The streetlights cast long shadows, and a paper cup rolled in the wind, echoing on each bounce. Across the street from us, a sanity-challenged person stood in a doorway. "It's eleven fifty-eight and thirty-two seconds," he shouted. "It's eleven fifty-eight and forty-one seconds. It's eleven fifty-eight and fifty-one seconds."

A second man appeared in the gloom, charging toward us, an amoeba-shaped hat pulled low over his ears, a long coat engulfing his burly bulk. It was two against one, but what if he had a weapon? I braced myself as he reached us. Before I could scream, though, he crossed the street.

"You're wrong, man," he said to the yelling man in the doorway. "Your watch is fast." After a short pause, the chanting started again. "It's eleven nineteen and nine seconds."

My stomach unclenched. I really did have an interesting imagination. Weyland led me to an apartment building close by with flimsy steps that shook as we climbed to a balcony that ran along the second story. He slipped a key into the lock.

"Shhh. We don't want to wake him." He opened the door slowly and switched on the light.

"Haaaaiiiiyaaaaa!"

The shriek came from a man wearing only boxer shorts, presumably Joel. He had a long, gleaming sword blade raised over his head. I ducked.

CHAPTER

21

Bad times lie behind you.
And some lie ahead.

The sword wobbled a little. "We're friendly," I squeaked in my best Rodent of Confidence manner. Weyland doubled over laughing, a kind of high-pitched chuckle that took me by surprise—a man-giggle.

Joel stood motionless, the sword still aloft. "I coulda split your head like a melon," he said, the words blurring at the edges. "That woulda sucked."

Weyland kept laughing, and Joel flicked the sword blade downward. "What're you doing here?" The room reeked somewhat unpleasantly. I noticed a Costco-sized liquor bottle on the kitchen counter that may have contributed.

"Borrowing your Wi-Fi," Weyland said. "Nice cats."

Joel looked down at the kittens frolicking across his boxers. "I'm going back to bed, loser. Keep your voices down and don't wake the kid." He pointed to a writhing bundle of sheets perched on one end of the couch. "Too late. Now he's your problem. Sing him a lullaby or something." He left, closing his bedroom door behind him.

"You could've warned me," I whispered.

"Joel is harmless. He learned everything he knows from the movies."

The sword blade looked real enough.

I gave Weyland my laptop, and he sank into the cushions at one end of the very-plaid couch. The room was sweltering, so I peeled off my hoodie and sat down between him and the bundle of sheets. A tuft of frizzy hair emerged first, and then a whole boy's head. Between his lopsided Afro, blond at the tips, and his round eyes, he looked like a troll doll.

"I'm Erin. Who are you?"

He yawned a long and shuddery yawn. "Lincoln."

"Like the president?" I asked.

He snorted air through his nose. "Like the car, dummy."

"Is Joel your dad?" They didn't look remotely alike, except it's wrong to assume.

He shook his head. "I live downstairs with Karina. She's at work."

"Who's Karina?"

Lincoln buried his head in the pillow. "My mom. In Latvia, everyone calls their parents by their first names." He seemed to go back to sleep, so I left him alone and looked around. The room had more in common with a storage locker than with your average living room. Three rows of freestanding shelves took up most of the floor, displaying crystal balls, a knight's helmet, weapons, robots, figurines, and antique dolls.

"Is Joel an artist?" I whispered to Weyland.

"He makes a living buying from estate sales and selling on eBay. I found the Sleepy Inn. Get me something to write on."

I wrestled a little spiral-bound notepad I always keep in my boho from the tangle of other things. When it came loose, something connected to it—Linny's skimpy bra, in fact—launched upward, and landed on Weyland's shoulder. Thankfully, he pretended not to notice while I snatched it away and stuffed it back in, blushing horribly.

"It's Linny's," I said in an attempt to explain.

Which clarified nothing.

Then, without warning, Weyland took my wrist and pulled me toward him. I drew in a breath, wondering if he meant to kiss me this time. "Don't move," he said, bending over my arm and writing the address to the Sleepy Inn on my skin. Sparks rose from the trail of ink.

I could've touched my lips to his hair right then, but something prevented me. Like common sense. Just because a force outside my control had caused an electrical disturbance that threw me into an unpredictable vortex swirling through the unseen fabric of the universe, that didn't mean I had to act crazy. Besides, the reality of having a boyfriend somewhat terrified me. Postponing any attempts at a relationship until later would be best for everyone involved, so I pulled away from him, and stood up.

Weyland didn't seem to notice. "I'll MapQuest it," he said. I pretended to examine Joel's collection of animal figurines, while watching him from the side. After a moment, his liquid eyes found my face. "Can I ask you something?"

"Sure."

"What's your natural hair color?"

"Light brown." With red highlights, but I kept that part to myself because it sounds vain.

He squinted as if trying to picture it. "Why did you dye it black? Are you going emo?"

"All my friends are Chinese." Did that make me superficial? Except what's wrong with wanting to fit in? My nature was Chinese, maybe because Mom drank too much Sang Ji Sheng tea to strengthen her blood when she was pregnant with me.

"You should grow it out," he said.

I snatched a felt fedora from Joel's shelf, squashed it over my hair, and turned away from him.

He got up from the couch. "I'm going to get gas. I'll be right back."

"Shouldn't I go with you?"

"It's not safe unless you have a black belt."

"You have a black belt?" The glint in his eyes made me suspicious.

"In Whac-a-Mole." He started man-giggling again, which I liked, actually, because it expressed so much happiness.

"What's Whac-a-Mole?"

Lincoln popped out from under the sheets again, fully awake this time. "It's an arcade game with a mallet and moles."

"Let me demonstrate." Weyland found some drumsticks in Joel's collection of amazing junk, buried his hand among the pillows on the couch, and pretended to thwack it every time it surfaced. His hand (the mole) always dove away just in time. "It's a useful skill. Especially if there's ever a zombie apocalypse."

I laughed, the temporary awkwardness between us gone.

After Weyland left, I collapsed back onto the couch, and Lincoln climbed halfway into my lap. "Is he your boyfriend?"

He weighed as much as a very large dog. "No, he isn't. I can tell you a bedtime story."

"But he likes you."

I sighed. "I'm not sure, actually. We just met. It's complicated."

Lincoln leaned his head into my shoulder and gazed up at me. "No, it's simple. Just French-kiss him. Boys like that."

"How old are you?"

"Nine, but I'm homeschooled, so I know a lot."

Which gave me an idea. I shifted him off my lap and grabbed the computer. "You know about love, huh?" I asked. "Because I'm an advice columnist, and I need help answering some letters. You can't tell anyone my secret identity, though."

Lincoln nodded. "I won't tell."

I loaded Miss Fortune Cookie. "Here's a letter about love."

Dear Miss Fortune Cookie,

I have a boyfriend that I adore. I also have a boy *friend* that I've known for years. Suddenly my boyfriend doesn't like my boy *friend* and wants me dump him.

But my boy *friend*'s parents are divorcing, and he needs me. Besides, my feelings for my boy *friend* are slightly more than friendly.

Why do I have to choose between them?

Stuck in the middle

Lincoln got all solemn, putting the tip of his thumb in his mouth to think. The rubbery skin between his eyebrows puckered a little.

"A tough one, right? Let's look for something easier."

He took his thumb out with a smack. "It's not hard. Just type what I say." So I did.

Dear Stuck,

Your boyfriend is being really mean to your boy *friend* because he's jealous. You have to choose or they will kill each other.

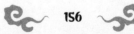

My mom says the only kind of boyfriend worth anything is nice to you and lets you wear your old clothes around him. Pick that one.

Lincoln

His letter made me smile, so I saved a draft for later and clicked on the next one.

Dear Miss Fortune Cookie,

An incredible thing happened this week. My daughter got into Harvard. Right away she told me she didn't want to go. Whenever I bring it up, she changes the subject.

She needs to be more independent. It would be good for her to be away from home. What should I do?

Concerned

I blinked a few times because I knew who'd sent in this letter. *Mom.* The next breath I took hurt like my ribs had burrs stuck to them. *I* needed to be more independent? The apartment makeover made sense now, and all the excitement about Harvard. She wanted to clear me out like debris from her closet. Salt stung my eyes.

"I liked the boyfriend/girlfriend one better," Lincoln said. "But I'll answer this one anyway." I suctioned back my tears and typed as he dictated.

Dear Concerned,

As soon as I can drive, I'm going to buy a VW van and convert it to solar and drive across Asia. It will have

robotic feet for sand and mud. When I get to Tibet, I will study with the Shaolin monks, because they can levitate.

My mom thinks it's a good idea. Tell your daughter about it, and she'll want to come too. It will get her out of the house.

Lincoln

I began to feel a smidgen better. Really, Lincoln's ability to get to the heart of the matter was near demonic. In a good way. My reasons for choosing Berkeley over Harvard remained solid—the cost, the distance, the joy of going to college with my best friend, et cetera. But Lincoln somehow turned the sad event of leaving home into a grand adventure. Maybe I shouldn't worry so much about Mom eating alone, cleaning alone, and shopping alone. Getting lonely alone.

Before I could digest it all, Lincoln had moved on. "Look for a letter with a kissing problem. Kissing is more interesting. Or we can play Whac-a-Mole online. I know the website for that."

I closed the laptop and stashed it away. "It's late. You should go back to sleep."

He started doing jumping jacks at high speed. "I'm not tired." Then he stopped, climbed into the couch, and rammed into me, breathing hard. "Tell me a story. Make it really scary. I only fall asleep to scary stories."

If subjected to intelligent scrutiny, his statement was ridiculous, but I fell for it anyway. "You want scary? Okay, hold on to me, then." He clutched me with both hands. "This is a Chinese story about water ghosts. They're sort of like zombies, the dead bodies of people who have drowned but want to live again. If anyone foolishly swims by, the ghost yanks them under the water and steals their breath."

Lincoln smiled at me. With clenched teeth. "Keep going."

"Once, a girl lived by the Yangtze River with her family. She worked hard, plowing, planting, and weeding the fields. Her greatest love was flowers. Even if every muscle hurt at the end of the day, one smell of jasmine would cure her.

"On Double-Seventh Day, the boy who loved her gave her a bouquet of jasmine. The village prefect, an older man who wanted her as a concubine, got jealous and threw the flowers into the river. Forgetting all about the water ghosts, she jumped in after them. Just as her hand closed around the stems, a dead creature clawed her ankle with its bony fingers, dragged her under, and—"

The door opened and Lincoln screamed. "What's going on?" Weyland asked.

Lincoln bounced from one end of the couch to the other. "Erin is telling me a story."

"I filled the tank. We should go."

Lincoln brought his hands together under his chin like he was praying. "Can I come?"

Weyland shook his head. "Sorry, little man. Why don't I tuck you in?" He held out the sheet as if to wrap it around him.

Lincoln scrambled behind the couch. "I can't go to sleep now! Joel's robot is haunted! It wants to kill me! It keeps saying *crush, kill, destroy!* Can't you hear it?"

Weyland shot me a look. "I'll put the robot in the bathroom."

While he was out of the room, Lincoln ventured from behind the sofa, crawled to me, and wrapped his arms around my legs. "Please, please, please. I'll wake up Joel if you don't take me." He wailed like a siren. Literally. Just as I clapped my hand over his mouth, Weyland came back out.

"What should we do?" I asked.

"It's not that far to the Sleepy Inn, and Joel's my cousin," Weyland said. "That hardly makes me a stranger. We can take Lincoln and bring him right back after you talk to Mei."

But if we both went to jail for kidnapping, who would bake the cake with the file in it?

I let go of Lincoln's mouth. "I guess. Maybe."

# CHAPTER

# 22

You will find love with a strange handsome.

Lincoln did a cartwheel to celebrate his victory over sensible behavior—he'd essentially blackmailed us into bringing him along—and knocked down a row of figurines with his foot. They fell unharmed onto the carpet. While I lined them on the shelf again, he wrapped himself in an oversized purple shawl, which made him look totally zepto.

$$Zepto = small^{-21}$$

"Let's go," I said.

Lincoln belly wiggled to the front door. "I'm hungry. Can we stop at the pancake house? It's only three blocks from here. Joel always gets them for me."

Ack. What started as a high-speed car chase had slowed to an event a decrepit snail could win. It felt like one of those dreams where you're running through honey, and your leg muscles become so feeble, you go about three feet a minute. I would never get a chance to talk to Mei. "If we keep it quick."

Weyland led us to the Mini Cooper and pushed aside the cloth bag to make room for Lincoln in the back seat. Lincoln sat down on top of it. "What's in here? It's lumpy."

"Just random body parts. Nothing to worry about," Weyland joked.

Lincoln's eyes widened. "Can I see?"

In traditional Chinese medicine, courage resides in the gallbladder, an organ about the size of a plum. Lincoln's was more like a grapefruit, I think. Weyland laughed. "Sorry to disappoint you, little man. It's just some costumes I put together for a play I'm in."

Lincoln rummaged through the bag. "I was a farmer in a play once. What are you?"

"I have multiple parts. A prince, an ogre, and ...," Weyland said, "a Bic lighter."

"Wow! Do you get to light your head on fire?" It doesn't take much to impress a nine-year-old.

"I wish," Weyland said. As Lincoln gave directions to the restaurant, Weyland drove at an annoyingly law-abiding pace. His sleeve had gotten a bit twisted, and I straightened it for him. After he pulled into Pancake World, he turned to look at me.

"It was crooked," I said before turning away from shyness.

While we waited at the counter for our order, Lincoln slipped his hand into mine. "Don't tell Karina about the chocolate chips. She only lets me get whole grain."

"I promise."

"Did the water ghost drown that girl in the river?"

"Yes. The jasmine girl became the new water ghost, and the old one got to live again. After that, the girl's true love drowned himself so they could be together."

Lincoln looked up at me with teacup eyes. "Tell me another water-ghost story."

I thought for a moment. "Okay. This one's true. When I was your age, a water ghost visited my friend Mei. She showed up one night in a soaked dress, water streaming off her skin, seaweed twined in her hair. She kept saying the word *love* and touching her heart. Mei showed me the wet spot on her carpet the next morning.

"Then I dreamed about an old letter in Mei's room. When we looked for it, we found a piece of paper stuffed into a crack at the back of her bookcase, all wavy as if it'd been wet."

Lincoln tightened his grip on my hand. "What did the letter say?"

The pancakes came. "Just a sec." After a short verbal tussle with Weyland, he let me pay for them with Mom's twenty, and we returned to the car. I made sure Lincoln buckled in before we pulled out into the road.

Lincoln huffed. "*Now* you can tell me."

"It wasn't a letter. The paper had two Chinese characters on it, *bi hai*, which together mean something like *sea of jade*. On the back, someone had scrawled a man's name and an address. I thought they might belong to the water ghost's lover, and wrote him a letter, even though Mei laughed at me. A few days later, I found a piece of green sea-glass on my dresser."

"That's the best story ever."

Which made me glad that I'd withheld the ending where Mei and I fought over the piece of glass. She thought it belonged to her because the ghost-girl had first come to *her* room, and we'd found the lover's address there. But *I* had written the letter, and the ghost-girl delivered the thank-you gift to *my* dresser. I kept the glass hidden after that, because every time Mei came over, I worried she might pocket it.

Weyland glanced at me, curious. Did he think I was weird for believing in ghosts?

"Can I have a cigarette?" Lincoln asked.

I turned around in my seat to admonish him. "You don't smoke. You're only nine."

"And three-quarters. Kids are allowed to smoke in Latvia."

I seriously doubted that. "Cigarettes cause cancer, emphysema, and heart disease. Do you know what emphysema is?"

"Holes in your lungs. Can I have the pancakes, then?"

Aha. I recognized the ploy—first ask for the impossible and then switch to something less forbidden that seemed almost reasonable by contrast.

"No cigarettes or syrup inside my car," Weyland said. "Besides, we're almost there. You can eat at the motel."

The Sleepy Inn sign came into view, and we turned in to the lot. Darren's van was parked in front of one of the rooms. Weyland reversed in next to it, and I hopped out, excited to be there at last. Before I could knock on the door, though, Weyland stopped me, put both of his arms around me from behind, in fact. Which startled me like a hug from an electric eel. In a good way.

"It's after midnight. They've turned off the lights."

"You're right," I said, though I could barely form words because of how it felt to be so close to him. If I woke up Mei and Darren, they would naturally feel crabby. And crabby people are harder to convince of anything. But what would we do while they slept? And how early could we wake them?

Lincoln sidled over to us, all agog, and Weyland let go of me. "Why don't we wait till morning? I'll get us a room."

Panic time. "What about Lincoln?" I rested my hands squarely on the little boy's shoulders. He stood between me and a motel room containing Weyland, our nano-chaperone. "Shouldn't we take him back to Joel's? We could hang out there till morning."

Lincoln piped up. "No! I love sleeping in motels. Can I keep the soap? You can have the shampoo. I don't like washing my hair. Just get me home by ten."

"Or we could sleep in the car?" I suggested. "I'm out of money."

Ignoring me, Weyland headed toward the office with Lincoln following. I stayed in the Cooper, listening to the wind sweep the parking lot, shaking the branches of a stunted tree nearby. A few drops of rain fell. When I lay down across the seats, Weyland's scent rose from the backrest, so I sat up and opened the glove compartment. Besides a manual, an insurance card, and a flashlight, I found a little book of Taoist sayings that I flipped through.

*Love is of all passions the strongest, for it attacks simultaneously the head, the heart, and the senses—Lao Tzu.*

*Attacks* was exactly it.

They came back. "We're in the room next to theirs," Weyland said.

I lowered my eyes. "Great. I'm going to stay here."

Weyland frowned. "This has to be the weirdest date ever."

A note rose inside me like the beginning of a happy musical. Despite everything, Weyland still considered this a date. Except the idea of sharing a motel room with a twenty-one-year-old near stranger scared me. A stranger who had seen me in my underwear, but still. What if Lincoln fell asleep and Weyland kissed me? Wouldn't that lead to other things? "I'll be fine out here."

"You should get some rest."

I hadn't even checked the expiration date on my ancient condom. "I'm fine."

Weyland tensed. "You don't trust me?"

I didn't trust *myself*. I might croon love ballads in my sleep, talk about my feelings, and unbutton his shirt. The subconscious mind can be a dangerous thing. "I need some time alone to think."

Lincoln snatched the bag of pancakes from my lap and ran off with them. "Come and get me," he taunted from behind a tree. So I chased him until he let me catch him. "Come on, Erin," he said, holding up the bag. "Let's go eat these in the room."

A low car rumbled into the lot with a woman at the wheel. She wore a towering hat with a huge bow that rivaled Aretha Franklin's at Obama's inauguration. It was bright pink. I tried not to stare when she got out.

"I'm not hungry," I said.

"Don't be stupid. I won't touch you!" Weyland said.

"I'm staying in the car!"

The woman in the pink hat came over to us. "Is this a****** bothering you?"

I covered Lincoln's ears, but he shook me off like a dog shakes off water. "I've heard worse. Way worse."

"We're rehearsing for a play," I said. So she turned around and went into the office.

"This is about the *S* word, isn't it?" Lincoln said.

"What do you know about the *S* word?" Weyland asked.

"I know about herpes."

I climbed into the passenger seat, leaving the door open. "I'll keep the keys and your phone, just in case."

Weyland nodded coldly. I watched his straight back as he walked away.

Lincoln must've noticed my forlorn expression, because he wrapped his arms around my neck and kissed my cheek.

"Good night," he said in a normal voice. Then he whispered, "Weyland's totally hot for you."

"Not anymore," I whispered back.

"You're wrong. Do you want to know what else I know?"

"Of course I do."

He winked so that one half of his face scrunched together. "You'll change your mind."

"Why's that?"

"I have the pancakes." He darted toward the room. "We're in One-oh-four."

CHAPTER

23

An adhesive adventure awaits you.

I slouched down into the passenger seat, ignoring the hungry gurgle from my stomach, shutting out the picture of the two of them eating chocolate-chip pancakes, Lincoln dripping butter onto the bedspread, syrup on Weyland's lips.

In other words, failing miserably.

I opened the car window, and a mist of drizzle blew in, cooling me as I combed through my thoughts. If I had any hope of dissuading Mei from eloping, I needed a solid strategy. The you're-too-young thing wouldn't fly, because Mei always thought she was mature for her age. I'd have to play the brokenhearted-mom card. After all, moms lived to plan, organize, and conquer their one-and-only daughter's wedding. I knew this from countless movies and TV shows.

The rain picked up a little, the occasional larger drop plunking on the roof. I heard, "F*** the f*** off!" shouted from across the parking lot and made out a man dressed all in gray standing alone near the road, his arms raised in the air like a kid having a tantrum. To be on the safe side, I closed the window, locked the doors, and sank down lower.

A city girl like me should be street-smart. I'm not, though. I spend most of my days at Lowell, where almost nothing ever happens. Two years ago, a fight broke out in the courtyard, but I missed it by being home sick that day. One time, a janitor got fired for giving a student his phone number, but he'd never even tried to talk to me. Mom drove me to school because of the SpongeBob pajamas guy, and the afternoon Muni riders consisted mostly of students and commuters.

The man stopped yelling. I finally relaxed enough to take out Dad's journal and touch the egg on the cover, tracing the funny bird feet with the tip of my finger, delaying the actual moment of truth. What if he had written something terrible about me, like he couldn't stand how I smelled?

Or hadn't written anything about me at all.

But my curiosity eventually won out, so I opened the journal and looked at his messy, slanted scrawl. Not wanting to turn on a light, which might attract the attention of Yelling Guy, I read by the infrequent and dim photons that managed to get through the wet window from the parking-lot lamps.

*May 22, 11:30 p.m.*
*Erin finally fell asleep after I rocked her for an hour. She looks like a baked potato wrapped in a blanket.*

So I *was* a beautiful baby. I skipped ahead a few pages.

*June 2, 3:00 a.m.*
*The nights are harder than I expected. Everyone is cranky. Erin, the cause of all the trouble, is*

*cheerful. Right now she won't stop flapping her arms and squawking with happiness like a bird in a birdbath.*

My night-owl side revealed itself early, then. It isn't fair for Mom to blame it on my homework schedule. I flipped to the middle of the journal and picked a long passage dated September 29—which made me almost five months old. Dad had taken me to a park in Shanghai, carrying me on his belly in a front pack. There was a long rant about some women mobbing him, all wanting to touch my face and hands, and how he worried about infectious diseases.

*I hid in a thicket, and finally we had fun. Erin grabbed for everything—leaves, twigs, flowers—she's so curious. She doesn't put anything in her mouth, though. I ascribe this to her superior intelligence. Erin's intelligence will let her do whatever she wants. She could figure out how to prevent tuberculosis or design a solar car—but all I care about is that she's happy doing what she chooses.*

I closed the journal and leaned back. Babies drool a lot, make funny noises, and look surprised that their hands can move. And still he recognized me as brainy at five months. Or maybe he just imagined it. But I was crying for another reason— his beautiful wish for my future. While I dried my eyes on my sleeve, his words enfolded me like an embrace.

Weyland's phone went off. It was Linny. "Hey. Where are you?" she whispered when I picked up.

"Why are you whispering?" I asked.

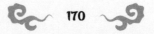

"Dub is here. I don't want him to think I'm gossiping."

"He's at your house? I thought you were tired?" My mouth went dry. I remembered seeing a water bottle earlier and reached under the seat to feel for it.

"He's helping me with the protest. Did you find Mei?"

After a quick sip of water, I filled her in about the car chase, Joel, Lincoln, the pancakes, and the Sleepy Inn parking lot. "I didn't think a motel room made quite the right setting for a first date. I'll wait in the car till dawn, then wake up Mei to talk."

"Sounds kind of boring. Don't fall asleep," she said. The rain came down harder, hammering the roof of the car. "I found someone to play 'Hava Nagila' on accordion tomorrow. And Mischa canceled, so you *have* to come."

My hand rose to loosen the tight scarf around my neck. Except I wasn't wearing a scarf. "I'll try."

She raised her voice a little. "You better."

"I'll be there." Probably. Most likely. Maybe.

Linny lowered her voice. "Thanks. Actually, I called because I think tonight's the night."

"For what?" I drank a lot more water.

Her voice changed. "Don't be dense. For me and Gio."

"Who's Gio?"

"God, Erin, Gio is Dub!"

Which started with a *G* instead of a *W*, by the way. I squeezed the water bottle until it crackled in my hands. "Why have you been calling him Dub then?"

"It's his nickname from his DJ days."

I swallowed. "He used to be a DJ? You haven't told me a thing about him since you met."

"I'm sorry. He doesn't fit into the Lowell mold, you know? He's Italian, born in Milan. He went to college here, and now he's in graduate school."

171

Which made him how old? "I bet he has a sexy accent."

"Incredible," Linny purred. "Tonight has been the most romantic night of my life. He brought tiramisu and helped me make a gazillion paper yarmulkes. It seems right for the big *S*."

I twisted the bottle too hard. Water poured out from a crack in the plastic, but I managed to lean forward in time, so that most of it landed on my feet. I took a deep breath. Here was my chance to prove my trustworthiness as Linny's friend by not arguing with her like Mei would. Even asking questions could sound judgmental. "Wow. I hope it's really . . . perfect and amazing. Well, and that he uses a condom."

Linny cracked up. "You're so funny, X. Call you later, 'kay?"

When I signed off, the rain let up a bit and then stopped altogether, which seemed like a good omen, but I couldn't stop myself from wondering if I'd been a true friend by suppressing my opinions. I opened my dad's journal to the middle and called her back.

"Hey, again," she whispered.

"I forgot the most important thing. Mom found this journal that my dad wrote about me."

"That's so great, Erin."

"Can I read you something from it?"

"I'd love that. Go ahead."

" 'Erin's intelligence will let her do whatever she wants . . . but all I care about is that she's happy doing what she chooses.' "

"That's so beautiful," Linny said.

"I know. So, I just wanted to ask you a question. And please, please, please don't take it the wrong way."

" 'Kay."

No more obscure advice like I gave her when she first mentioned the Big *S*. No more tangents about eagles, rodents, and jet engines. "Do you love Gio?"

Pause. "I think so."

"Does he love you?"

Linny sighed noisily into the phone. "I don't know. It's just that after taking nine AP classes in the past four years and killing myself with homework, I feel like I'm living inside a dry-cleaning bag. Gio is like real life for a change. Fresh air."

Right then, I decided there would be no more sincere lies between my friends and me. "I want you to be happy, like my dad wanted for me," I said. "But will Gio make you truly happy? What about volunteering for that program in Africa? Micro-loans for women. Wouldn't that be real life?"

"It *would* be cool to go to Africa. But I don't think it kisses quite the same as Gio," she joked. "Anyway, you and I are going to have the best time together at Berkeley next year. I feel it."

But what if I decided to go to Harvard?

$$\int college / \infty friendship = 0$$

In other words, complicated. "We *will* have the best time. Still, I could survive without you. You should consider working in Africa, that's all I'm saying," I reasoned most reasonably.

"Thanks." Her whispering had gotten huskier.

"Sweet dreams. I love you," I said.

"Love you, too."

When she hung up, I relaxed my clenched muscles and enjoyed the feeling of blood flowing to where it belonged in my body. We'd had a real talk this time, whatever she decided. Just as my eyelids grew heavy, the phone went off again. "I forgot to tell you something," Linny said. "Mrs. Liu came by my house to talk to Mei. I told her you went out for ice cream and I didn't know where."

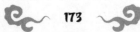

"When was that?"

"Forty-five minutes ago, around midnight. She was totally worried, naturally."

Ack. "I should call her," I said.

"Maybe, maybe not. I should go."

Even Linny could be indecisive sometimes. I considered what to do next.

The poor man from earlier had returned, because I heard the f-word again in various forms. He was probably cursing his wet clothes. At least his yelling would keep me awake. "Good night," I said to Linny.

I pressed end and straightened up to peek out the windshield. The scene in front of me banished any last bit of sleepiness. The woman with the pink hat was sprinting toward her car, the man in gray chasing after her. He caught her before she could get the door open. "Get away from me!" she roared.

Still partly hidden from view, I dialed 911.

"Give me the f***ing purse!" He yanked at it while she protected it with her body like a football player getting tackled, her pink hat coming off and rolling across the pavement. Before the 911 dispatcher picked up, I hit the end button. She needed help right now. There was no time to ponder the best kind of assistance, either.

I slid into the driver's seat and honked the horn, but, misfortunately speaking, nothing happened, not even a squeak. So I turned the key in the ignition, pressed the gas pedal to the floor, and started the engine. Flashing the headlights did nothing to dissuade him either. He hit her in the face, in fact, and she teetered.

As I gunned the engine and lifted my foot from the clutch, my skin prickled. The sound of the Cooper's tires screeching against the pavement finally got his attention, and he turned

toward me at the exact same moment that the motor stalled. While I fumbled with the shifter, he charged the Cooper with his head down, a Bull of Pamplona. Though big and hairy didn't describe him, I still felt like a scrawny beach ball, especially when he thumped into the front hood.

Luckily, by the time his pounding fists made it to my window, I'd figured out how to propel the car forward, and I swerved around him, zoomed across the lot, and jammed on the brakes without running over the woman. The engine stalled again. Still, I had the presence of mind to lean across to the passenger side and fling open the door.

The woman scrambled into the seat and slammed the door behind her while I restarted the car. When I tried to engage the clutch, though, metal ground against metal, and the Cooper jumped forward in crazy leaps. The man got to his feet to run after us. My eyes were glued to the rearview mirror.

"You're in third," the woman said calmly.

I jiggled the shifter, my hair follicles contracting with fear, and we took off toward the exit at megaspeed.

"Slow down, Speed Racer," she said.

Just as we shot into the street, I managed to lift my foot from the gas pedal, which seemed to have no effect.

"Hit the brakes!"

Your past misfortunes will be
overshadowed by future bad luck.

Fortunately, I turned the wheel in time to miss the curb.
Unfortunately, the curb I missed happened to be on the
far side of the road. Fortunately, the road was empty of other
cars. After bringing the Mini Cooper to a stop without hitting
a single thing, a rush of euphoria hit me, bathing me in happiness. I'd never rescued a damsel in distress before.

"Wake up, s*** for brains." Except the woman didn't talk
like a damsel. "You can't just park in the middle of the effing
road." Only she didn't say effing. "Hello, anybody home?"

The woman's face, medium dark and freckly with pink
cheeks, looked almost sweet despite the bruise. She had two
braids that turned her into an African-American Pippi Long-
stocking, in fact. I loosened my death grip on the wheel. "Would
you like to drive?" I offered.

"Push down the clutch with your left foot. Hold it there.
Now touch the gas with your right foot. No. Lightly. Lift your
left foot. Slowly!"

After we started rolling, I changed into the correct lane, made a wide turn at the first corner, and pulled almost all the way into a parking spot in front of an SUV to shield us from view. The engine stalled.

"Natty car. Too bad you can't drive worth s***."

My heart slowed from *allegro* to *andante moderato*. "I'm Erin."

She squinted at me. "Shanice. I thought little Asian girls like you ran away from trouble. Got a phone?"

She thought I was Asian, which meant I had no choice but to love her with all my heart. I handed over Weyland's cell.

Shanice entered a number. "It's me," she said. "The meth guy is back. Lock the door and call 911." She gave the instructions as calmly as if she were ordering pizza. Seriously. After ending the call, she fixed her bright eyes on me. "Drive me back to the motel."

Only then did I realize how much my hands were shaking. Though my heart rate had returned almost to normal, the adrenaline from before still gummed up my system. Instead of grabbing the key like I meant to, I hit the windshield wipers, and rubber screeked across the glass at hyperspeed.

Shanice dismissed my incompetence with a poof of air through her lips. "You're the worst driver in the history of the world. I should carjack this sweet baby. She needs a real woman at the wheel." Then she laughed. "Put your eyes back in your head, girly. I'm only teasing. What's a delicate thing like you doing out in the middle of the night?"

"A friend of mine is eloping. I'm trying to talk her out of it."

"Is that right?" She fired off a bunch of questions, and when she'd gotten the whole—albeit abbreviated—story from me, she huffed through her nose. "I get it."

"Get what?"

"The Chinese mom thinks the Filipino boyfriend is too brown for her daughter."

Which made me squirm, because some Chinese-Americans *can* be somewhat racist. But not Mrs. Liu. I didn't think so, anyway. Most of the time. "Mrs. Liu has nothing against Darren specifically," I said. "She just wants Mei to attend Harvard, the Holy Grail."

"The Holy what?" Shanice said. "Never mind. Take me back. How long you been driving, anyway?"

"Um. Since never. I have a learner's permit, though."

"Then I better learn you something."

She reviewed the basics with me—shifting, stopping, and turning. As my body reabsorbed the adrenaline, a feeling approaching confidence came over me. I'd done something brave back in the motel parking lot, crazy and risky. I'd done the right thing. Learning to drive was easy by comparison.

Shanice put her hand on my shoulder. "Take me around the block."

I pulled out without a hitch, avoiding the windshield wipers, and accelerated to fifteen miles per hour. Then twenty-two. The engine whined.

"Shift up," she said. Which I did without grinding the gears. "Damn! I hope no one messes with my hat while I'm out here fooling with you. I love that hat."

In truth, the pink hat with its gargantuan bow made Shanice look like a cake with too much icing—a fact that distinctly called for a sincere lie. "Pink goes well with your complexion." We drove a long, long way before reaching a traffic light. "Should I turn here?"

"Yeah. That's the way back to the motel."

I slowed down. "But that man will be waiting for us."

Shanice bared her teeth. "Watch it, Hoity-toity. My cousin's

178

working the front desk, and we have to make sure she's okay. The police will have scared him off by now. Anyways, I'm in a hurry. I'm dead tired after working twelve hours, and my son's going to wake up the second my head hits the pillow." She looked at me. "Don't be making no faces, Hoity."

I tried to arrange my features into a neutral expression. She *did* seem a little young to have a son. "What's his name?"

"Jason. He's four and never stops moving."

Which might've sounded like a nightmare, except Lincoln somewhat fit that description too. And I liked him a lot.

"What's bubbling in that overprivileged head of yours, Hoity?"

"I'm not overprivileged." I lived in a tiny bedroom inside a tiny apartment with a thousand well-fed cockroaches. My cell phone had run out of minutes, my computer had died, and my mom had just lost the Hubei Chop Suey account. A homeless guy was replacing our kitchen floor tonight in exchange for a place to sleep.

"Going to college?" she asked.

I braked at a stop sign, coming to a halt about thirty feet too soon. I tried again, this time stopping just past the line. I *was* going to college, without question. I could even choose to attend the best university in the country if I wanted to. The idea made me flush. Was that from excitement or embarrassment? "Yes."

"Turn right. How you going to pay for that?"

"A loan?" If my scholarships and financial aid package didn't suffice. "You could go to college too."

"Who's going to raise my baby, then? You?"

"Um."

"I'm only ribbing you."

Her lighter snapped as she lit a cigarette. Thankfully, she

lowered her window and exhaled. "You're some kind of busybody. First you run your friend's life. Now you're running mine. How long you known me for?"

"Is it bad to care what happens to people?"

She took another drag. "That don't give you the right to act like no bulldozer. Even Jason can't stand to be pushed around." She blew more smoke out the window. "When he puts on his fire-engine shirt with his green pants, I tell him my eyes might go blind. But does he listen? No. His life is his life."

"He must adore you."

She laughed and threw her burning cigarette out the window. "That's true."

A whooping noise startled me, accompanied by abrasive red lights whirling in the rearview mirror. Fines for littering in California can be as high as a thousand dollars for a first offense, but cigarettes are pretty tiny, so maybe we'd get off for a few hundred. My hand hit the wiper control. Screek. Screek.

Shanice turned them off for me. "Damn. That's a patrol car. You best pull over. He came out looking for that meth guy, I bet, and now he's pissed off because he got nothing."

I lurched toward the curb too sharply and knocked over a garbage can, spilling thousands of dollars' worth of litter onto the ground. In a flash, I had my seat belt off and started to open my door. Shanice leaned over, shut it, and buckled me back in. "Don't be a fool. Put your hands on the wheel where he can see them. Let me do the talking."

When I took *qigong* last year, my teacher claimed that regulating one's breath restored the purity of the lung metal, but when I tried this now, nothing happened. Maybe because I didn't know what pure lung metal felt like. Maybe because my breathing had stopped altogether.

The officer tromped over to the driver's side and shone a flashlight in my face.

"Lower your window and be quiet," Shanice hissed. I did what she said and returned my hands to the wheel. Between my badminton accident and her fresh bruise, we made quite a pair.

"How are you ladies doing this fine morning?"

"Okay," Shanice said for the both of us.

His jeering expression reminded me of a movie I saw once about a serial killer impersonating a police officer. Why do they even make movies like that? "You're probably wondering why I pulled you over. May I see your license?"

"Of course." My voice came out a little high-pitched due to a prolonged pharyngeal spasm. "Can I take my hands off the wheel?"

He laughed. "Go right ahead."

As I dug through my bag for my expired learner's permit, my fingers felt like bananas, and my eyes wouldn't focus. Which possibly explained why I handed him my fake ID by mistake.

CHAPTER

**25**

You were born under a confusing star.

He looked from me to the photograph and back again. "Erin McFerrin. Your name rhymes. You must hear that a lot. I see you're from Arizona, Erin McFerrin." The booming of his voice echoed in my heart. "Which part?"

My fake address happened to be printed on my fake ID, which happened to be in the police officer's hand. Since I have a nimble understanding of probability, I chose the largest population center in Arizona. "Phoenix." It took all my willpower not to end the assertion with a question mark, though.

"Why does your license say Tucson?"

"We moved?" I said.

Fortunately, Shanice could think fast under pressure. She smiled at the officer. "Erin never gets to live anywhere for more than four months. Her dad works for a telecommunications company."

He nodded at Shanice.

She went on. "Now they shipped him to California. I'm

reviewing the traffic rules with Erin so she can apply for a new license."

The officer turned over my fake ID. "Looks like you girls were in a barroom brawl. Have you been drinking?"

"No, sir. I got a hockey puck in the eye this afternoon. My four-year-old hits hard, but he doesn't have good aim."

"I got hit by a badminton birdie," I said. Of course, it sounded like *I* was the one lying.

The officer chuckled. "I was hoping you were professional mud wrestlers."

Ew. I opened my mouth in disgust until Shanice poked my calf with her foot. "Are you going to give us a ticket, Officer, sir?" she asked.

He tapped my fake ID with his flashlight. "You need to get yourself a proper license."

"Yes, sir," I said. I'm a quick study.

"Your emergency flashers were on. That's why I pulled you over."

"I understand, Officer, sir. I'll be more attentive from now on."

He passed my ID through the window. "You can go. Drive safely."

When he returned to the squad car, I reached for the ignition, but Shanice stopped me. "Wait till you're calm, girly, and he's drove off." So I nibbled on my sleeve to pass the time. After his car disappeared down the street, I started up the Mini Cooper and pulled out.

"Woohoo! He didn't even ask for your registration or nothing!" Shanice shouted. "We're free."

"You sure knew how to talk to him," I said. Then, I drove without mishap for several blocks in a row, negotiating two turns and three oncoming cars.

As we entered the Sleepy Inn lot, Shanice put her hand on

my arm. "Now don't be forgetting what I said about meddling in other people's business."

Despite my best intentions to keep my mouth shut, a little sound escaped my throat—the sort of indignant squeal a rodent might make.

Shanice glared. "Don't start with me, Hoity."

I pulled up the hand brake and turned to face her. She had no idea how scared I'd been before. "My meddling saved you." Which came out rather more pompous than I had meant it to. I hate it when that happens. "I'm sorry. It's just that maybe you should think of looking for a safer job."

Shanice shoved my shoulder. Hard. "Who made you queen of effing Oprahtown? Is that what they teach you at your uppity private school? How us low-rent losers can better ourselves?"

"I go to public school," I said. An uppity, hoity-toity public school, but still.

She opened the door and got out, then turned on me, wound tight as a stretched spring. "Well, for your information, Hoity, I just got me my GED, and I'm going someplace better soon. You, on the other hand, you'll waste yourself trying to fix other people's lives. Let your own life fall into a mess. I know the type."

The injustice of what she said, combined with the underlying truth, burned me. Like in chemistry, when you mix two innocent liquids, and they change color and start smoking.

$$\Sigma indignation + \Delta\, insight = \int transformation.$$

"Maybe I shouldn't tell Mei what to do with her life. You're right. Still, should I have let that meth guy beat you up? Admit it. I was brave to go after him, and I saved your butt."

I waited for Shanice to slam the door in my face, but she

laughed aloud instead. "You've got some fire, girly. There's hope for you yet."

"Thank you."

"Now haul your a\*\* out of that seat and help me look for my hat."

As I climbed out into the moist night air, my skin tingled all over. The motel was deserted, no sign of Meth Guy anywhere, or even the Zodiac Killer II. I felt awake, 100 percent alive. Shanice thought I had potential. We scoured the lot, looking behind light poles and under bushes. Nothing.

Shanice went into the office, and I followed her. "Maybe Mandaline found it." The lobby smelled of air-conditioned air and mildew. A young woman, taller and thinner than Shanice, stood behind the counter talking on the phone. When she saw us, she said, "Hang on," and covered the mouthpiece. "Did he hit you? You better go home and put ice on that."

Shanice grimaced. "Everyone wants to boss me tonight."

"You need bossing."

Shanice gave Mandaline a sour look. "Good night. And lock the damn door."

"Good night." Mandaline resumed her phone conversation.

Shanice wrote something on a scrap of paper and thrust it into my hand. "My number. Call me. I want to know the end of Mei's story."

"Me too," I said.

She pursed her lips. "Thanks for rescuing me, Hoity."

My eyes misted a little. "It was nothing." And by nothing, I meant the crowning achievement of my life.

After Shanice left, I considered what to do next. The wall clock said 1:47 a.m. Mandaline had her back to me. "He should

buy himself a disco ball," she said. Pause. "But a disco ball would sparkle up the luau." Pause. "It's not a luau? What's the theme?" Pause. "Beer is not a theme!" Pause. "No, *you're* a sociopath." She twirled a bracelet on her finger. "A nice one." Finally, she noticed me and hung up. "Can I help you?"

"I'm in One-oh-four, but I don't have a key."

"With Weyland Ching?"

"Um." The truth sounded like a fabrication: *He's just a friend of a friend helping me find another friend who's eloping.* No sane person would believe that, so I kept my lie simple. "He's my brother."

Mandaline stared. I guess I looked less Asian under fluorescent lighting, or else Shanice needed glasses. "Just tell me your name, *hermana*, not your life story."

"Erin Kavanagh."

She winked at me. "What you do in your room is your own business. But I know one thing: That sweet-looking boy in One-oh-four is not your brother."

The urge to confess overcame my need for dignity, maybe because Mandaline had such a warm smile. "You're right, he's not. We only met on Friday, but I think I'm in love. Is that even possible?"

She turned down the volume on the TV, an infomercial on colonic health. "Why not?"

"We hardly know each other, and I'm only eighteen." Minus one week. "I don't really have time for Mr. Right, anyway, because I'm going to college."

She leaned across the counter toward me. "You think too much, *hermana*." Which was probably true. "Go for it."

"Well, thanks." I took the key card and hurried to the room through the dark night. Though light shone through the curtains of Room 104, I entered quietly in case they'd fallen asleep. They had. When I saw Weyland lying on top of the bedspread, stripped down to a pair of boxer shorts, sweat shining on his bare skin, I averted my eyes. Then I remembered what Mandaline had said and really let myself look at him, savored looking, in fact, appreciating his well-defined arm muscles and the contours of his chest. One of his socks was black and the other navy blue, but it didn't bother me.

Without thinking it through, I took a picture of him with his own cell phone, framing it in such a way as to exclude Lincoln sprawled out next to him. Which made no sense, because I couldn't send it to my email anyway. But before I found the delete submenu, the screen went blank. Ack.

I switched off the light and fell into an overstuffed chair, quietly panicking. If Linny were here, she would tell me it didn't matter. Try to convince me to climb into the bed next to Weyland, even. Tell me to go for it, just like Mandaline had. She was a good friend. I fogged the window with my breath and wrote *ai*, the Chinese word for *love*. In the middle of the character, a tiny roof shelters a heart.

Friendship means being that roof. A lump grew in my throat. If I went to Harvard, saying good-bye to my friends would be the hardest part.

A fierce gust shook the window by my ear, which reminded me where I was. And that Mrs. Liu had probably called Mom by now, told her that Mei and I had disappeared while going out for ice cream. Rather than risk waking Mom up unnecessarily, I plugged in the laptop and opened my email. Luckily, I didn't need a password to connect to the Wi-Fi.

Hi, Mom! Mei is here with me at the Sleepy Inn in Oakland. We're in 104, if you want to call. Tell Mrs. Liu not to worry. Nothing has happened. We'll come home in the morning. ~E

After that, I signed into Miss Fortune Cookie and reread all of Lincoln's advice. He would make an excellent assistant. Then I took off my hoodie and scanned the next letter in my inbox.

Dear Miss Fortune Cookie,

All my friends are in couples right now. Do you know how annoying that can be? Why do boyfriends make your friends forget that you exist? I don't want them to break up or anything. I just want friend time. You know what I'm saying.

Single

I glanced over at the bed. In the silvery light, Weyland's chest rose and fell, smooth and inviting. Some girls like hairy boys, but not me. I imagined my cheek against his skin.

Dear Single,

~~What you need is a boyfriend.~~ Bad joke.

So I deleted that and tried the opposite approach.

Dear Single,

Love is sentimental measles.

How could I compose a sympathetic answer with Weyland in the room, so good to look at and perfect for me? Though I

sort of thought of him as a stranger, I actually knew a lot about him. He was considerate and acted calm in a crisis. He liked to laugh at himself, and had gotten goofy with Lincoln. He wanted me to be myself around him. His eyes slanted downward when I hurt his feelings. Once he fell asleep, nothing seemed to wake him, even a girl wrecking the clutch on his precious car.

Dear Single,

**Miss Fortune Cookie says: Riding two horses at the same time can be painful.**

Don't be too mad at your friends. Sometimes romantic love overwhelms a girl's senses, turning her into an obliviot.

Tell your friends that you miss them. Invite them to do something with you without their boyfriends. But get to know their boyfriends, too.

Miss Fortune Cookie

Meanwhile, Weyland looked more and more like a piece of dim sum sprinkled with sesame oil. I wanted to inhale him on the spot. Resolutely, I opened the next letter.

Dear Miss Fortune Cookie,

This really hot dude asked my best friend to the school dance. I should be happy for her, but I'm soooooooooo jealous! I want someone to ask *me* out. I keep waiting, and no one does. It's really hard to act supportive when my friend is always talking about how awesome her guy is.

Jelus

Exactly. Mei had Darren. And Linny had Gio. No wonder I felt left out before—the lesser third. Except the whole lesser-third thing had somehow evaporated in the last twenty-four hours. Mei had apologized for rejecting me in eighth grade. Linny had finally confided in me about Gio. I'd gotten into Harvard.

And Weyland said I was beautiful. I wanted to run my hands across his bare chest. Feel his lips pressed against my neck.

Had I really just thought that?

Focus, Erin.

Dear Jelus,

**Miss Fortune Cookie says: No one feels more helpless than the owner of a sick goldfish.**

Sometimes it seems like all the good things happen to everyone else. The thing is . . . your sick goldfish *will* recover.

Luck changes fast. Or you can change it yourself. Maybe there's a hot dude you've had your eye on that you could ask to the dance.

Miss Fortune Cookie

I closed the laptop and lowered myself onto the bed next to Weyland. The springs hummed. Confucius had a lot to say about duty, family, and the proper way to live. But love—both the kind between friends and the kind between lovers—well, he ignored that. Whereas Lao Tzu had written about love attacking all the senses.

Somehow I don't think he was talking about a crush on a boy in a motel room when he wrote that.

Or maybe he was.

Weyland turned onto his side so that the tips of his fingers brushed against me, sending shivers across my skin. His breathing slowed, and warmth came off his sleeping body in waves.

## CHAPTER

# 26

Good luck or bad is waiting just around the corner.

I was lying next to a boy I liked *on a bed* inside a motel room. (!) An asleep boy, but still a momentous event for someone like me. I inched toward him to smell his hair. My eyes closed by themselves, and images played across my eyelids—sweaty dancing, running a red light, a Blade of Death, and Lincoln's impish face. I kept returning to one in particular, Weyland smiling playfully at me. We were floating in a pool of warm water while gardenias rained from the sky, rippling the glassy surface. Weyland held me against his chest. Drums beat in the distance.

I opened my eyes. Dawn light filtered into the room through a gap between the curtains. I'd been dreaming. But my cheek actually *was* against Weyland's chest. Bliss. He filled my entire view like a landscape, his heart beating in my ear, his arm resting across my waist. From my vantage point, I could survey the most valuable real estate in the world. His chin alone would sell for a million dollars an acre.

Weyland shifted, and that woke me more fully. I raised myself over him, looking mostly at his mouth, and then lowered myself until my lips brushed softly against his. With his eyes still closed, he circled me with his arms, pulling me on top of him, and kissed me back, even better than the fantasy. And amazing.

My hand moved to his face. He slid his palms along my waist and gently up the sides of my tank top. Every inch of me trembled with an unfamiliar giddiness, tumbling, as if inside a clothes dryer. Except the sensation felt more delicious and more overwhelming than that. I wanted it to last forever.

His lips left mine to explore my ear, my neck, my shoulder. Each spot he kissed tingled and sparked, even after he had moved on. One finger traced the soft curve at the edge of my rib cage, exploring upward. My heart went bonkers then, and I rolled off of him to sit up. Cold air rushed into the places he had just occupied.

He propped himself onto one elbow. "What is it?"

"It's just . . ." I lowered my eyes. How could I tell him I'd never really kissed anyone before? That fact about me had to be weirder even than believing in ghosts. Like I was some middle school girl pretending to be a senior.

Lincoln sat up too, apparently deeply awake. Weyland scooted to the end of the bed, with his back to me, and pulled on his pants. "When did you come in last night?"

"Around two," I said, reaching for my hoodie.

He fastened his shirt buttons. "You didn't get much rest."

Lincoln somersaulted across the bed. "Neither did I." Chocolate, presumably from the pancakes, rimmed his mouth, and sleep had shaped his hair into a pinecone. He started jumping on the mattress. Boing. Boing. When Weyland went into the bathroom, he whispered to me, "I told you so."

"You're wrong."

Boing. Boing. "I saw you kissing."

"He was just dreaming about some other girl. I don't even know how to kiss."

Lincoln changed things up by landing on one knee every second bounce. "I've seen a lot of movies. Should I teach you?"

I laughed. "Nice try."

When Weyland came out, Lincoln dropped onto his rear end, launching himself from the bed to the floor. "You want to be Erin's boyfriend, don't you? I'll cover my eyes so you can kiss her again."

Weyland avoided looking at me. "Your hair's a disaster, little man. Here, borrow my comb."

I held my breath against the flood of pain. He'd liked me for a while, but I had somehow ruined it. Fortunately or misfortunately—depending on how you look at things—a series of loud thumps on the door interrupted my misery. Through the peephole, I saw Shoe Fang, stiff as a spike of rebar, boring a hole through the wood with her eyes.

Before I had the door half-open, she stormed in. "Where is Mei?" she demanded. "This is no good occurrence." She scowled at Weyland and Lincoln.

I found the Mini Cooper keys in my hoodie pocket, along with Weyland's dead cell phone. He took them from me and went out, dragging Lincoln with him.

The door clicked shut.

*"Ta zai nar?" Where is she?*

I opened the curtain a bit and then pulled it shut again. Darren's van hadn't moved from its parking spot. "I'm not sure."

She sat down on the end of the bed, her back ramrod straight. "No yank my chain." Her natural expression tends toward melancholy, like the heroines in Chinese movies—the

kind where a young girl's father dies, forcing her mother to sell her to a wealthy family. Today, Shoe Fang looked more unhappy than usual. And by unhappy, I mean angry. "Your ma say you have eye on her."

"I fell asleep. I'm sorry." Did concealing Mei's whereabouts constitute a sincere lie or an insincere one? Either way, Mei trusted me, and I couldn't betray her like that.

*Sweet-talking Mei ≠ strong-arming Mei*

"Darren is the best. I mean really, really incredible. Smart, polite, caring..." Goofy. "...supersmart..."

Shoe Fang sagged and buried her head in her hands. I sat down next to her and rested my arm around her hunched shoulders. She lifted her head and turned her eyes on me, clear and distant. "You like ghost stories. Let me tell story."

More than anything I wanted to warn Mei. Still, I listened patiently.

"There is girl in China with very poor parents. They scrape together every last *yuan*, send her to school to learn so she bring honor to her family. At school, girl work hard. After school finish, she meet man. Her heart recognize his heart. Maybe they know love together long, long time before. Girl very happy.

"Family find work for girl in America. Her heart friend cannot go too. She is very sad, but she obey parents. Responsibility to family most important thing. Next year, her heart friend visit America. He is ghost. She cry bitter, but he comfort her with love."

Her shoulders narrowed a little, as if she were shrinking.

"Ghost-lover tell girl to marry. On wedding day, he stand between girl and new husband like thick silk cloth. After baby arrive, husband go away. Ghost-lover go away too."

Suddenly all business, she shook me off and spread her arms. "Mother give everything to make baby smart and strong."

"Baby Mei," I said.

Her story was a paradox, illustrating two opposite points of view simultaneously:

*Mrs. Liu understood true love and loss*

and

*True love must be sacrificed for family honor*

Either history would repeat itself, or it wouldn't. Ack.

She slapped my arm. "No more dawdle around. Where is Meihua?"

In that instant, I knew what I had to do—talk to Mei one last time without Shoe Fang present. "Mei could still be here, but I don't know which room she's in," I said. "We can ask at the front desk to see if she checked out. Just let me use the bathroom first."

My ploy worked. As soon as I finished talking, Shoe Fang zipped outside and jogged toward the office. When she'd disappeared inside, I hurried to 103, Mei's room. While knocking, I looked at Weyland in a sidelong sort of way. He was leaning against the Mini Cooper. Next to him, Lincoln danced on his toes, Shanice's Barbie-pink hat perched on his hair, his mom's large purple shawl wrapped around his body. "Erin! Look what I found."

"You look gorgeous," I said.

As I waited for Mei to come to the door, the cleverness of my current scheme dimmed. And by dimmed, I mean I suddenly recognized it as an act of lunacy. Before I could waver, though, she appeared, wearing a silky, white knee-length dress with beads along the neckline and hem, a vision of loveliness

except for the shock on her face. I pushed past her and closed the door behind us.

"What's going on?" Darren said. He had on mere jeans and a Super Mario Brothers T-shirt, not what I'd call appropriate elopement attire.

But I had zero time to squander on fashion commentary. Or on long explanations. "Weyland and I followed you last night. Sorry. Your mom is here, too."

Mei looked at me accusingly. "How did she know where to find us?"

I sucked air through my teeth and then talked even faster. "It's my fault. I left a message with my mom. I didn't tell about your plans, though, because you know how moms are about weddings. Anyway, I know my mom would lose her mind if I eloped. Seriously. I'm talking institutionalized."

Mei looked wistful, the exact reaction I'd hoped for. "Ma loves to tell the story about a wedding in China where they ate special cookies," she said, "and the bride wore a red dress. They threw winter-melon candies to represent bad habits and burned coal to ward off evil spirits." I could see her softening right there in front of me.

Still, I didn't want to be the bulldozer Shanice accused me of being. "You still have time to run for it," I said.

Mei pursed her lips at me. "You didn't need to follow us here. Last night Darren and I made the decision not to elope."

"But at the Elbo Room, Weyland said . . ." The look on her face suddenly made me feel foolish and immature. Weyland hadn't known for sure. Still, what about the inconsistencies? "Why are you wearing that dress, then?"

Mei blushed and glanced at Darren. "We . . . wanted to see how it looked."

Darren checked her out and whistled. "You're one sexy bride."

Mei smiled at him. Then she inhaled and straightened her spine. "Are you ready to go face her?" Darren nodded and Mei opened the door. We both followed her out.

The moment Mrs. Liu spotted us, she came marching over.

"I found them," I said to her, in a meek attempt at artifice.

Ignoring me, she clamped Mei by the elbow. "Why you dress for funeral?" Without waiting for an answer, she dragged her toward the car. "You must come home now!"

Mei pulled free. "I'm eighteen. An adult."

Shoe Fang's mouth turned downward, more scary than melancholy, a frown that could dam the Yangtze River, in fact. "Eighteen is just number. I am your ma."

I could see Darren puffing up like a potato in a microwave, wanting to defend Mei. Still, he kept his mouth shut. He's tactful like that.

"I think they need their privacy," Weyland whispered to me, getting into his car. When I didn't move, Lincoln grabbed my hood and towed me to the passenger side as if I were an uncooperative pet.

"I try to be a good daughter, Ma," Mei said. "I want to be. But *my* feelings matter too. I should be allowed to go to Stanford."

"Family is most important thing. My name is Liu Shufang," Shoe Fang growled. "Family name first, then second name."

"This is America. I'm Meihua Liu here."

While Lincoln tried to shove me into the back seat, I directed every kilojoule of energy I could muster to Mei, sending her strength to stand up to her mom.

Shoe Fang noticed us. "You do enough, Erin. Go. Scram," she commanded.

So I let Lincoln win our push-me-pull-you war. After I'd

made it halfway inside the car, he jammed the backrest into my knees, dove into the front seat, and slammed the door behind him. Weyland started the engine and shifted into reverse. Despite the g-forces, I managed to sit up enough to see Shoe Fang and Mei walking to their car.

Without Darren.

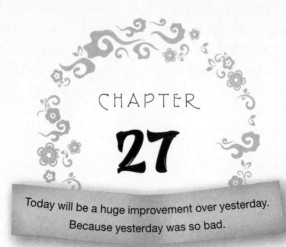

CHAPTER

**27**

Today will be a huge improvement over yesterday.
Because yesterday was so bad.

As Mei and Shoe Fang disappeared from view, anxiety snaked through me. I pushed it aside. After all, Mei had stood up to her mom in the Sleepy Inn parking lot. I felt a little sorry for Mrs. Liu, actually. She had raised a singularly determined daughter.

"All that fighting made me hungry," Lincoln said. "Let's get pancakes!"

Up ahead, a traffic light changed from green to yellow, and Weyland zoomed through the intersection too fast, narrowly avoiding a car inexplicably parked in our lane. The costume bag rolled to my side of the back seat.

"Sorry, little man," he said, "I'm late for class. Erin, can your mom pick you up from Lincoln's apartment?" He kept his eyes on the road.

I was late for class too. In an effort to quash my hurt feelings, I blinked at the giant cloth bag, directing all my attention to the blond wig poking through the top, smoothing a ringlet around my finger. "Sure."

"How many TVs do you have?" Lincoln asked.

Thank you, Lincoln. He had a gift for perfectly timed non sequiturs—glorious changes of subject—and my heart filled with gratitude. I could've hugged him right then but contented myself instead with reaching around the backrest to pat his head. "Just one."

"Lucky you. Karina thinks TV rots your brain. We go to the library a lot." He twirled Shanice's hat on his fist.

I should've taken the pink monstrosity to the Sleepy Inn office before we left, but I could hardly ask late-for-class Weyland to turn around now. Besides, I had Shanice's phone number. "Have you read any of the Diary of a Wimpy Kid books?" I asked Lincoln.

"Years ago. I'm reading the classics now."

"What, like *Oliver Twist*?" Weyland asked.

"That's too easy. I'm reading *Eragon*. It's seven hundred and sixty-eight pages long."

Weyland giggled, which reminded me of laughing with him last night. Rather than gazing with futile longing at the back of his head, though, I dug through the costume bag to amuse myself, pulling on a bit of filmy fabric. A white cape with a hood slid out, and that gave me an astoundingly good idea. "May I borrow this?"

Weyland looked in the rearview mirror to see what I meant. "What for?"

"A freaky hate group called Westboro plans to picket Lowell today. Linny is helping organize a counterprotest to balance things out."

"She told me. I still don't get why Westboro chose Lowell."

"It's a mystery," I said.

Lincoln climbed into the back seat with me. After I buckled him in, he emptied the entire bag onto my lap and handed me a rubber mask depicting a former presidential candidate replete with melting jowls. The inside smelled of dried fish, but I squeezed into it anyway.

Lincoln made a face. "Ew. Gross. Let me try it on."

"What are you doing back there?" Weyland asked.

Suffocating inside the stinky head of a Republican? I peeled it off, ripping out a few hundred hairs in the process. "Trying a few options." After Lincoln shoved his head into it, I wedged Shanice's hat over the rubber hair. Then I arranged the white cape around my shoulders and raised the hood.

"How do I look?" Lincoln asked.

"Creepy," I said.

Weyland's eyes were on me. "Lovely." Which hardly sounded indifferent, and suddenly it hurt to breathe. "Why do you need a costume for the protest?"

"Linny wants me to sing a song about love." As if that explained anything.

"A love song? Like 'No Air'?" He sang, then, his tenor voice rippling through me, " 'I'm here alone, didn't want to leave. . . .' "

I joined in. "My heart won't move, it's incomplete. . . ." My throat constricted to the width of a drinking straw, and I couldn't continue. Maybe I still had a chance with him. "I can't sing in front of people."

Weyland giggled. "How's that going to work?"

"I'll hide under your cape and pretend that nobody's there."

Lincoln plunged forward and thumped Weyland's arm with his fist. "Slow down. That's my street."

Weyland spun us to the left. "I know where you live. I'm Joel's cousin, remember?"

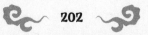

Lincoln clapped his hands to his head. "Oh no! There's Karina."

"Where?" I asked.

"The car in front of us."

Karina's little Jetta turned in to the lot by the apartment building. Weyland pulled in next to her, the Cooper's brakes squealing a little as he came to a quick stop. She was a thin woman with long blond hair, and when she hopped out of the car, she gave Weyland the finger. Lincoln flung open his door. "Mom! Let me introduce you to my new friends."

"Lincoln! What are you doing in some stranger's car?" But her face went tender as his body sank into hers. Besides, she wore pink plastic barrettes, and that gave me hope.

I quickly took off the cape. "I'm Erin. We borrowed Lincoln for a little outing. Sorry."

Lincoln butted my stomach with his head, a slow-motion cannonball. "Shush, Erin. Let *me* tell the story. After you left for work, Mom, I didn't watch one minute of TV with Joel." He executed a series of dramatic leaps while he talked. "Or eat a bag of candy corn. And I brushed my teeth really well." He stopped to pantomime furious scrubbing. "I went to bed on time until some intruders broke in and Joel almost cut their heads off."

"We weren't intruders. I'm Joel's cousin."

"Don't interrupt, Weyland."

So we let Lincoln tell the rest of the story. The rain had washed the leaves on the trees clean, and I appreciated the fresh scent. When Lincoln mentioned whole-grain pancakes, I nodded my head to corroborate. Though he omitted *the kiss* in the motel room, he included enough other stuff to upset his mom, and Weyland kept interjecting explanations to smooth things over.

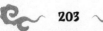

Karina pointed at me. "You should've left Lincoln with Joel." The nail on her index finger appeared rather sharp to my eyes.

Lincoln hugged her from the side. "Don't be mad, Mom. I *made* them take me. Joel's apartment smelled disgusting." He fished a greasy napkin from his cargo-pants pocket. "I saved you a pancake."

Ignoring it, she waved her angry ballerina arms. "You could've told him no."

Lincoln cupped a hand over Karina's ear to whisper, and by whisper, I mean shout into her eardrum without using his vocal cords. "Joel was as drunk as a skunk."

Poor skunks get no respect.

Karina got all soggy then. "This is my last week of nights, sweetie, I promise. I'm starting my new job at the doctor's office on Monday."

I smiled at her. "Lincoln is awesome. Maybe we can hang out again sometime."

Lincoln flapped his arms. "Why not today? Erin promised me a game of Parcheesi. It's more fun with two players. I can skip school whenever I feel like it."

Oops. "Sorry, I can't. In fact, I'm really late for school already. I should call my mom to pick me up. Can I borrow a phone?"

*breakfast at home + long shower + clean clothes = Erin's Shangri-la*

"You don't need to call your mom," Lincoln said. "My home-school group meets in San Francisco at Alisha's house. We can drive you there. Right, Mom?"

Karina rested a hand on his head. "I guess we can. Don't you want to change into clean clothes first?"

"Nope."

"What about the syrup on your shirt?"

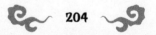

"Syrup is clean."

Weyland raked his fingers through his hair, oblivious to the effect the gesture had on my nervous system. "Did you leave anything in the Mini?" he asked. Lincoln grabbed the purple shawl.

"I have everything," I said. Feeling shy now, I lowered my eyes, not seeing anything above his chin. "I'll give the cape to Linny when I'm finished." His shirttails hung outside his pants, and a button had come undone on his cuff. I darted forward to refasten it. "Well, bye."

He looked like he might say something else. *Nice knowing you.*

Karina got into her car, and Lincoln opened the back door. "Take shotgun, Erin."

Except I couldn't leave Weyland without knowing how he felt, exactly. I ignored the skittery bits of myself and focused on the solid part. "I guess this is it."

He gazed steadily at me, without saying a word.

"Is it something I did?" I asked.

He shuffled his feet in the dust. "I'm not really into playing games," he said softly.

"And *I* am?"

He stood there, arms akimbo, looking at his shoes. "First you're sweet to me at the club, but you don't want to slow-dance. But you flirt with me in the car. Then you act hot and cold at Joel's. Then you kiss me in the motel room. Then you pull away."

Without warning, Lincoln ran forward and thwacked Weyland with Shanice's hat, hard and repeatedly. Which was really chivalrous of him.

Karina leaned out the window. "Can you talk about this later?"

I let the tension in my vocal cords subside before trying to talk. "I wasn't playing games. At first I thought you were Linny's boyfriend. And the rest . . ."

Weyland's eyes went dark. "But in the room you . . ."

"I'm sort of a nerd. I've never had a . . ." Never had a boyfriend or even kissed a boy I liked before. ". . . I never . . ."

Karina leaned on the horn. Lincoln grabbed my hood, somewhat choking me. "Uh-oh. She's mad!" He yanked harder. "Bye, Weyland."

So I stumbled after him, climbed into the front seat, and stared at Weyland through my window. He looked back at me, mystified, one finger resting on his bottom lip.

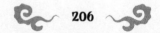

# CHAPTER 28

If an onion rings, answer it.

Weyland possibly liked me.
Probably liked me.

Maybe.

Unfortunately, I didn't have the luxury to debate this with myself in peace. Since the air pressure in an enclosed space increases proportionally to a decrease in volume, and a compact car has less volume than your average bathroom stall, Karina's impatience pervaded every air molecule trapped inside with us.

Fortunately, Lincoln had a supertongue, and it could fly faster than a speeding bullet. "See? I was right. I knew it all along. Weyland likes you." Talking was his superpower. "Promise me the next time he kisses you, you'll post it on YouTube."

He could've chosen something less embarrassing to talk about, though. "Why?" I asked.

"So I can outdo him when it's my turn to kiss you."

I laughed it off, but my cheeks flared up.

Karina didn't seem to mind. She must've been accustomed to Lincoln's crazy ideas by now. While we drove across the bridge, she warmed up to me even, sharing personal details from her own life, like how Lincoln's dad embezzled money from his employer but the bastard didn't go to jail for it. I considered what to say.

*Did he move to the Bahamas?*

Or *Cute sandals. I wish I could wear styles like that, but my feet are too wide.*

Instead, I told her about Lowell and my classes and my plans for the future.

"You'll love it at Berkeley," Karina said.

Okay, so I relayed one possible version of my future, keeping Harvard a secret because I hadn't made up my mind yet. Besides, I wanted Karina to like me. Some people are put off by people who've been accepted to Harvard. Shanice had nicknamed me Hoity without even knowing I might matriculate at an Ivy League college, like she could smell the odor of academia clinging to me.

And people can't stand people who use the word *matriculate*. Why did I have such an annoying brain?

I managed to stick to safer topics the whole way home. By the time Karina had rolled in to our alley in Chinatown, I'd already entered our phone number into her cell so she could reach me to babysit Lincoln. Not that I said *babysit*. I invited Lincoln to *hang* with me. When I climbed out of the car, he followed, hugging me like a lovesick boa constrictor. "I won't say good-bye."

"You have to," Karina said.

Armageddon Guy was bearing down on us, which made me think fast. "If you don't go with your mom, you'll have to come to calculus with me, where you're required to differentiate

quadratic equations. If you fail, the teacher throws you into a pool full of ice cubes. But . . . if your mom says okay, you could stay at our apartment for the next few nights." I glanced at Karina. "Just until her new job starts." Of course, I hadn't cleared it with *my* mom.

Karina's eyes got damp. "Why don't I meet your mom first, then we'll see."

After she promised to come by the apartment when Lincoln's homeschool group finished for the day, Lincoln finally hurled himself into the car again, bouncing on the seat like a Ping-Pong ball. "See you later, elevator. In a while, TV dial."

As they drove off, Armageddon Guy yelled, "The end is near! Buy some toothpaste!" Poor guy. Dental hygiene really stressed him out.

When I entered the apartment, the first thing I saw was Cigarette Willie on the couch, sleeping at a high decibel level. The night hours had wrought dramatic changes in his appearance. His blanket, his shoes, and a lot of his hair were gone. His tan and leathery skin gave him a handsome outdoorsman air, like Hugh Jackman, especially if I somewhat blurred my eyes.

The apartment had undergone serious changes too, the drop cloths over the furniture removed and most of the boxes put away. Pretty blue tiles brightened the kitchen floor. One wall in the living room was now a cheerful yellow in the morning light. By the looks of things, the two of them had pulled an all-nighter.

Mom appeared in her bedroom doorway, her hair a rhomboid from having slept on it funny. After hugging me for a very long time, she whispered, "I was getting worried. Tell me everything. Is Mei okay?"

I flopped onto her pillows, and they sank down nicely. "She's fine. She's home."

Mom scooted in next to me, and I told her about Weyland, the fake ID, the Elbo Room, the virgin martini, and Mei's plan to run away, leaving out the elopement part because I didn't entirely trust Mom to keep it a secret. I also utterly deleted Meth Guy, since I didn't know how I felt about that.

Except proud and exhilarated by my dashing rescue. But Mom might not see it in the same light.

Likewise, I edited out the interactions between Weyland and me. If you have to know the juicy details of other people's love lives, read the tabloids. Still, Mom got all inappropriately curious. For instance, she asked me, "You spent the night in a motel room with a strange boy?"

I covered my warm cheeks with my hands. "He's not strange. Nothing happened! We just slept until Mrs. Liu knocked on the door this morning."

Mom patted my face. "I'm sorry I gave you away. Shufang was so sure that something terrible had happened to Mei. I couldn't leave her in the dark."

I wasn't entirely annoyed at Mom for ratting us out. Mrs. Liu, despite her fierce demeanor, probably gets scared like the rest of us. I blame it on all the reality TV cop shows she watches.

"What happened after that?" Mom asked.

"Mei and Mrs. Liu went home together."

"Thank God!"

Now that I thought about it, though, Mom's reaction *did* bother me, and by bother, I mean it somewhat sandpapered my nerves. "Mei would never have run off if Mrs. Liu hadn't forbidden her from having a boyfriend."

Mom sighed. "I've talked to Shufang about that, tried to get her to lighten up on the rules a bit. You know how she is.

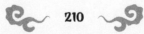

Family first. Work first. Duty first. I don't think she's even been on a date since the divorce."

Which reminded me about Mom's letter to Miss Fortune Cookie. I sat up and hugged my knees. "Can I ask you something?"

"Always."

"Are you fixing up the apartment so that I'll stay here with you? Or would you rather I left, because . . ."

"Of course I want you to stay with me!" She pinched my cheek like a zealous grandma. "Forever! But you should know something too. You can move out without worrying that your crazy mom will fall apart two seconds after you leave."

Oh. She hauled herself out of bed and started hanging up clothes with brisk, vigorous movements. While she worked away, her words sank in.

$$(Worrywart + daughter)^{clueless} \pm (smothering + mom)^{mistake}$$
$$= misunderstanding$$

Her Miss Fortune Cookie letter made sense now. She loved our life together but wanted to give me breathing room, a chance to grow on my own. That also explained why she'd kept quiet about Harvard, though I imagined the question itched like a heat rash you can't scratch. I appreciated the time she'd given me to figure it out on my own. "Thank you, Mom. I'm ready to try to be more independent, actually."

She stopped fussing with the buttons on a blouse to look at me sadly. "I know you are."

"Even if I move out, we'll see each other all the time. Especially if I go to Berkeley."

She came over to where I was sitting. "Maybe not so much. Picturing life without you in this apartment really made me

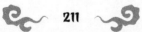

think hard about what comes next. I decided to go to graduate school. Linguistics at SFSU."

I stared up at her. "Why didn't you tell me?"

She grinned. "I just found out that I got in."

"I mean, why didn't you tell me you applied?"

"I worried about stealing your limelight, I guess." She pulled me up by the hands and danced me out the door of her room. "As if that could've happened. You got into Berkeley and Harvard!"

She had managed to work Harvard into the conversation, after all, which made me smile. I hugged her. "Wow, Mom. That's great. Better than great. You'll learn cool new stuff. Meet cool new people. Do cool new things. Land a cool new job."

"So you're *cool* with it?" She laughed so hard at her own joke that I had to hit her with a couch pillow to get her to settle down. Still, all our giggling and squealing failed to wake up Cigarette Willie. Mom looked at him and yawned. "You should get some sleep before the protest. Me too. Linny called to say it starts at one. I'll set an alarm and we can go together."

Ack. But at least she had a life of her own now. After tucking her in, I locked myself in the bathroom to wash away the accumulated grime from my adventures, emerging from the shower only when the hot water ran out. Then I ate a large can of mandarin oranges I found on the kitchen counter.

Climbing under the soft covers in my soft bed was a slice of heaven. Still, sleep eluded me. The leftover coffee I'd drunk to wash down the mandarin oranges probably had something to do with it, plus another, less-controllable stimulant— disconcerting boy thoughts. I'd sent Weyland mixed signals and would have to unmix them somehow. Which sounded as

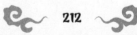

hard as unstirring fruit-at-the-bottom yogurt. In search of the guy perspective, I opened Dad's journal to a random page.

> *January 22, 3:13 p.m.*
> *Erin can crawl. She refused to go more than a few feet until I tied a string around her favorite stuffed animal's neck and dragged it slowly across the rug. When I wiggled it right, she crawled like crazy.*

Okay, then. I thumbed through the last quarter of the book to see if he had anything to say about boys. Finally, I found this.

> *June 10, 4:45 p.m.*
> *We borrowed a little boy from next door for a toddle date with Erin. When she tried to give him a plastic ring, he shoved her, and she hit her head on the table and cried. I took the little hooligan back to his apartment. I've come to a decision. No more dating till she's an adult.*

Which made me laugh, but I still had no idea how to fix things with Weyland. I would have to ask my more experienced friends, except they were in no position to talk about my nano-problems. Linny had to run a protest, and Mei had to battle with Shoe Fang. Neither one was online, in any case. So I sent a message to Mei from the laptop.

> Hi, Mei! Are you okay? Stay strong. Your mom will give in eventually. I feel sure of it ~E

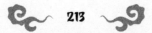

Then I signed in to Miss Fortune Cookie.

Dear Miss Fortune Cookie,

I'm a senior, and dying of frustration because everyone keeps asking me what I'm doing next year. They want me to go to college or culinary school. But I can't decide! *head thunk*

The thing is, despite my double x chromosomes, I know my way around an engine and can manage money well. My uncle offered me a job at his racetrack. I'm really smart, so my friends and parents think I will be wasting my brains there.

Can you please tell the world that there is nothing wrong with me!

Tangled

I was too tired to stand on my head, so I fell back into my pillows to think. I could relate to *Tangled*'s problem, the subtle yet intense pressure exerted by those around us. Linny had pretty much picked Berkeley for us, which seemed like a good idea at the time. It has a stellar reputation, and zillions of majors, it's relatively inexpensive and close to home. But was I dying to go there? I hadn't given it much thought, to be honest. Until I got in to Harvard.

Dear T,

**Miss Fortune Cookie says: Don't take advice from people missing fingers.**

I have all my fingers, so you can take my advice, actually.

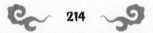 214

Most people do what everyone expects of them. ~~It's really cool It's really awesome~~ It takes grit to follow your own path when others disapprove.

Tell people that your job at the racetrack does require brains. It's called spatial and logical intelligence. A lot of people don't have those.

Listen up, world! *Tangled* has her head on straight. Give her your support.

Miss Fortune Cookie

I envied *Tangled* for her single-minded passion, actually. Everything interests me. Except extreme sports. How would I ever narrow all the choices down to *one* major in college? So I did a Google search of my favorite advice columnist, Carolyn Hax, to find out what she'd majored in, and got a megatesla-shock. She went to *Harvard*. Which seemed too big a coincidence to ignore, so I sent her an email.

Dear Carolyn,

I'm a little high school student with a big problem. I promised my best friend I'd go to Berkeley with her before I knew that I got into Harvard.

Your amazing wisdom over the years inspired me to start my own advice column. Still, I don't know what advice to give myself!

I somewhat want to go to Harvard, but I'm afraid to let my friend down.

Erin

PS—What did you major in? Do you think going to Harvard might help me become a famous advice columnist like yourself?

I can be spontaneous like that.

CHAPTER

**29**

When you till the soil, unexpected things will sprout.

My burst of spontaneity quickly lost momentum, like throwing a ball underwater. After writing Carolyn Hax, I reread the letter a couple of times, and by a couple, I mean at least a dozen. If you thought about it, my question—just like Mei/*Desperate*'s question to Miss Fortune Cookie—was kind of immature. I wanted someone else to make the hard decision for me.

The truth: Linny and I needed to talk.

But since we couldn't talk right now, I opened the next letter.

Dear Miss Fortune Cookie,

My forever boyfriend will be leaving soon for a program in a remote part of Sweden. He'll be gone for ten months. I can't go with him. He is my first big love, and I am his. We're both about to lose it.

I think I should break up with him to save him from the pain of missing me and ruining his experience in Sweden. He'll be sad for a week and then get over it. If we both still love each other when he returns, we can get back together.

Tyler

Hmm. *Tyler* planned to break up to save his boyfriend from missing him. He wanted him to have an adventure free from prior commitments. But was this selfless, or an act of crazy martyrdom? Mei would side with Tyler. Linny would get POed at him. And which side was I on?

Dear T,

**Miss Fortune Cookie says:** ~~Don't climb a tree to look for fish.~~ **Don't swat a fly that's landed on a tiger's head.**

Ack.

*Tyler*'s problem had gotten me all disoriented. Twisted around. I wanted to tell him no but couldn't pinpoint the reason. Like if Shoe Fang prevailed and Mei went to Harvard, Mei would never break up with Darren in advance. Then again, missing each other really *could* wreck their first year of college.

Mei might have a shoulder to cry on, at least. (Mine!) Sometimes truth is stranger than science fiction. I reached for the album Mei gave me on Saturday and studied a picture of us with Fruit Roll-Ups dangling from our mouths, the elongated tongues of the kind of ghosts that live in the rafters. At Harvard, would we go back to that kind of friendship? If Mei went to Harvard, that is. And if I did.

Next thing I knew, Mom's alarm went off in her room. Light streamed through the batik tacked over my window, and I smelled bacon, which Mom never cooked. I sat up. Eeep. I needed to get dressed for Linny's protest.

Weyland's white cape had gotten wrinkled from being wadded up inside my boho. I shook it out, because ironing it would take too long, and wrapped it around my shoulders. My pale reflection in the mirror gave me another idea. I smeared white goop from last Halloween onto my face, and cream blush under my eyes, transforming myself into an other-worldly creature.

In full regalia, I tiptoed through the living room, sneaking up on Cigarette Willie, who was standing in a column of smoke by the stove. When he looked up from jabbing the bacon, he let out a little scream and dropped the fork. Seriously. It was a proud moment for me.

"Good morning," I said.

He picked up the fork. "You startled me. Do you want some soy bacon? It's delish."

I looked at the wall clock. Noon—technically lunchtime—though my stomach couldn't quite relate. "Sure."

He set a piece of dry toast onto a plate, drizzled it with sesame oil, and laid two strips of bacon-oid on the diagonal. It tasted better than expected, maybe because I'd only eaten an olive and some mandarin oranges since dinner last night. After I'd polished it off and had seconds, Mom came out of her room in drapey hippie clothes—a tunic top, a flowing patch-work skirt, and beads. "I'm ready," she said. "You look great."

"Thanks," I said. She didn't ask me what was up with the costume, and I loved her for it. "Cigarette Willie made us lunch."

"Erin! His name is Will."

*Will* made her a plate too, and she sat down to eat it, but my incessant tapping and shifting must've gotten to her, because she ate fast, stopping only once to laugh at his joke about humanely raised soybeans.

While *Will* started on the dishes, we dashed to the car. Right away, Mom floored it, zipping up to the rear bumper of the car in front of us, in fact.

I held on to my seat. "I read a little of Dad's journal last night," I said. Mom looked over at me and then, thankfully, returned her attention to the traffic. "I never pictured him staying up at night so you could sleep."

"He was wild about being a father," Mom said. "Before he died, he worried about you growing up without a dad."

"Did he ask you to remarry?"

"He didn't have time." Mom's face went pink, and she slowed down. A little car squeezed into the narrow space between us and the truck ahead. She braked some more. I hoped she wouldn't cry. "Will and I are just friends, if that's what you're asking."

"I didn't mean *that.* I just wondered. Have you ever met someone . . . since Dad . . . who you could imagine spending the rest of your life with?"

Another aggressive driver crowded us into the right lane, and suddenly we found ourselves sandwiched between two Munis. "Chill, Mister. Can we talk about this later, Erin, when I'm not driving?"

"Sure," I said.

She put on her blinker, and after twenty cars ignored us, a guy on a motorcycle let us in. "Are you excited about the protest?"

"Of course I'm excited." If, by excited, she meant as

nervous as a hamster on a street corner in a city full of cats. "What should I do if I get arrested?"

Mom smiled nostalgically, clearly liking this question better than my earlier ones. "Back in my day, protesters used a technique called passive resistance. If an officer caught you, you'd let your body go limp, making it hard to haul you off to the police van."

Except that wouldn't work for me. Some down comforters weigh more than I do.

"You won't be doing anything illegal, anyway," Mom said. "Just holding a sign on school property, listening to a few speeches, and dancing. Let's get in the proper mood for the event, shall we?" She stuffed a Beatles tape (our car was as old as Darren's van) into the slot and started to sing along. I joined in with her, which was fun.

We parked behind Lowell, and on our way to the flagpole ran into a group of boys wearing bright pink leis and carrying signs for the protest. A girl from the Gay-Straight Alliance was giving out white paper yarmulkes on the catwalk. My costume fit in with the whole crazy scene, except for the fact that I happened to be walking with my mom.

"I'm going to the bathroom," I told her. "Meet you out there?" After we parted ways, I took a long minute to reoxygenate, and a second minute to feel okay about ditching my mom. She'd just told me to stop worrying about her, right?

Cheers echoed off the walls, and a girl I barely knew high-fived me in the hallway. She had a rainbow-colored flower on her sign: BEING DIVERSE IS NOT A CURSE. At that precise moment, I loved my school.

A throng had gathered outside—students from every social group, parents, teachers, our hip Japanese-American

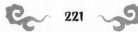

principal in a natty dark suit, and a camera crew from a local TV station. I stopped to talk to a boy I knew from Key Club last year. He sported a polka-dotted bow in his hair instead of his usual baseball cap. Clearly today counted as a special occasion. His sign read WE ARE NOT GOING TO HELL. WE ARE GOING TO DANCE. "Where are the picketers?" I asked him.

"Way over there." He pointed across the street.

I went to get a closer look, weaving through a group of girls shaking it up to music from a boom box; one in a black bowler twirled her white feather boa at me and lured me in to dance with them. When the song ended, I made my way toward the Westboro people. Their messages of hate were written in bold black letters against bright pink and neon green backgrounds, making them easy to read. Temporary metal fencing and yellow tape barred them from our school. The commotion on our side of the street drowned out the actual words they were shouting.

Almost. Not enough, because my skin began to crawl.

Still, I loitered there, pinned like an insect to a collector's display. The scene behind the barricade reminded me of those portable carnival rides that look bright at a distance but rusty up close. The cruel words spewing through the megaphone, calling us vile names and damning us all to hell, began to work a spell on me, shutting me down.

Just as I felt myself curling into a ball inside, a school bus arrived, and the police moved aside the barriers across the Lowell parking lot to let in a flood of newcomers. "They came from other high schools to support you," a parent next to me said. He was holding a sign that said GOD LOVES BAGELS.

My insides unfurled a bit. I turned my back on the Westboro people to rejoin the party in the Lowell courtyard. The

crowd had swelled. A woman with gray, curly hair played the accordion, while another demonstrated steps to a Jewish folk dance. I spotted Linny on the far side and skirted the edge of the circle to reach her. She had put together a wild outfit—suede knee-high boots, a tie-dyed mini, and a baby-doll top. As I approached, I studied her for clues of how last night had gone with Dub. I mean Gio.

No idea.

When I joined the circle next to her, she beamed at me. "You're here!" If you hooked her smile to the power grid, it would've lit up San Francisco. "You look awesome, Erin. What are you?"

"A peony spirit," I said.

"Very cool. So what happened last night?" she asked.

"No," I said, raising my eyebrows suggestively. "What happened *with you* last night?"

She bumped me with her shoulder. "I asked first."

"Okay, okay. Mei decided not to elope. Mrs. Liu showed up at the Sleepy Inn this morning and yelled at Mei, then they went home together."

Linny's wattage dimmed. "Oh well."

"Don't say that. You didn't want Mei to elope, did you?"

"I just liked that she was finally rebelling."

"She stood up to Shufang this morning," I said. "In a respectful way. Who knows what will happen next."

"That's true."

The dancing started, slowly at first to accommodate all the beginners, and then faster and faster. Sometimes I crossed over in the wrong direction or did an extra step by mistake, but nobody cared. When the song ended, we danced another and a third, until I thought my feet might skip away on their

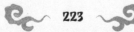

own. We were a big family under a big sun, no divisions, no cliques, just camaraderie. Even everyone's sweat smelled good.

Finally, I dragged Linny out of the circle and straightened the hem of her top. We stood there for the longest time, arm in arm, listening to the speeches that followed, soaking up the golden rays and magic all around us.

She grinned at me. "I love this protest so much, I want to marry it."

"There's so much love here," I agreed, closing my ears against the ranting from the megaphone across the street. "Is there something I should do in case I want to sing?"

A peony spirit can do anything, after all.

"Yes!" She grabbed both my hands and twirled me till the cotton-ball clouds spun in the sky. When she let go, I skittered off and sat down. "Let me go tell the sound girl," she said, sparking with excitement. "What song? Are you ready right now?"

Um. "'All You Need Is Love.'"

She dashed off and came back in what felt like fifteen seconds, holding up her phone to take a series of pictures of me. After that, she took another of a dude, his sleeves rolled up to show off his biceps, and a piece of paper taped to the back of his shirt that read I'M NOT GAY OR JEWISH, BUT I SUPPORT MY BROTHERS & SISTERS. I heard clapping.

"You're up," she said.

My tongue felt dusty. "Water. My kingdom for a glass of water."

Linny handed me a bottle, and when I'd downed the whole thing, the liquid sloshed inside me, not a pleasant sensation. My stomach contracted, in fact, which—as any doctor can tell you—may lead to spontaneous vomiting. I followed her to the microphone and managed to grab the bulky thing by the

throat, my heart doing a Lamborghini, zero to sixty in three seconds.

"Hello? I mean, testing, testing." I expected screeching feedback, something that always happens in teen movies. But my words came out crisp, and a few people looked my way. "I'm going to sing 'All You Need is Love.'"

Linny leaned into the microphone next to me. "Written by John Lennon. Join in if you know the words."

I waited for the music to start.

Linny covered the mesh with her hand. "I forgot to tell you. We're having technical difficulties. You have to sing a cappella."

CHAPTER

**30**

Get ready! Good fortune comes in bunches.
So does bad.

Luckily, I had some experience singing without musical accompaniment, like in choir with fifty-zillion others. And alone in the apartment. With my eyes closed, I pictured myself in our kitchen, dirty pots in the sink, crumbs under my bare feet. "'Love, love, love...'" The dent in the cupboard door from an unfortunate mopping accident. The shiny new floor. "'There's nothing you can do that can't be done. Nothing you can sing that can't be sung.'" My last note wobbled.

Then some people from the audience joined in, and the most amazing thing happened. Their energy flowed into me like a warm river, and I could open my eyes. As their voices grew stronger, it made me strong too, like they were feeding me particles of electrified essence, light itself. "'Nothing you can say but you can learn how to play the game.'" Every last one of my hairs stood on end. I threw off the hood. "'It's easy.'"

I felt powerful. I was spreading joy.

"'All you need is love.'"

My classmates made human chains and swayed together. It seemed as if everyone in the courtyard was singing with me. By the end, the buzzing in my ears had gotten so loud, I could barely hear the clapping. Next thing I knew, Linny's arms were around me, leading me away from the microphone. Maybe she worried I'd turned into a ham and would try a Lady Gaga imitation next.

"How do you feel?" she asked when we made it away from the stage.

"I missed a note or two, but..." Linny slapped my hand, and not gently, either. "What did you do that for?"

"The twenty-five-cent fines aren't working," she snapped.

I pursed my lips in fake indignation. "You didn't let me finish. I was going to say... I rocked out there."

"You totally rocked."

"And I need to wash off this makeup." I felt too alive to be a ghost any longer. "Right now."

On our way to the bathroom, we plunged through a troop of Star Wars Jedi with lightsabers in hand. Lowell can be surreal and wonderful like that. While I rinsed my face in the sink and Linny scrounged for some clean toilet paper to dry me off, I thought about our future together—living in an apartment the size of a closet, helping each other daily, hanging out between classes, working at a café, eating café leftovers, sharing textbooks.

Basically, perfection.

Except for one little thing.

Harvard.

Now that I'd had time to think about it, the idea of hanging out among the bottom third of my class at Harvard seemed tolerable. Pretty great, actually. Magnificent. I could shine in areas that had nothing to do with my GPA. Maybe

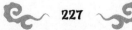

write an advice column for the *Harvard Crimson*. Join the fencing team.

Linny and I went back out, and she spun me under her arm. "Aren't you going to ask me about last night with Dub?"

I shook off my self-absorption to look at her. "I already did, but you blew me off. Well?"

Despite the dark circles under her eyes, a lovely expression spread across her face. Then she yawned loudly, kind of laughing at the same time. "You won't believe it. I thought last night would be *the night*, you know? Then I fell asleep before anything could happen, *while* Dub was cuddling with me. Is that your mom?"

It was. Her turquoise tunic top and skirt billowed around her as she danced. "She's everywhere."

Linny started dragging me in her direction. "Let's go dance with her."

I dug in my heels. "Actually, can we talk? I mean, really talk?" When she agreed, I led her to my favorite spot, under the giant ponderosa pine, and sat down cross-legged among the needles, swerving just in time to avoid a piece of used gum, a big ugly red wad like a kidney with teeth marks.

Linny dropped down next to me. "Is this about Gio?"

"No."

She ignored my answer. "Because I thought a lot about what you said last night. I don't know if we're in love. For instance, he doesn't own a single pair of underwear. That's kind of weird, isn't it? I like the idea of underwear. And he has three piercings in his left ear. That's fine by me, but he did them himself with a sewing needle."

Did I really need to know that?

She shook her ponytail at me. "The thing is, he never pushes me to do stuff. He sees past the BS to the real me

underneath. And wait for the best part. Wait. Wait. Here it comes. He's totally devoted to his grandma. I can *so* trust him. You understand, right? When I'm ready to take things to the next level, I need you to be okay with that. The decision has to be mine."

I scooted toward her and farther away from the wad of gum. "I wasn't judging you. It's just that sometimes I keep my opinions to myself to be polite. Last night I kind of realized I should stop doing that."

"That's great, Erin." She leaned against me, resting her head on my shoulder and closing her eyes. "Too many late nights in a row."

"If you invite Gio over tonight," I said, "you might die from lack-of-sleep stroke."

She straightened up and narrowed her eyes at me. "I'll invite him if I want to. What other opinions have you been keeping to yourself?"

"I don't know." I hesitated, but then pressed forward. "Okay, this is not an opinion. Being boyfriendless around you and Mei makes me feel immature, like I'm your little sister eavesdropping on your big-girl conversations."

"Really?" Linny said. "I don't think of you that way. You're so wise."

"I kissed Weyland at the motel, and I feel weird talking about it because it sounds so middle school."

Linny smiled. "I have a good feeling about Weyland."

A bird hopped toward us, and I shooed him away so he wouldn't eat the gum by mistake. "So, here's another thing. When I'm really into one of my classes, I kind of tone it down because you're not so into school right now. Sometimes I even fake-complain about homework, though I actually like it."

"I love who you are, X."

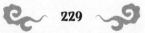

It was a perfect friendship moment, an intimate conversation illuminated by beautiful, evergreen-filtered sunlight and enveloped in warm resin smells. Too bad I had more to say. "There's something else."

Linny drew her eyebrows together. "No secrets between us."

"You know how you're always a little down on Ivy League schools? I don't really feel the same way." My voice quavered. No more lying to Linny. "I'd kind of like to go to Harvard." I kept my gaze on her face as I said it.

She stirred the needles with her hands, never once looking up. "Is that why you begged me to go to Africa last night?"

"No!" I shook my head till my neck hurt. "I didn't even decide to go till this morning." While I waited for her to believe me, a tall, skinny man, one of the picketers, holding a green and orange sign, started creeping along the wall of a building in our direction. It freaked me out. "Look," I whispered to Linny. "Should we hide?" But there was nowhere to go. It felt like the scene in *Jurassic Park* where a velociraptor traps some children inside a kitchen.

Linny stood up, scooping a handful of pine needles as she did so. They seemed an unlikely defensive weapon to me. Still, I grabbed a handful too. We were in this together. "What are we going to do?" I asked.

She looked at me sharply. "I don't know what you're going to do," she said, throwing the needles against the tree. "Thanks for crapping all over my perfect day." She strode away.

"Linny! Wait!" *You're the independent one. You don't need me.*

But she didn't wait. Instead, she sprinted across the grass toward the picketer, screaming at the top of her lungs. He dropped his sign. Without the prop, he looked almost ordinary, a regular man in jeans and sneakers. When Linny got close, he turned and started running the other way so fast, his cap came off. Which would've been almost comical on any other day—a tall man running away from a petite girl—except I didn't feel like laughing. Or crying.

Or even breathing.

When they disappeared from view, I wrapped the wad of gum in a leaf, put it in my bag, and left.

CHAPTER

31

Sweet, sour, bitter, and pungent all must be tasted.

The entire drive home, Mom bubbled over about the counterprotest, going on and on about how Lowell students were the most mind-blowing teens on the planet—how loving and diverse and playful they were. How they accepted people different from themselves. She might've drawn the opposite conclusion if she'd witnessed the scene between Linny and me under the ponderosa pine. I stared straight ahead as she talked. Mom finally noticed. "Did you have a good time, Erin? You didn't tell me you were going to sing."

"I didn't know until the last minute."

"You did that spontaneously? You were incredible up there. I'm so proud of you."

I softened then, let myself bask in Mom's praise for a few blocks, even, until my thoughts snapped back to Linny. What had started as a sincere lie to protect her feelings—neglecting to mention my true feelings about Ivy League schools—had curdled with age. In the end, I hadn't protected her at all. On the other hand, her strong opinions made honesty unpleasant sometimes.

Gah! Why did the pure and simple truth have to be so murky and complicated?

Mom swerved to avoid a mammal in the road, a cat maybe, or a small raccoon. "Does Berkeley have a choir? You should sign up for it first semester."

I would have to tell Mom about Harvard too. Obviously someone had designated April 4 as National Confession Day.

I drew in a breath. "Mom? I've been thinking. About possibly going to Harvard? I know it's far away—I mean really, really far away—and there are a lot of issues, the cost for instance, but I would like to try, anyway—"

Mom's eyes bugged out, and she failed to notice a car that swerved into our lane until we were right on top of it. She slammed on the brakes. The street slanted precipitously downward, and my head bumped the windshield. Just softly, but still. "Sorry, Erin! Are you okay?"

The swerving driver flipped us off. "I'm okay," I said. "Bad timing. Sorry."

When we started rolling down the hill again, Mom paid more attention to the traffic. "Wow, Erin. You seemed dead set against Harvard just a few days ago. This is huge." Her voice rose as she spoke. It occurred to me that my tendency to squeak under pressure might have a genetic component.

I tucked a rebellious strand of her hair behind her ear. Her expression changed from flabbergasted to determined. "Of course you should go. Don't worry about the money. Uncle Mark might help with the tuition. I told you that, right? Maybe I didn't. I'll be fine." Her knuckles, white from gripping the steering wheel too hard, told another story.

Still, we made it home alive. When we got there, we saw

that Will had painted a second wall of our living room. A wave of exhaustion crashed into me, and I would've collapsed into bed, except Karina and Lincoln arrived with a sleeping bag and Parcheesi set. I'd totally forgotten my promise to let him spend the night. Luckily, Mom reacted the same way she had when I brought home Cigarette Willie, ushering them in with a smile. We all squeezed into the living room to get acquainted. Before the tea finished steeping, Lincoln got jumpy. "Can we play in Erin's room?" he asked.

"Go right ahead," Karina said.

I led the way. While I made room on my bed, he closed the door and jammed the game into my closet. "Youngest goes first," he shouted. "Your roll!" Then he switched to whispering. "Did Weyland call yet?"

Lincoln has an interesting future ahead of him, an exciting career in acting or espionage.

I sat on my bed. "I think we can talk in regular voices. They're making a lot of noise out there. And, no, Weyland hasn't called me. Do you think he will?"

Lincoln lay down on his stomach. "Do you have his phone number?"

"No."

"Who has it?"

"My best friend, Linny."

"Then give me her number."

"She's kind of mad at me right now. She needs time to cool off."

"Okay. Let's write some Miss Fortune Cookie letters," he said. So I checked my inbox on the laptop. Ugh. The one from *Tyler*, whose boyfriend was going to Sweden, still needed to be answered. Lincoln looked over my shoulder while it loaded. "Tyler's not the brightest bulb in the socket, is he?"

"What do you mean?" I asked.

"How does he know that his boyfriend will be sad for a *week* after they break up? Maybe his boyfriend will be sad for two months. Or more."

"Good point."

"Do you have any better ones?" he asked.

So I clicked on the next letter.

Dear Miss Fortune Cookie,

I wanted this guy I like to notice me, so I pretended to be in love with his favorite band, Gagging Maggots. I made a book cover from their concert flyer and passed him my earbuds with a GM song playing.

It so worked! He asked me out, and now we spend every minute together. But I think his music is giving me permanent brain damage. What should I do?

Sorry I Lied

I looked at Lincoln. *Sorry* had told a sincere lie, and I wondered what he would think about that. I watched as he squinched his face into a raisin of concentration. "Here goes," he said. Then he started talking so fast, my typing could barely keep up with him.

Dear Sorry,

Tell your boyfriend that you're a fraud. Maybe he'll like you afterward. Then you can kiss and make up.

Maybe he'll get really, really mad and tell you to get lost.

I stopped tapping the keyboard. "You're being a little rough on *Sorry*, don't you think? It's kind of more complicated than that. She really liked this boy and just wanted him to notice her."

Lincoln grabbed one of my donkeys by the neck, a little one with a curly forelock. "Yeah. But maybe that guy only loves the Gagging Maggots and not that girl. I know how to juggle. Do you want to see?"

I couldn't let Lincoln change channels now. I needed to know. "Haven't you ever lied?" I asked.

"All the time." He threw the donkey in the air with his left hand, and caught it with his right. After that he transferred it to his left again, and repeated the maneuver. "I lie when I don't want to get in trouble for breaking things or making messes or eating pancakes. I never lie about important stuff."

Like lying to your friend about who you are? Then again, should I, a senior girl of superior intelligence, contemplate the deeper significance of pronouncements made by a mere kid who deludes himself about his juggling skills? I closed the laptop firmly. "We'll finish the letter later. Show me more tricks."

While I buried myself under the blankets and let my eyelids droop a bit, he selected another donkey from my shelf. "Watch carefully."

Actually, it kind of bugged me that he was right about truth and lies. In a good way. "I'm watching," I said.

He held one plush animal between his chin and chest, threw the other two into the air at the same moment, and then caught them both, which made me slightly less annoyed. Giggling does that to a person. "Show me again," I said.

When he did, my eyes got even heavier. The next thing I knew, an unfamiliar whooshing noise woke me. In the dim

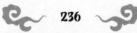

light from under my door, I made out the shape of Lincoln lying on my beanbag, bundled in a blanket. When I slipped out of bed to check on him, he appeared to be snoring. The next time I woke, light shone through my window and the beanbag was empty.

I heard voices in the living room. After changing into fresh jeans and a clean top, I went to investigate. Before I was able to get my bearings, a Super Ball hit me in the head. I captured it and tossed it to Lincoln, who bounced it off the coffee table toward Will. Will raised his foot, kicking the ball into the air, Hacky Sack meets Smashball.

Mom came out of her room too, dressed and ready for the day. Wednesday, I think. "What's going on in here? Oh. Sleeping Beauty is awake."

I caught the ball and stashed it in my pocket. Lincoln puckered his lips at me. I shook my head at him. "I'll take breakfast over the handsome prince today. I'm starving."

Mom smiled at me. "I made your favorite, rice porridge with duck and green onions. Let me heat it up for you."

It was almost eight-thirty. "I'm late for school."

Mom wrapped me in her arms and squeezed tight. It felt like when you try on a dress two sizes too small and you're afraid to breathe because a seam might rip. "Why don't you take the day off?" she suggested. "We can talk about everything."

Lincoln lit a burner on the stove. While Mom hurried over to turn it off, he found a carton of eggs in the fridge. "I have a special recipe. Do you have any chocolate chips?" He poured half a cup of oil into a frying pan.

Mom put my rice porridge in the microwave. "No chocolate chips. Do you want me to crack an egg for you?"

"I know how to do it. How about paprika and mayonnaise?"

When he banged the egg against the edge of the pan, the insides bobbled onto the stovetop and slid into the burner. He tried to pick it up with a kitchen towel, but Mom intervened.

"Why don't you have some of my congee?" I said. "Oh, wait. Only people with sophisticated palates would like it. Sorry."

"I have a sophisticated palate," Lincoln asserted.

Which he proved by eating half of my breakfast. Will joined us at the table, setting his unlit cigarette next to his mug of coffee. After Lincoln finished eating, Mom tossed Will her car keys. "Time to go to your homeschool group, young lad."

"I have to tell Erin a secret first." Lincoln cupped his hand over my ear. "Check MFC ASAP." He grinned at me, clearly up to something. Like maybe he'd posted a bunch of inappropriate letters in my name. "You'll see."

Will jammed his old hat onto his head and headed toward the door.

"What was that all about?" Mom asked, after they left.

"Lincoln kind of has a crush on me, I think."

"That's cute."

Luckily, Mom got a work-related call right then, allowing me to dash into my room to check my blog. At least Lincoln only had one night and a morning to mess up my professional image. While signing in, I mentally prepared for damage control, and that made me totally unprepared for the first letter in my inbox.

Dear Miss Fortune Cookie,

I met *the one*. She has black hair. No, brown. Her hair color doesn't matter, because I've been dreaming about

her all day. I even forgot to take notes in my philosophy class! She has bewitched me.

When can I see her next?

W

I had bewitched him.
Just as he had bewitched me.
Bewarlocked?
I hugged the laptop to my chest and then kissed the *W* at the end of the letter, which left a big smear on the screen. Lincoln must've gotten Linny's number from Mom and Weyland's number from Linny, called Weyland up, and revealed my identity as Miss Fortune Cookie. He had a substantial talent for intrigue for a nine-year-old. And three-quarters.

After reading the letter again and again, the thumping in my chest only got worse. How could Weyland know that I was *the one* after a single weird date? Then again, if you tallied up the Elbo Room, Joel's apartment, our fight in the parking lot, and our kiss in the motel room, plus all the time in the Mini, maybe that counted as five dates. Then again, *again*, hadn't I just decided to move to a faraway town called Cambridge?

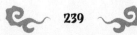

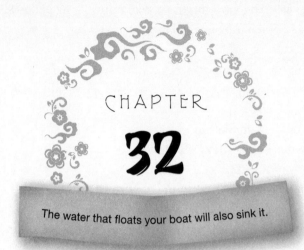

CHAPTER

**32**

The water that floats your boat will also sink it.

Mom and I sat together on the couch, ostensibly talking about my future at Harvard, though my mind kept wandering back to Weyland's letter. A girl can give herself vertigo considering every option, angle, and possibility while under the dizzying influence of love. It was a miracle that I didn't float up to the ceiling and stay up there, spinning like a ride at Great America.

Mom kept petting my hair while we talked, though she refrained from tickling my chin or scratching me behind the ears, at least. "I realized something the other day," she said. "I've been hanging on to you too tightly."

I shifted a little. "But now you're going back to college. I'm so excited."

Mom gave me the once-over. "You look dazed."

"I kind of am, actually. Remember the boy I told you about earlier, Weyland?" I said. "The one who does theater, is very considerate, and has a great sense of humor?" Who isn't *that* much older than me? And writes letters like he kisses—mesmerizingly. Which isn't a real word, according to Merriam-Webster, "He asked me out."

"That's awesome, Erin," she said, trying to knuckle-bump me. She pulled me into a hug, and this time it felt exactly right.

Will entered the living room, a can of yellow paint in one hand. "Time to finish this off, eh?"

I stood up. "Do you mind if don't participate? I'd like to go upstairs to talk to Mei if she's home, and if Mrs. Liu will let me."

Mom put on the kettle in the kitchen. "Why wouldn't she?"

"Because I didn't notify her immediately when her daughter ran away?"

"Don't be silly. She's very understanding."

I suppressed a snort of disbelief. Though I loved Mrs. Liu with all my heart, *understanding* did not describe her. *Inexorable* was closer to the truth. *Ferocious.*

"She gave Will a temporary job as assistant chef at Hay Fat," Mom said.

"She did? Congratulations, Will."

Will laughed. "You look a tad horrified, young miss. You think she might eat me for supper? But, you see, I won her over with a top-hole ghost story. I've had many interesting encounters with ghosts."

That shut me up for a moment—thinking about his dead family, and how they'd perished in a fire that he had started. Who knew that the hum from the malfunctioning light in the kitchen could be so loud? "So your wife and daughter visit you, then?" I asked.

Mom discreetly jabbed me with her elbow, which I took to mean, *What the hell are you talking about?* I put some distance between us. "Sorry. I don't mean to pry."

"No offense taken," he said. "Anna, that's my daughter, disapproves of my vagabond life. She has made it her mission to get me to make something of myself."

"That's so sweet of her," I said, liking that Anna's spirit had lived on to be concerned for her father.

Will growled as he spread a drop cloth under the last un-painted wall. "If you like bossy daughters. The news about my job will delight her, even if it's temporary. She's studying art history in Edinburgh."

Oh. "That's . . . neat." Ghosts might haunt their homeless dads, harass them to move off the streets, even, but they don't usually study abroad. It occurred to me just then that Will had, in fact, *not* started a fire with a cigarette that burned down a building with his sleeping wife and daughter inside. I felt like a box of rocks. A dork slap. Then I fined myself fifty cents. On the other hand . . .

$$gullible\ fool \div cynic = 1$$

If I had to choose to be one or the other, I'd go for gullible fool any day.

Will cleared his throat. "I take it you've heard the urban legend about me?"

"Mmm," I said, a little embarrassed.

"What are you talking about?" Mom asked.

Will stirred the paint, setting the gooey stick onto a piece of newspaper when he finished. He didn't seem angry. "I bet you're curious why I keep this around." He drew the cigarette from his pocket, placed it between his lips, and inhaled. "I miss how it feels."

"That's why you should never start smoking in the first place," Mom said.

Will flourished his cigarette. "Cliché."

"You mean touché," Mom said.

"Not so much," he said, adopting an American accent and rolling his eyes like one of my classmates. He has a great sense of humor.

I went to my room, and after checking various class blogs for homework and arming myself with textbooks to lend credibility to my visit, I climbed the stairs to Mei's apartment. When Shoe Fang opened the door, her expression changed from grim to glowering. I hate having that effect on people.

"*Ni hao ma?*" I asked. *How are you?*

She pressed her lips together and shook her head.

My next words came out all in one breath. "I'm sorry. I should've called you on Monday night. Can I see Mei to give her the homework she missed at school?" I lifted the books in case Shoe Fang wanted to inspect them for authenticity. Or skin them, maybe, with a fillet knife.

"She no can talk now." Before I could ask why, she shut the door in my face.

I tromped down the stairs again, said hey to Will and Mom as they painted the living room, and retired to my room to call Linny. After leaving a mere four messages, I tackled my calculus problem set, polishing it off in record time. Relaxing would just lead to worrying, so I began the paper for the AP English sub. Only when I'd completed a decent draft did I allow myself a little Miss Fortune Cookie time as a treat. Except Weyland's letter made me too happy and too nervous because, if I mentioned Harvard, would he lose interest? So I warmed up on the one from *Tyler*, who wanted to break up with his boyfriend to save him future pain.

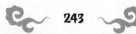

Dear Tyler,

**Miss Fortune Cookie says: Do not kill the fly on your boyfriend's head with a hatchet.** There has to be a better way to deal with the problem. I don't know, like using a flyswatter?

Seriously. Instead of breaking up, you should ask him how he feels about long-distance relationships.

Miss Fortune Cookie

Not bad. It made me realize that I'd have to be honest with Weyland. Still, I delayed the moment of truth by calling Shanice about her hat. She refused to trust the precious pink confection to the U.S. Postal Service and suggested picking it up on Friday afternoon, the day of our college acceptance party at Hay Fat. So I invited her to come. Just as I hung up, someone knocked on the front door. Mom and I used to live a quiet life, but in the last few days, the apartment had become Grand Central Station. Which I kind of relished, actually.

"It's unlocked!" Mom yelled.

Mom and Will were sitting on the couch in the living room, eating pizza. A box lay open on the coffee table, with two slices missing. The door opened, and in came Mei with a manila folder under her arm. "Hey, it's me." Seeing Will, she said, "I'm Mei."

Will stood up. "Cheerio, I'm Will. Would you care for some pizza?"

Mei watched my mom taking a huge bite. "I thought you didn't like pizza, Mrs. Kavanagh."

Mom blushed. "I'm just not overly fond of pepperoni."

"It's a Vegan Delite," Will said, "spinach and soy cheese. Delish."

"Thank you," Mei said. "I'm not really hungry."

We all exchanged a few more polite pleasantries, until Mei plunged into my room and I followed her, closing the door behind me. After setting the manila folder on the floor, she plopped down on my beanbag, while I gleaned her face for signs of tragedy—redness, puffiness, water damage. Or fury. Nothing. "Your mom's new boyfriend is cute," she said.

"They're just friends." Except Mom had blushed about the pizza. "Anyway, he's funny and way nicer than Pete-the-Accountant."

"I only have a few minutes before Ma comes back. Listen, Erin." She stopped, possibly to give me an opportunity to fall to my knees and knock my head against the floor. After all, she'd reached out to me, made an album of our best friendship years, and then I'd betrayed her when she ran away.

"I really *am* sorry about Monday night," I said. "Telling your mom."

Mei looked serious. Older. "I could've been nicer to you when you barged in. It just surprised me to see you at the motel." She nibbled on her pinkie knuckle.

She wasn't mad. I twirled the butterflies she'd given me. They had gotten dusty over the years. "Is your mom wavering about Stanford?"

Mei hugged her knees to her chest. "No."

I sat down on the floor by the beanbag. "Is she still angry with you?" We'd entered a new phase of friendship, a level beyond dressing up and pretending to be other people. Now we were being real with each other.

"My whole life is crazy with a capital C," Mei said. "Remember my cousin from China? He stayed with us for a month in fifth grade."

"Sort of."

Mei grabbed my hand and squeezed it. One of her newly grown nails dug somewhat into my skin. "He's going to sell his house to help pay for my tuition."

"That's intense." Ow.

Mei put on her donkey face. "Darren and I will make it work. I know we can. We'll see each other during vacations, we'll talk on the phone every day."

My finger, the one with her nail embedded in it, wiggled on its own. She let go, springing up with sudden energy, kneeling on my bed to examine the poster print on my wall, the one of the three of us together by Lake Merced. I got mushy inside imagining Linny, Mei, and me as old ladies together. Linny would surely have forgiven me by then.

"We should take that same picture every year, don't you think?" I said. "Until we're wrinkled and lumpy and like to wear slightly ugly but practical shoes."

Okay, so I was trying to get Mei to laugh, and failing miserably. She looked distracted in a way that didn't match the tone of our conversation. "Uh-huh," she said, like she was far away.

I threw a donkey at her to bring her back to the room. "I have something to tell you. It's kind of big news," I said. "I got into Harvard too. We're going to be freshmen together."

Mei spun around and flung her arms around me. "Erin! That's great!"

Was that fake enthusiasm I detected? "I'm so thrilled too."

When she let go, she said, "I have something for you," and stooped to retrieve the folder from the floor. "I started collecting these a long time ago, hoping it would make up for . . . you know. How I treated you in eighth grade."

The folder was thick with Carolyn Hax letters cut from

newspapers and printed off the Internet, maybe two hundred of them. "Oh my . . . gosh! I love this. Thank you. Thank you. This is amazing." A warm tide rose in my chest.

Mei seemed almost detached about the gift and my reaction to it, though. "I would've put them in a binder—" She stopped talking abruptly and paced the few steps from my dresser to the door, back and forth like a trapped animal. "I should go. Don't be too happy, because there's something I haven't told you."

I waited.

Her eyes were a flat black, unreadable. "Linny was at that sleepover. You know the one I'm talking about. I said you couldn't come because I didn't want you to meet her." She spoke matter-of-factly, as if listing rivers in the Amazon basin for a teacher.

"I don't understand."

"I was afraid she'd like you. Too much. I just thought you should know." She left me there with my jaw hanging open.

CHAPTER

33

Your bad plans may yield good results.

The Carolyn Hax letters were dog-eared, messy, and in no particular order. Mei's printer had run out of ink half-way through one, and some others had been ripped from the newspaper instead of cut out neatly with scissors. Inky finger-prints streaked the folder they came in. A gift of love. And guilt.

No wonder Mei had acted strangely just now in my room. Surreal images from the past played in my head, warped and distorted—my overnight bag bizarrely enormous, Mei's mouth opening in slow motion. Yet a sliver of me (not the best sliver, either) understood why she'd done it. I didn't always dance with ecstasy at the idea of sharing Linny, either. Still, the deliberate way Mei had knocked me out of the running somewhat took my breath away.

Not that her nefarious plan had worked.

I stood on my head for a while to see the world upside down. It really helped. All these years, I'd somewhat blamed the past on myself, imagining that Mei had gotten fed up with me. I'd also blamed it on Mei—for the wrong reason—thinking she cared too much about my non-Chinese DNA. In a way, this new understanding filled me with relief. Though I don't believe that the cosmos revolves around me, it felt as though the universe had shifted over an inch or two. In a good way.

I called Linny sixteen more times—perpetually going to voice mail—not to blab about what Mei had just confessed, but rather to make things right between us again. Though important exchanges should never be done by text (apologies, I love yous, breakups, insults), pleas for communication are okay, I think.

**hi lin, pls call me. x**

Then I focused a beam of my purest mind-energy onto the phone, channeling it like a magnifying glass concentrating the sun's rays, willing Linny to respond. But she didn't. Hell on rye. Another potential superpower down the toilet. Luckily, Karina came to drop off Lincoln, who barreled into me so hard that Shanice's hat, which had been stuck onto his head at a rakish angle, flew across the room. I welcomed the distraction.

"Did Weyland write you like he promised?" Lincoln asked.

I pretended to shake him by the shoulders. "He did, you scoundrel."

Lincoln's chest expanded with pride. While the adults talked, he dragged me off to my room, shut the door, and took a running leap into the beanbag. "I told him you were Miss Fortune Cookie," he said, delighted with his bad behavior.

I scowled. "I know. Don't tell anyone else, or I'll have to scrobble you."

"What's that? It sounds fun." He bounded off the beanbag

to open the laptop. "Did you post Weyland's letter? Can I see it? Have you written back?"

"Not yet, but if you settle down, I'll show it to you."

Lincoln read the letter thoughtfully, pinching his chin between his fingers. "He said you bewitched him."

I flushed. "I noticed that."

"I know how to answer," he said. "Type exactly what I say. 'Dear W, Come over right away so we can kiss. Your kisses are better than Justin Bieber's. I would like more of them, please. Your lips on mine. Your—'"

I interrupted him midrhapsody. "I'm not going to say that. Make it rated PG, okay?"

"Write him some *boring* letter, then."

So I attempted to, though it took me forever to achieve the exact degree of ambiguousness I wanted to convey.

Dear Weyland,

I like you a lot, too. You should know that I got into Harvard and have decided to go there. Maybe it's for the best that we don't start anything, even though we had a lot of fun together.

Lincoln wrenched the computer away before I finished. "You can't send *that*." He held his nose with one hand and pressed down the delete button with the other till the laboriously considered paragraph had disappeared. "You sound exactly the same as that dumb guy."

"What dumb guy?"

Lincoln pounded his forehead against the wall to demonstrate my utter dim-wittedness in the face of his contrasting brilliance. "The one who wanted to break up with his boyfriend so his boyfriend could have fun in Switzerland?"

 250

"Sweden," I said. "You think I'm acting like *Tyler?*"

"Hello, Captain Obvious."

In the end I let Lincoln help me write Weyland a more encouraging letter, though we fought over every word.

Dear Weyland,

What a crazy night! I am smitten too.

You should know that I got into Harvard and have decided to go in the fall. It was a hard decision to make.

Still, I'd like to see you again. A lot. Since I don't have any minutes on my phone, you can email me back.

Btw, have you ever played Pokémon? And do you have a favorite character?

Erin

I somewhat cringed from shyness after hitting send. Should I really have said *smitten?* But Lincoln insisted, and now it was too late. Fortunately, my little friend never left my side all evening, so when Weyland failed to write back or call, I didn't freak out to the same degree I might have on my own. Instead, I introduced Lincoln to all my donkeys, from Abigail to Zenobia, the queen of Palmyra. Then I explained to him about my Pokémon theory of dating, and how favorite characters spoke volumes about a boy's personality. He totally got it.

In all that time, no texts came from Linny, either, rounding out a perfect evening of wretched electronic silence.

One amazing thing happened in the middle of the night, though. Lincoln zonked out early. I remained hopelessly alert, on the other hand—wired, in fact—stalking my blog, email,

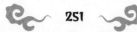

and Facebook while hiding under my covers, hoping to hear from someone. Finally, Mei showed up on my Facebook chat.

**Mei:** hi!
**Erin:** hi hi
**Mei:** Do you think I'm still mean?
**Erin:** noooo!

Kind of, but not really. Maybe a tad self-centered. Anyway, Mei *had* changed a lot since eighth grade and it's not like I thought of myself as perfect either. The ropy tangle in my chest loosened.

**Erin:** it was forever ago
**Mei:** thanx. don't leave. sending a link.

Something I did in middle school weighed on my conscience, too—a girl without friends asked if she could eat lunch with Mei and me one time. I didn't like her and convinced Mei to tell her no. She changed schools before I got to apologize. Thank God middle school only lasted three years. Though it felt like an eternity at the time.

**Mei:** http://www . . .
**Erin:** what is it?
**Mei:** you'll see. congrats on the big h!!!!!
**Erin:** thanks
**Mei:** ttyl
**Erin:** bye

When I clicked on the link, a YouTube video came up, a clip of me singing at the protest. The cape and face makeup

made me eerie, and no girl looks her best with her mouth open wide, but I saw something else.

Poise.

After watching a couple of other protest videos, and by a couple, I mean every last one posted online, my eyes grew heavy, and I went to sleep.

The next morning, Mei didn't knock on our apartment door to catch a ride, and I couldn't find Linny at school. On the bright side, I'd missed so many assignments in the last two and a half days that working through lunch made sense. It conquered my loneliness, anyway. Besides, my classmates were still abuzz about the protest, and all the residual excitement spilled over onto me. Especially when I got complimented on my singing. When I made it home, Mom had on her coat, ready to pick up Lincoln from his homeschool group. I offered to drive.

Yep. Erin 2.0 in action. Erin-Xtreme. That was me.

Mom graciously agreed to let me take the wheel, with a single grimace as evidence of her true feelings. After I navigated twenty blocks without a problem, her shoulders relaxed a little, which allowed mine to fall some too. Really, a person's scapulae should remain well below her earlobes while operating a motor vehicle.

"My daughter at Harvard!" Mom said. "I can't help wondering if I've taught you everything you need to know to make it on your own."

"You've taught me plenty, Mom."

"But you'll be in new situations, and I won't be there to guide you."

"We'll talk all the time. It's not like I'm moving into a tent in the Gobi Desert." Though they probably had cell service in central Asia, too.

"I don't know how to Twitter. Should I learn how to Twitter?"

"Tweet. Talking on a phone is better, anyway."

During the entire drive across the city, I activated the windshield wipers only once and got honked at only twice. One time by a cute guy hitting on me, I think. I pulled into the narrow driveway, and Lincoln ran out to meet us, his pants pockets bulging. "Can Weyland come over this afternoon?"

"What's that in your pockets?"

He climbed into the back seat. "Orange peels. I collect them."

I used my turn signal and checked my mirrors before pulling out. "Why?"

"They're cool and smooth, and they smell good. Everyone was just going to throw them away. Do you want one? Why can't Weyland come over? He said he wanted to in his love letter."

Mom somewhat smirked at me. "Weyland wrote you a love letter?"

"You should've seen the way Erin kissed him in the motel room," Lincoln said.

If the steering wheel hadn't occupied both my hands, I would've slapped a strip of duct tape over Lincoln's mouth. As it was, I could barely stay in my lane.

Mom laughed. "Tell me more. Erin claimed that you all just *slept* in the motel room."

"Mom! We kissed. End of story. You've taught me about protection and STDs and boys who don't respect you in the morning. None of that applied. Did Lincoln tell you he's reading *Eragon*? Lincoln, my mom would like to hear a thorough summary of the plot." Luckily, the novel had more than just a plethora of pages. It had a storyline that took half an hour to explain.

When we got home, I took Lincoln on the town with me to buy a present for Mei because it seemed safer than leaving him to gossip with Mom. Lok, the orange-eared Pekingese came, too, because I liked his company.

Lincoln commandeered the leash right away. "Are you mad at me?"

Yes. "I don't like it when *people* tell the whole world every detail of my life."

"Sorry." Lincoln looked close to tears.

Which made me feel bad. A homeless man with long, stringy hair and only one foot happened to be leaning against the wall two doors down, and that gave me an idea. "Tell you what. Take a dollar to that man, and I'll consider forgiving you."

"Really?" Lincoln brightened in an instant, snatched the bill from my hand, and hopped over to the man. After they talked for a while, Lincoln returned. "I showed him how to walk. He said he was going to call you."

"He did?"

"Not *that* guy. Weyland! I called him today."

"You called him?" A nine-year-old boy had taken control of my love life, and Shanice had called *me* the busybody. Except I appreciated Lincoln, because I didn't dare call Weyland myself. "Which number did you give him?"

"Your mom's phone."

After buying Mei's gift and cleaning up after Lok, I hurried us back to the apartment to check for calls, but Mom had left, taking her phone with her. Lincoln squeezed the oil from the orange peels into a candle flame, which sparked and crackled. Before he set anything on fire, I got him started with online Whac-a-Mole on Mom's computer so I could do my homework. And by do my homework, I mean refresh my email and Miss

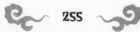

Fortune Cookie inbox every thirty seconds. Later that evening, Mom came home, Will returned from his first shift at Hay Fat, and we all sat elbow to elbow around the kitchen table.

After dinner, Lincoln wanted to write more letters, but I wasn't in the mood, so he read through my archives while I sifted through the papers on my desk, looking for something to wrap Mei's gift in. "You give really good advice," he said.

"You think so?"

"People ask a lot of stupid questions, but you're always nice to them."

I found a piece of origami paper with only two folds in it. "But I'm kind of a busybody, telling everyone how to run their lives, don't you think?"

"No. You don't *make* anyone. You give them new eyeballs, like when I put on Karina's reading glasses. Everything looks huge and fuzzy through them. It's so cool."

The scissors I'd been holding fell to the floor. Really?

The truth had been right there in front of me all along, like Dorothy and the shoes that could take her back to Kansas. I had a mind of steel, and fresh points of view more powerful than a locomotive, able to leap tall problems in a single bound.

I had a superpower to call my own.

CHAPTER

34

Plan for many troubles and pleasures ahead.

ate Thursday night, Linny finally called. Her voice was entirely unrecognizable. A talking duck would've been easier to understand. Luckily, I had caller ID. "What happened to you?" I said.

"I got the flu and slept for thirty hours straight."

Which explained her scary hoarseness. I kept a joke that popped into my head about duck flu to myself, laughing nervously on the inside. Ha ha ha. The flu also provided a possible explanation for her icing me out since our fight. "Did you get my text?" I asked.

"I can't find my phone," she rasped. "Did you get my Miss Fortune Cookie letter?"

Um. "No."

"Of course you didn't, because I just sent it. I'll hang on while you read it." So with slightly shaky fingers, I signed in to my blog.

Dear Miss Fortune Cookie,

My friend decided to go to college where we can't be together. It hurt my feelings, and I totally went off on her.

I'm always telling her to be adventurous, but the truth is, I like taking care of her. Then she grew up without me. How annoying is that?

A friend

I waited a moment to give myself a chance to absorb this. To give my lungs a chance to de-gum from all the sweet feelings trapped inside me, actually. Finally I was ready. "That's it? You're not mad at me anymore? I love you, Linny!"

"I'm not mad. I'm furious," she quacked.

"I'm sorry."

"You should be. I can't believe you're going to abandon me like this."

"I'll miss you too," I said.

"Can you hear that yelling? Mom wants me to hang up because my bathwater is getting cold." I really *could* hear it. "I might have to move to somewhere with unreliable phone service to escape her. You know, like Africa."

Minishriek. "You're really considering it?"

"Maybe. That doesn't mean I forgive you."

We kept talking until Adele made her hang up, and by then I felt sure she'd forgiven me despite what she said.

That night, I slept deeply for the first time in forever, forcing Lincoln to jump on me and stick his finger up my nose to wake me the next morning. Well, probably not, but that's what he did. Who knows why?

On Friday, my classes crawled by at a glacial pace. The clocks were running backward, I think. Whenever I drifted into a daydream, say of kissing Weyland while reclining on a soft cloud in the troposphere, I pinched myself awake. Imagining the frenzy in Mrs. Liu's kitchen this morning helped some. The lavish volume of spirit money alone required for the occasion boggled the mind. Yet Mrs. Liu said the ancestors expected nothing less. At least she hadn't insisted on Mei making her entrance riding in a palanquin carried by eunuchs.

The ride home on Muni added some bizarreness to my day. I sat next to a balding man talking to a smiley face drawn on a piece of paper. The conversation was so engrossing that he ignored me. One stop before Union Square, a group of men in their twenties got on board, all without pants, possibly a performance-art piece, though I didn't ask.

When I arrived at our empty apartment, I threw on the dress Mom had laid out for me (she knew I'd take forever choosing otherwise), flattened my hair, and speed walked to Hay Fat. Mom, Will, Lincoln, and Mei were shoehorned into the kitchen on top of Mrs. Liu. Darren and Karina tried to help too, and by help I mean step on each other's feet and bump into things. In all the craziness, I noticed something—the mess of spices, seeds, and dried fungi on the shelves. I'd always planned to alphabetize them but never got around to it, and maybe never would. It hurt to think about it.

Mrs. Liu shouted commands, all the while hurling things into the wok and stirring like a cyclone combined with a tornado. Combined with a hurricane. You'd think we were part of the staff preparing for a British royal wedding. Something wet went into the wok, and oil splattered in all directions. Mei jumped back to protect her clothes.

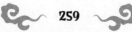

"Now I know why it's called Hay Fat," Darren whispered, cleaning his glasses on his shirt. I'm guessing his mom still does his laundry.

Mrs. Liu overheard of course. "Name is good advertisement. No oil mean no taste."

"I love oily food. That's the only kind my mom cooks," Darren said.

She stopped stirring to give him a pained smile. But when Karina knocked over a bucket of shrimp, the tender moment faded, and she booted us all out. The adults moved into the dining room. Before Mei and I left, though, Mrs. Liu shook her spatula at me. "You go to Harvard. You are good daughter." She frowned at Mei.

Just the kick our friendship needed.

I smiled awkwardly, then seized Mei, hauling her to a place behind the Dumpster, where the vegetable peels rotted and the general foulness afforded us a modicum of privacy.

"I'm sorry about *that*," I said, pointing my chin toward the kitchen.

"Whatever. Are you going to tell Linny?" she asked. It took me a moment to understand. She was worried I'd blab the real reason she'd dumped me in eighth grade.

"I won't if you don't want me to." I smiled. We had turned into co-conspirators. "Anyway, you've changed since then."

"You're nicer too."

That took me by surprise. "I am?"

"Don't you remember? You used to say mean things to me all the time. Like when I bought those skinny jeans, and you said they made my legs look like Popsicle sticks. And you didn't want me to grow out my bangs because my forehead was too wide."

Now that she mentioned it, I kind of did, except I hadn't

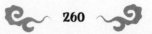

meant to hurt her. Which made me reconsider my ban on lies. The *sincere* kind still protected people's feelings. "I didn't mean to be mean."

"Really?" But she said it with a grin.

A fly kept bombarding my face, and we fled into the restaurant. Hundreds of crimson helium balloons—Harvard's color—drifted along the ceiling, clashing with the red lacquer shelves, the pink lanterns, and the green tablecloths. Blue and yellow crepe-paper streamers to honor Berkeley added to the color mash-up.

Linny had arrived and was sitting with Darren and Lincoln at a banquet table. When Mei and I came over, she stood to hug us. Everyone behaved sensitively, refraining from making comments about the significance of the party decor. Everyone except me. "No red and white for Stanford. At least you have three weeks to wear her down," I said to Mei. College acceptance forms were due on May 1.

Mei sucked her lips into her mouth. "Optimist."

Darren gave me a sad smile. "Congratulations on Harvard, Erin. You'll be seeing a lot more of my girlfriend than I will." Then his smile changed to goofy. "Don't forget she's taken, okay?"

"I won't," I joked back.

Lincoln moved to the seat next to Mei to stroke the shoulder of her blue silk *qipao*, a Chinese tailored dress with cloth buttons that run diagonally across the chest. Darren whacked him with a napkin. "Watch yourself, bub."

Lincoln's eyes went round, turning into saucers of innocence. "I'm only nine."

I set a little box in front of Mei. "A present for you. Lincoln helped me pick it out."

It was a beaded butterfly barrette. She had a thing for

butterflies. After all these years of giving her donkey things, I finally got it right. Besides, donkeys don't look that good in your hair. "It's beautiful," she said. Then she noticed another thing inside the box—the sea-glass given to me by the water ghost. "Erin! I've always, always, always wanted this. How did you know? You're so . . . What's the word?"

*Perceptive. Generous.* "Nice?"

"Thank you!"

Next I gave Linny a scroll tied up with a bow. She ripped it open and stared at the photograph of a woman with a small ruminant on a leash. "You bought me a goat? Is this *my* goat?"

"I named it Ninny," I said.

Linny cracked up. "Linny and Ninny! That's perfect!" She hugged me so tight that some of her voluminous hair ended up in my mouth. "I got you something too," she said, still holding me. "It's from my mom mostly. But Mei and I both chipped in." She let go, and I disengaged from her hair.

Mei handed me a small package. I could tell she'd wrapped it because of the quantity of tape involved. Darren offered up his pocketknife to help me. Inside, I found a familiar object. "My old cell phone. Um. Thanks."

"With like a gazillion minutes on it so you can call me all the time."

Oh. It was a double whammy gift: Linny giving me her blessing to go to Harvard *and* Mei encouraging me to stay friends with Linny. "Thank you!" I turned it on. "I'm going to make my first call right now." I looked at Linny. "Do you have Weyland's number?" A low ooooh sound started up around the table, like I'd suggested a round of strip poker.

"It's not activated yet," Mei said.

Mrs. Liu had confiscated Mei's cell, Linny's was still AWOL, and Darren had forgotten his, so I decided to use the pay phone half a block away. And told Lincoln he couldn't come with me.

Phone booths in movies have a romantic air, but this particular one was covered in silver and blue graffiti, and the mouthpiece smelled of moldy lemons. After I punched in the number, a shadow fell over me. I turned to find Weyland standing behind me with his cell pressed against his ear. My heart skipped a beat, more than one, maybe, as his voice entered my phone ear and my free ear at the same moment—a most savory sensation.

My hand lost its grip, and the receiver dropped, dangling on its snaky metal cord. Weyland put his arms around me. For a moment, his embrace felt awkward, all bones, elbows, and uncertainty like I had my face pressed against the chest of a stranger I'd met in a BART station. But then I saw his slightly unmatched socks, and our long crazy night together came back to me in a rush.

I tilted my head toward him just to say something, I swear. Before I got out a word, he brushed my lips with his. This slight touch sent goose bumps down my spine and raised shivers all over my skin. Or something like that.

He slid his hand into mine and started walking. "I got your letter."

His shoelaces looked new. "Everyone says that long-distance relationships don't work," I said. It came out dry and flat, like an old newspaper.

He stopped in the gilded doorway of a shop selling wax umbrellas and jade dragons, tightening the grip of his fingers entwined in mine. "Who are *they*, and what do *they* know? I don't have to stay at Berkeley forever."

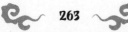

"What do you mean?"

"What I mean"—he smiled at me in that heart-stopping way of his—"is this."

He pulled me into him. Slowly, we came together like when the sun rises over the horizon and its warmth increases by degrees. Our lips touched. And then we were moving at five times normal speed, kissing with our bodies crushed together, his nose against my cheek, his hands sliding along my waist. He stepped back for a moment and set my palm against his chest. Hot toaster.

"Keep going," Lincoln said. The kid was part ninja, I think.

Weyland ignored him. My fingers fluttered against his chest, feeling the pounding of his heart through his shirt. "How do you say *that* in Chinese?" Weyland whispered.

"*Wo ai ni*," I said. *I love you.*

"Whoa eye knee," he whispered.

Despite his atrocious pronunciation, and the fact that I'd kind of tricked him into saying it, a delicious tingling whirled through me.

"Translation?" Lincoln asked.

"It means mind your own business," Weyland said.

Lincoln persisted. "Did you tell Erin your favorite Pokémon yet?" Which kind of broke the mood.

Still, his answer mattered to me. I held my breath. *Please don't let it be that bully Machoke.* Or Jigglypuff. And definitely not that crazy Psyduck. Or a hundred other Pokémon I didn't fully appreciate.

Weyland looked mystified. "I was wondering about that. Why do you want to know?"

"Just tell her!" Lincoln shouted.

"I can't remember. Poliwhirl? Dragonair?"

Poliwhirl had a spiral at the center of its round, purple

body. Dragonair was intensely loyal. Neither one dominated by being obnoxious, aggressive, or nasty. I sighed. Then Weyland kissed me again for an eternity, except it wasn't long enough.

Lincoln tapped my shoulder. "Ahem. It's 6:13."

I pulled back from Weyland. "The party stuttered fifteen minutes ago!" I checked my hair. "We butter get moving."

"At least wait until you're coherent."

"I ma hocarent." I dragged him down the sidewalk toward Hay Fat, stumbling over a box of brass Buddha statues in the way.

"At least wait until you can walk," Weyland said.

CHAPTER

**35**

In the garden of your dreams,
good things will bloom.

Weyland and I entered through Hay Fat's alley entrance, still holding hands, with Lincoln nipping at our heels. I floated across the kitchen, buoyed by the savory scents in the air. Ingredients most Americans consider marginally edible, things discovered during times of famine—tree bark, roots, and small sea creatures—came together as an epic feast in Mrs. Liu's capable hands. The array of shumai on trays near the door seemed to be having a party all their own. I drifted over to introduce myself.

Linny swatted me before I could taste one. "I'm supposed to protect these with my life until it's time to take them out. Have you written your speech?"

Which plunged me down to earth in a hurry. "Speech?"

"It's on the program."

"You need time to prepare," Weyland said. "Let's go, Lincoln." They left me alone by the shumai, except for Linny, who remained on guard.

The moment her attention flagged, I popped a shiny beauty into my mouth, closing my eyes to better appreciate the symphony of flavors. "Did you know that certain compounds in shrimp and green onions improve cognition and creative abilities?"

Linny followed suit, and we chewed together in happy silence. Until she swallowed. "I think I *will* go to Africa this fall." A wave—no, a tsunami—of happy sadness overcame me. In a few months, we could be living on different continents.

"Where in Africa?"

"They're looking for volunteers in Mali."

Which had to be at least a few light-years from Massachusetts. The tag on her blouse was sticking up, so I tucked it back in for her. "What's it like there?"

"Hot and dusty and really poor. It used to be a colony of France, so I'll get to practice my French. They're really into music and dancing. Maybe I'll become a drummer."

"Anything is possible." My lungs expanded until the truth of it filled me up. I could do anything with my life too. Whatever I wanted.

"I have to figure out how to tell my mom so she doesn't panic," Linny said.

Mrs. Liu scurried over and grabbed us each by the elbow, dragging us into the restaurant. "Come help find chair for guest." Some things would never change, at least.

While Linny and Mei seated people and served tea, I hid behind the register to compose my speech, but in reality kept staring at Weyland, and the page remained stubbornly blank. Only yesterday, I'd believed that going off to Harvard would be a grand adventure. But then he showed up today. I wrote down the first thing that came into my head. *Love is loony.*

As I pondered the second bullet point for my speech,

Shanice walked in. I grabbed her hat from behind the aquarium, put it on, and sauntered over. Before saying hello, even, she had it off my head and cradled in her arms. "My sweet baby. I thought I'd never see you again." She kissed me on the cheek. "Hi, Hoity. Thanks for inviting me. I'm starving. Where's the food?"

"It's coming."

"I'm going to have me a few of these appetizers while we wait." She grabbed a handful of fortune cookies from a box. I led her to the table where my friends were, and introduced her. Shanice passed around the fortune cookies.

"Fortunes are more accurate if people choose their own," I said. I'd developed this theory during AP physics when I learned about particles, atoms, molecules, matter, and antimatter, and how everything is connected to something else. Despite the apparent chaos, the universe is not random.

Shanice rolled her eyes but gathered up the cookies again and heaped them in a pile at the center of the table. "Let's read them aloud to see if Hoity is right. Me first." She picked one and extracted the little slip of paper. "'The rubber bands are heading in the right direction.' What the hell? Explain that one, Hoity." Except she never stopped talking to let me. "I get it. It means I've changed something and my life will get better. Damn, it's true. I decided to go back to school like Hoity told me to. Effing busybody."

Lincoln made eyes at Shanice. "I wish Karina would let me swear like that." Then Weyland gave him a doofus slap on the back of his head.

"That's awesome," I said. "What are you going to study?"

"Mechanics. I'm good with my hands. I'll be specializing in those uppity European cars. That's where the money is."

Mei opened hers next. "'With a mind like yours, who needs a body?'"

"That's definitely true," Darren said. "Still, I'm glad you have a body."

"I agree," Lincoln said, which earned him a second doofus slap, this time from me.

Mei blushed. "Ma just switched cookie companies. I should warn her."

Lincoln waved his fortune like a flag. "Me next. 'You will meet a handsome stranger who will come and go.'" He shook his head. "I think this one's for my mom." We all laughed.

While Lincoln grabbed for another, Darren read his. "'Everything is not lost. You still have your faults.' Ha ha. Lucky for me, Mei overlooks them all."

Lincoln wrinkled his nose at his new fortune. "I don't think this one's mine either. 'You will marry a hobo.' Unless you're going to grow up to be a hobo, Erin." Weyland slapped him yet again. Gently, of course. Lincoln smacked him back, not quite so gently.

I looked over at Mom sitting next to Will, laughing, with her hand on his arm. "I can think of someone else that might apply to," I said. "Why don't you open another? Third time's the charm."

Linny went next. "'Something normal will happen tomorrow.' Hey! That's sucky. I want a new cookie too." Since I still had a pen from writing the speech, I took the fortune from her and changed *normal* to *abnormal*.

"Is that better?" I asked.

"Thank you. Did I tell you what Mischa said in class the other day?" Linny asked. "She said after she graduates, she's going to buy some lingerie, seduce a rich old guy with a heart

condition, and marry him for his money. Can you believe it?"

Um. "Really?" I said.

"Yeah, really," she said.

Lincoln read his third fortune through a mouthful of
cookie, "'You will win friends and influence people.'"

Would he ever. Too bad Dale Carnegie died without getting a chance to meet him.

Weyland cleared his throat, but Lincoln snatched his fortune away from him. "This is what it says." His smile stretched
like a balloon about to pop. "'The boy who kisses all the time
is smarter than the one who doesn't.'" Weyland scooted his
chair closer to mine and leaned toward me. I blushed for the
zillionth time and waited to catch on fire, but he just gave me
a peck.

"That won't make you smarter," Lincoln said.

Shanice rescued us. "What does yours say, Hoity?"

"Mine is the truest one of all," I said. "'There will be
tomorrow in your future.'"

Everyone laughed, and that's when I realized that Mei and
Weyland had the same giggle. No wonder I like him so much.

In the midst of all the joking around, Shoe Fang snuck up
on us. "What is this rigmarole?" she barked. "Party take work.
Come serve guests."

We all stood at once, even Shanice, and followed her to
the kitchen. When Lincoln staggered toward the first table
with a tray—the little plates of dumplings clinking together—
the dining room fell silent, everyone hoping that he wouldn't
drop it. By the second course, though, whole steamed rock
cod, Lincoln gained confidence. And by the third, bamboo
pith over vegetables, and the fourth, scallops with yellow fungus, he had mastered the job. We of the younger generation

had less time to eat than the other guests, but we still ate too much.

At banquets in China, the soup is served last because it's made by tossing all the feast leftovers into a broth. Mrs. Liu broke with tradition by making a masterpiece of sweet lotus. As I took my first sip, a raucous banging from the kitchen and copious swearing rudely interrupted me. Smoke poured through the door.

"Stay calm, everyone!" I shouted. "The kitchen is on fire."

The guests scrambled up, colliding into one another in their haste to escape. The smoke burned my eyes while I helped a group from a nearby table to the door. After every last guest had made it outside and the kitchen staff had put out the fire, Will sat down on the curb with a guitar and started playing seventies rock tunes. Lincoln wanted a turn, so Will obliged, guiding his fingers over the strings.

Mrs. Liu bustled over to me. "Good time for make speeches," she said, ever the practical hostess. "I speak first. Mei second. You last. Linny say no." She stepped onto an overturned vegetable crate and bored holes into her guests' skulls with her X-ray eyes. After a long moment, we all quieted down.

"Fire is out."

A few people clapped until Mrs. Liu frowned them into silence.

"Everyone know Harvard accept my daughter, Meihua."

Everyone clapped this time, and someone whistled.

"She only medium smart and only work medium hard. Lazy girl. She only get 3.9 GPA." In traditional Chinese culture, overt praise invites bad luck, so Chinese moms everywhere learn how to brag in underhanded ways. "I surprise when number one school in America take her as student.

"I am young before, in China, like Meihua. I try hard to

bring honor on my family. I come to America for family long ago. My Meihua is stubborn girl. *She* want to go to Stanford number four school to be with boyfriend. In China, good daughter must obey mother."

Mei's face went still, and Darren tightened his arm around her shoulders. It hurt my heart to think of them separated by thousands of miles.

Mrs. Liu raised a finger. "China and America not same country. People in America think true love more important than family love." A second finger went up. "America movie always have happy ending." She lifted yet another finger. "I have problem. My heart become like America heart because I like happy ending movie too." Mrs. Liu paused to give Mei a hard look. "I say to my difficult daughter, Meihua, work hard at Stanford. After finish Stanford, go to Harvard graduate school."

If the kitchen fire had caused a stir, Mrs. Liu's pronouncement threw us into pure pandemonium, like we'd won a vacation to Rio, a new luxury car, *and* a living room furniture set. Then Mrs. Liu, still standing on the crate, smiled directly at me. "Lucky for Meihua my number two daughter go to Harvard this year."

When she stepped down, Mei rushed in to hug her and kept on hugging her though Mrs. Liu stood like a telephone pole throughout. We crowded around the pair of them, pestering them with more hugs, good wishes, and even some tears. By the time Mei took the podium/crate, she looked watery and disheveled.

She cleared her throat. "My mother, Ma . . ." she said, tearing up again. We all waited for her to find her voice. "Ma always puts family first. She learned how to cook professionally for her family and created a top restaurant for them. She still sends money home.

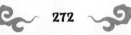

"Ma raised me to value hard work and has given me every opportunity to shine. I hope I can repay her someday. I love you, Ma."

A low *awww* rose up from the audience.

And though it's clearly wrong to gloat, I let myself enjoy a brief twinge of self-satisfaction at the turn of events. I *had* been right to trust Mrs. Liu all along. My smugness was short-lived, though, because our impatient hostess jerked her head in my direction, ordering me to the crate to make a speech. And I still hadn't written one.

My bladder felt full, and my tongue turned to fur in my mouth, which could indicate Fanconi syndrome. Or not. I stepped up, my eyes on the nearly pristine piece of paper in my hand, hoping for some words to appear. Mrs. Liu clutched a broom as if she might sweep me off any second if I failed. I smoothed my hair to keep my cerebrum from turning into loofah.

"Love is loony," I said. This earned me a few strange looks. "And by loony, I mean that love doesn't follow normal rules. Love encourages a person to take risks." I paused to wipe my forehead with the back of my hand. "The power of love starts when a parent raises her child through every hardship without considering the sacrifice. Like Mei's mom. Like Linny's. Like mine."

Mom and Adele beamed at me. Perhaps somewhere my dad was smiling too. Mrs. Liu looked melancholy. Then again, she usually did.

"Love is being there for a friend. Love is knowing when to let go."

I locked eyes with Linny, and then Mei. They were my people, the ones I protected with sincere lies. The ones who had my back.

"I'm not always the world's most confident person, but I usually understand a little how others think and feel. In fact . . ." I paused to gather strength for what came next. "In fact, I've had a secret project for a while, an online advice column. It started small but keeps growing each year. I am Miss Fortune Cookie."

Mei stared. From the elevation of her eyebrows, I could see she hadn't guessed. A lightbulb went off in Mom's head, and I sensed another conversation in our future. Shanice huffed and looked at the ceiling.

"The advice I give to everyone boils down to a few basic truths. Appreciate and respect your family and your friends. Be grateful. Follow your heart. Trust your intuition. Be honest with those you love." In the important ways, anyway. I took a deep breath. "And never, ever . . . ever . . . mind your own business."

When the laughter died down, Mei raised her glass. "A toast to Erin!"

Linny joined in. "To my wise friend. To X."

Weyland's eyes were warm. "To Miss Fortune Cookie."

As others took up the toast, someone lit a brick of firecrackers behind me. I covered my ears against the onslaught of noise, closed my eyes tight, and smiled.

# PRONUNCIATION AND TRANSLATION GUIDE FOR CHINESE WORDS AND NAMES

(Visit http://www.chinese-tools.com/tools/dictionary.html
to hear someone say them)

*Ai* [EYE]—love

*Bai tou* [BUY TOE]—Foreigner; literally white head

*Bao* [BAO (rhymes with *cow*)]—Bun

**Bi hai** [BEE HIGH]—Sea of jade

*Chi fan* [CHIRR FAHN]—Eat

*Dousha bao* [DOE SHAH BAO]—Buns filled with red bean paste

**Eren** [UH RUN]—Transliteration of Erin

*Gaosu wo ta de mingzi* [GOW (rhymes with *cow*) SUE WO TAH DUH MING DZUH]—Tell me his name.

*Hen qiguai* [HUHN CHEE GWAI (rhymes with *eye*)]—Very strange

**Lao Tzu** [LAO (rhymes with *cow*) DZI]—Taoist philosopher

**Liu** [LEE-OH]—Mei's last name

**Mei** [MAY]—A girl's name that means "beautiful"

**Meihua** [MAY HWAH (rhymes with *schwa*)]—A girl's name that means "beautiful flower"

*Ni de zuichun hen hao kan* [KNEE DUH ZWAY CHUN HUHN HOW KAHN]—Your lips are very beautiful.

***Ni feng le*** [KNEE FUHNG LUH]—You're crazy.

***Ni hao ma?*** [KNEE HOW MAH]—How are you?

***Ni shi lao*** [KNEE SURE LAO (rhymes with *cow*)]—You are the elder *or* You are old.

***Ni zuo*** [KNEE ZWOH]—You sit.

***Pang zhu*** [PAHNG JOO]—Fat pig

***Qigong*** [CHEE GOHNG]—Energy or life force+work=a kind of exercise

***Qipao*** [CHEEBOW (rhymes with *cow*)]—Tailored dress

***Renao*** [RUH NOW]—Lively, fun

**Sang Ji Sheng** [SAHNG GEE SHUHNG]—Tea to strengthen the blood

***Shenme?*** [SHUN MUH]—What?

***Shi bu shi?*** [SURE BOO SURE]—Is it true? (Literally, "is no is")

**Shufang** [SHOE FAHNG]—Mrs. Liu's first name, meaning kind, gentle, and sweet

**Shumai** [SHOO MAI (rhymes with *eye*)]—Delicious steamed dumplings

*Si* [SUH]—Four *and* Death

***Ta zai nar*** [TAH DZAI NAR]—Where is she?

***Wei*** [WAY]—Hello

***Wo ai ni*** [WHOA EYE KNEE]—I love you.

**Xiao bi** [SHE-OW BEE]—Small nose, Linny's nickname for Erin

***Xie xie*** [SHI-EH SHI-EH]—Thank you.

***Xihuan Meiguo ma?*** [SHE HWAHN MAY GUOH MAH]—Do you like America?

**Yuan** [YOU-EN]—Chinese money

***Zaijian*** [DZAI (rhymes with *eye*) JEE-EHN]—Good-bye

**Note:** These pronunciations are approximations. My Chinese professor at UC Davis told us nonnative speakers, "If your mouth feels comfortable saying something in Chinese, you are saying it wrong."

## A NOTE TO READERS

In January 2010, members of Westboro Baptist Church came to Lowell High School in San Francisco to picket with their message of hate. At first, school administrators asked the students to ignore the picketers. But when a group of students and faculty got together and made an impassioned plea for creating an event that would balance out the hate with love, the administration and the entire school got behind it. My novel contains a fictionalized account of these true events that I hope reflects the amazing and joyous spirit that lived at Lowell that day. To see a video of the actual event, please go to http://www.youtube.com/watch?v=hjV06XZ1PUk&feature=relmfu.

# ACKNOWLEDGMENTS

The characters in this story are fictional, as are the majority of the locations in San Francisco and Oakland—Hay Fat, Donatello's, and the Sleepy Inn. Lowell High School, though, is a real public school. While in the midst of writing *Miss Fortune Cookie*, I learned that Westboro Baptist Church had picketed Lowell and saw on YouTube the modern-day love-in the students organized to counteract their hate. The positive energy of the Lowell students inspired me to include a fictionalized account of this event in my novel.

Heartfelt thanks to the incomparable Katie Gong, Lowell class of 2011, for sharing her blog, answering my many, many questions, and reviewing my manuscript for accuracy. I am forever in your debt. Thanks also to Kevin Dinh for providing details about planning the Westboro counterprotest, and kudos for your part in it. Appreciation goes to Katie's friends—Jeanette, Karissa, Samantha, Karen, Mirabella, Amy, Sophia, Derek, Priscilla Y, and Priscilla. Thanks to my cousin and Lowell graduate, Leon Sultan, for telling intriguing stories about his alma mater.

Thank you to everyone at Henry Holt who has devoted time and energy to this book. I especially appreciate Kate Farrell for her guidance, perceptive suggestions, and many readings of the manuscript. Thanks also to Catherine Drayton for keeping her faith in me throughout.

My critique partners and beta-readers deserve a lot of credit too—Danielle Joseph, Megan Crewe, Janet Gurtler, Heather McDougal, Miriam Goin, Jennifer Grais, Todd Wynward, Alex Sternhagen, and Dorothy Chen.

Thanks also to my close friend and high school classmate, Rachel Golden, for sharing her experiences applying to Harvard.

Anyone who posts fortune cookie sayings online, please take a bow for adding to my enormous (but woefully inadequate) collection used in the writing of this book.

Some real-life events inspired vignettes in the novel—thanks to my sister, Jolene Welch, for lending me her ID to go dancing with the love of my life at eighteen; to John Lennon for writing amazing protest songs that never go out of style; to my uncle Tom Patty, who ghostwrote a celebrity advice column in the '70s; to Bonnie Katzive for her funny story about a former classmate; to Eliana Goldstein for saying "what the what?" in my living room; to Simon Aldana for collecting orange peels that would otherwise be thrown away; to Karl Adler for introducing me to the Elbo Room; and to the real Cigarette Willie, resident of Key West, Florida, circa 1973.

Last—and most of all—love to Pelle for sharing his appreciation of Chinese poetry, history, language, and food. As always, thanks to my sons for allowing me the time to write, and to my family and friends for your constant support.

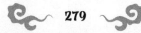